MURDER IN HELSINKI

JOHN SWALLOW

Copyright © 2022 John Swallow

All rights reserved

The characters and events portrayed in this book are fictitious. Any similarity to real persons, living or dead, is coincidental and not intended by the author.

No part of this book may be reproduced, or stored in a retrieval system, or transmitted in any form or by any means, electronic, mechanical, photocopying, recording, or otherwise, without express written permission of the publisher.

ISBN-13: 9798359774116

Cover design by: Art Painter
Library of Congress Control Number: 2018675309
Printed in the United States of America

CONTENTS

Title Page
Copyright
Sauna ... 1
Frozen ... 8
Neighbour ... 12
Shock ... 17
Investigation ... 23
Coffee ... 32
Petra ... 37
Stefan ... 44
Salonen ... 50
Meeting ... 61
Interview ... 67
Aimo ... 76
Discovery ... 85
Courage ... 94
Prison ... 101
Search ... 109
Attraction ... 118
Unexpected ... 129
Birthday ... 137

Money	141
Missing	148
Safety	155
Haven	163
Trouble	169
Attack	177
Chase	185
Evidence	196
Escape	204
Arrogance	215
Suspect	221
Enough	228
Surprise	236
Action	247
Flight	254
Revenge	258
Success	265
Departure	273
Beginning	279
Ending	282
About The Author	287
Books By This Author	289

SAUNA

"It's freezing out there," Petra exclaimed as she opened the back door leading to the terrace.

"What did you say?" a voice asked from within the house.

"I said it's freezing out there," she shouted, louder this time.

"What's the temperature?"

"Bloody cold," replied Petra, shuddering and closing the door.

She returned to the relative warmth of the living room and wrapped a woollen throw around her shoulders. It was cosier inside, but even those few moments had chilled her bones.

"You exaggerate sometimes," the unseen voice complained as it approached.

Petra glanced across the open-plan living space as her husband, Tommi Heikkinen, appeared from the direction of the bathroom, shaking his head.

He strode to the window and peered through the ice-crazed glass of the living room window at the thermometer, which read minus fourteen degrees.

"Hmm. You're right. It is bloody freezing. According to the forecast, it wasn't supposed to get as cold as this tonight. We should do something to keep warm."

"I might have an idea," Petra said, her mouth slowly widening to a grin.

Petra Heikkinen had a smile that was so wide it seemed to stretch across her whole face, just managing to curl up at the edges to fit. This endearing feature, among other things, had initially attracted her husband, as it had others before him.

"That would be nice," replied Tommi, guessing where her thoughts were leading and agreeing with their destination.

"But what about my sauna first? I switched it on over an hour ago, and it'll have reached the perfect temperature."

"It's not like you to postpone my invitations," remarked Petra, with a twinkle in her eye.

"I know, but I spent most of today on the construction site, outside in the snow, and I need to warm up a bit. Besides, you know that I can never waste a good sauna."

Tommi changed the tone of his voice to an excited storyteller and explained his plan for the evening.

"Tonight, I want to relax in our wonderful sauna, drink an ice-cold beer or two, and finally go to a nice warm bed with you in it."

"It might not be so warm if I'm already asleep," she warned. "I'm whacked."

"You won't be when I arrive," he replied, grinning.

"You're pretty confident in yourself tonight," Petra replied, raising her eyebrows in mock affront. "Alright, let's go to the sauna, and I'll join you for a while."

The couple went to their shower room and undressed. Each chose one of the four available showers in the black and white, square-tiled space.

When ready, they entered the sauna area; it was indeed

warm. Tommi immediately threw a ladle of water onto the hot stones. A second later, they felt the burning yet relaxing sensation of the resulting steam penetrate deep into their bodies.

The initial heat was overpowering and took their breath away for a moment. The couple sat back against the wooden bench to enjoy the sauna's soothing feeling in silence. Petra gently rubbed her ears. They'd been roasted more than usual due to a recent haircut that had exposed them.

After the steam subsided, Petra picked up a small bottle from a shelf and added a few drops of incense to the water bowl they'd brought. The next ladle of water surrounded them in steam infused with lavender and rosemary. They both breathed deeply in appreciation.

The sauna was Tommi's pride and joy. After marrying and buying the house together, he had spent weeks stripping everything down until the room was bare. Next, he painstakingly constructed his dream: the perfect sauna space.

His renovations included fitting the interior with new wooden planks and installing three benches along the walls—the remaining wall comprised of a full-length, single glass panel with a view directly to the showers. The seats were stained black, contrasting against the fresh wood finish of the walls. A shiny stainless-steel sauna stove, a kiuas, was inserted into the centre of the space. The ceiling was also black but embedded with a hundred tiny LED lights that sparkled like distant stars.

Anyone in Helsinki or Finland would have been delighted with such a luxurious facility. However, to Tommi, it meant much more: it was his sanctuary.

Every night, he spent at least an hour there, barring some urgent appointment or disaster, which had ever happened to a level that would disturb his peace. Like many other Finnish men and women, he didn't just enjoy a sauna; it was an essential element of life for him. And this evening would be no different.

The other half of the young married couple, Petra, also enjoyed the sauna experience regularly, just not to quite the same degree as her partner. They had been married for three years now. However, she was still not yet accustomed to his unfailing commitment to the custom. Hence it was no surprise that she gave up after a short while that evening.

"Hey, I'm not up for any more of this tonight," Petra informed Tommi after thirty minutes of immersion in the hot steam.

Her husband nodded as she made her way to the door. He knew his wife didn't appreciate the benefits of a sauna quite as much as he did; he could never understand why.

Petra placed a towel around her shoulders and made her way to the back door, opening it to allow access to the terrace. She was still glowing from the heat but knew the ground would be ice-cold, so she slipped on her sandals and padded to the end of the deck. As she walked, steam rose from her body as she strained to see beyond the gloom of winter.

The main terrace area was illuminated after switching on an outside light, which only shone as far as the rear boundary. Petra walked to the end of it and leaned against the fence. It was pitch-black beyond, and she couldn't make out anything despite the snow on the ground. She knew that twenty metres ahead lay the start of the woods, which she often enjoyed walking through.

The proximity to the forest had been one of the reasons for buying that particular house: the privacy it afforded them. It allowed them to enjoy their sauna traditions, which usually took place naked. Even on light summer nights, Petra was known to enjoy the freedom of lying under the warm sun without a stitch on. It wasn't summertime now, though, and she felt the chilly air envelop her as she watched the blackness, her breath turning to steam ahead of her.

"Okay, That's it. Too cold," Petra informed the night.

She bumped into Tommi as he exited the shower room at the same time she entered through the back door. He was heading towards the kitchen, where she knew he would go straight to their enormous fridge to take a cold beer. That was another of his customs: he believed you couldn't enjoy a sauna without drinking a beer, sometimes several, and there was always plenty of stock available. Therefore, despite a previously trim figure, he was beginning to develop a slight paunch around the midriff. Petra hadn't commented, choosing to ignore it.

"Are you having one of these?" he inquired, popping the bottle's cap and taking a sip.

"No, I'm fine. I'm finished now. I'll see you in bed. Don't be too long, will you?"

Petra winked at him, and her smile broadened once again.

She headed to the shower room, and Tommi returned to the sauna. He sat down on the seat and took a drink of ice-cold beer, but didn't throw water on the stones yet. Instead, he sat savouring the glass panel's view of the shower room and his currently naked wife. Tommi watched her shower and wash her hair meticulously under his appreciating gaze. It always took so much time for her to wash her hair, as it was so long.

After a while, he enjoyed the steam once again. Deep in thought, he sat there for some minutes, after which he realised the moisture had subsided. At that point, he decided to get some fresh air.

That might clear my head, he thought to himself.

Tommi left the sauna, lightly smacking Petra's behind on his way to the terrace.

"Hey, you!" she playfully scolded as he grinned at her.

She completed her ablutions and dried herself thoroughly. At the same time, her partner enjoyed his cold beer outside on the frosty night.

Petra walked across the living room, taking care not to slip on the shiny wooden floor with her bare slightly-wet feet, and entered the bedroom.

She took her new pyjamas from the wardrobe, which were red with a pattern of tiny white hearts. The soft material felt warm and cosy next to her skin, and despite the underfloor heating, she pulled on thick woollen socks to keep her feet warm.

Next, she visited the bathroom, where she continued her night-time routine by brushing her teeth and slowly combing her long blond hair under the hair dryer's heat. She rechecked the mirror, pondering her reflection, and wondered if her hairdresser had cut it too short over her ears.

Still, everyone else seems to like it, she mused.

Petra took a cleansing pad and wiped her face, after which she inspected her appearance; she approved. The final touch was spraying perfume in the air, under which she turned around; her well-practised ritual of achieving an all-over scent.

With her night preparations complete, Petra climbed into bed. After a few moments, she decided to slip off her pyjamas in anticipation of her husband's arrival and placed them neatly under her pillow for later. She also dropped her thick woollen socks on the floor, deciding she would warm her feet on Tommi instead. Petra preferred to have bare feet whenever possible.

She felt sleepy now.

In an effort to stay awake, Petra took her book from the

nightstand, snuggled under the duvet cover and opened it at the bookmark. She began to read and was soon engrossed in its pages. It was her favourite kind of novel: where a single girl travelled to a far-off land and found romance with an unlikely character: in this case, in Italy. The book also contained somewhat steamy content, making her look forward to Tommi's arrival even more.

After a few chapters, though, Petra felt her eyelids grow heavy and drowsily turned to the clock to check the time.

What's he doing? she wondered.

Petra turned her head back to the novel and tried to continue reading. However, after a few pages, the soft and fuzzy weight of sleep wrapped around her, and she put the book down and laid her head on the pillow.

He's going to have to work hard to get my attention now.

Petra's eyes closed as she drifted softly into a blissful sleep.

FROZEN

It was some hours before Petra awoke. When she did, she wondered why she felt so cold. Pulling the duvet around her shoulders helped, but it wasn't enough. It was then that she realised she was still naked, as she had expected her husband to find her in that condition and wake her seductively when he came to bed. She instinctively turned to Tommi for the warmth she craved, but a quick check revealed his conspicuous absence.

Where is he?

Still groggy from her slumber, she glanced at the clock on the bedside cabinet. It spelt out 2.20 am in glaringly red LCD. She shook her head to try and focus.

"Tommi?" she called.

She tried again.

"Tommi?" louder this time.

Petra waited for a few moments, but when there was no answer, she pushed the duvet cover away, swung her legs off the bed, and placed her bare feet on the floor.

"Brrr."

The wooden floorboards were surprisingly cold.

What's happened to the heating?

Petra felt around and located the thick woollen socks she

had kicked off a few hours before, which she now pulled up to her knees. She took her pyjamas from underneath her pillow, dressed and made her way to the living area.

The first thought that entered her mind was that Tommi had fallen asleep watching television; it wouldn't be the first time. A small lamp they always left switched on at night illuminated the living area with a dim glow, but there was no sign of her husband. Everything was eerily silent.

She noticed the open door that led to the sauna area and felt an icy draft coming from that direction. Shuffling over in her socks, she observed the exit door to the terrace was ajar.

"Tommi!" she exclaimed, closing it.

No wonder it's so damn cold in here. Has that door been open all night?

She opened the shower room door and peeked inside. The dimmed under-bench lights of the sauna were still on, and she could see the LED lights shining from the ceiling. She entered the shower area and opened the door to the sauna, expecting Tommi to be there, but he wasn't. Why he would still be there wouldn't make any sense to Petra anyway, as she had left hours before. However, knowing his love for the sauna, it felt like the right place to check, just in case. It was warm inside the space as the door had been closed, at least better than elsewhere in the house.

He's not here either. Weird.

The only place left to check was the bathroom.

Of course. Tommi must be in there. The idiot forgot to close the back door. He probably had too many beers and is now relieving himself.

Petra entered the living area again and, after crossing it, opened the unlocked toilet door. It was also empty.

I don't understand. Where's Tommi?

Then, another thought came to her.

Surely, he can't be outside at this time, can he?

Petra hurried back across the living room, through the doorway, and reopened the back door.

Outside was dark, pitch black. Just as it had been before. Petra switched on the light at the rear, and it began to illuminate the area. After a couple of seconds, she became accustomed to the change from dark to light.

As the wintry scene outside began to take shape, she stood still to ascertain what was in front of her.

A strange form was draped over the fence at the very end of the terrace, just by the barbeque. Before Petra could investigate, something else on the floor nearby caught her eye: a pool of darkness spread out over the pristine white snow. As the light was now at its full brightness, the likeness of the shape was now more apparent.

"Tommi?" she half-whispered, with more than a hint of disbelief.

With Petra's gaze fixed on the figure by the fence, she slowly moved towards it. As she approached, it didn't move, apparently motionless in its chosen position. She made out the back of a head, confirming it was definitely human. Petra had suspected this at the outset but wasn't brave enough to admit it. It was a body, clearly naked. She stopped walking.

Petra was paralysed with a fear that gripped her entire body. All thoughts of the outside temperature were now gone, and all she could do was stare at the figure, unable to move.

After what seemed like an eternity, she dug deep and found the courage to override her fear. Pushing herself forward, she approached the figure, and as she drew closer, an appalling realisation swept over her.

Is that blood on the ground? Oh my god. It can't be. It's Tommi.

Still in disbelief, Petra touched her husband's body. It was indeed frozen, like a block of ice. She tried to scream Tommi's name, but no sound escaped. Something had taken her voice: a mixture of horror, disbelief and the freezing-cold air.

Petra sank to her knees, trembling, feeling sick. Her head was spinning, and her throat wretched as if to throw up but failing to do so. She was panicking now. She tried to breathe deeper to combat the feeling and managed to calm herself after a few seconds.

Then the adrenalin kicked in. Petra had to do something; get help. Taking one more look at the body, to be sure she hadn't imagined it, she sprang up and half-walked, half-ran, quickly back into the house.

Petra hurried across the living room, through the hallway and straight out and across the front garden toward her neighbour's house, where she began to ring the bell and bang on the door, crying hysterically.

NEIGHBOUR

Stefan had worked hard that day. He'd been busy scraping wallpaper from his living room wall in readiness to replace it the following day. Unfortunately, what should have been a simple, straightforward task had gradually evolved into a significant challenge, primarily due to the multiple layers of older paper lurking underneath.

After spending most of the day on his redecoration project, Stefan resigned himself to the fact that it would take much longer than expected and finally took a break later that evening.

It didn't matter, he had lived alone since his divorce, and there was no reason to rush anything. Besides, he'd arranged a few days off from work, so there was no issue; he would take his time.

Following a survey of his handiwork, he switched on his sauna at 9 pm and looked forward to relaxing there later. While it was warming, Stefan prepared a light dinner for himself. He heated the remainder of the previous day's salmon soup in the microwave. Next, he roughly shredded dill over the soup to add flavour, adding a twist of black pepper to give it a 'zing', as he called it. Stefan loved his black pepper.

As it was partially prepared already, his meal was soon on the table, and he opened a well-deserved cold beer to accompany his late dinner. He congratulated himself for making a large pot of the soup previously, meaning little effort was involved after his hard day's work.

Despite his frustration and exhaustion, he felt good about his toil, and there was visible progress. As someone who worked with computer programs in an office during the day, Stefan could often be found deep in 'coding mode' for hours on end. Conversely, when he wasn't working, he enjoyed working physically, doing something with his hands. This type of activity gave him a different feeling from that of his day job. To look at something he had crafted or visibly improved was a mile away from reviewing a lengthy amount of data.

Stefan found his meal delicious and just what he needed, making short work of the bowl-full and taking a second helping.

After eating, he smoked a cigarette, and the sauna was ready.

Good timing.

Before entering, he stripped off his clothes and took a quick shower to wash away the worst of the dirt and sweat earned from his day's labour.

How many showers will it take to get rid of this stuff? Stefan wondered, running his fingers through his hair disapprovingly in the bathroom mirror, trying to remove stubborn, clinging flakes of plaster.

It was almost ten o'clock when he entered the sauna. The heat was at its optimum—hot and dry enough to produce a refreshing blast of steam following a generous application of water directly to the stones.

"Ahh," Stefan moaned as the steam touched his body, permeating his aching muscles.

He covered his ears for a moment and held his breath due to the ferocity of the heat.

I must have left it heating too long.

Still, he knew this treatment was exactly what was needed and stretched the muscles in his legs across the bench, placing a small pillow that he kept there under his head.

Perfect!

Stefan had no idea how long he'd been in the sauna, just relaxing there, but he suddenly felt thirsty. He left the room, wrapped a towel around his waist, and took a can of gin and grapefruit juice, one of a variety of Finnish 'long drinks' he kept in the fridge. Refreshment in hand, he opened the back door and went out onto the terrace to enjoy the fresh air.

The winter night was clear and studded with stars, a nice change from the day's task of studying patterned wallpaper. If it wasn't for the amount of light in the area, he could imagine the northern lights dancing across the sky, just as he had seen in Lapland the year before.

While admiring the view, he noticed one of his neighbours, Tommi, leaning over his rear-facing fence.

"Terve! (Hello)" he called out, planning on exchanging casual greetings, as they occasionally did. "Looks like we have the same idea again."

His neighbour didn't reply and continued to lean against the fence, motionless.

Okay.

Stefan shrugged his shoulders; it seemed Tommi wasn't feeling social tonight, although he never was especially so. Unfortunately, there was no sign of his pretty young wife either.

That's a shame.

Stefan was used to encountering Petra during the day.

In the summer, he found their meetings delightful. She

tended to wear revealing bikinis on the terrace and was happy enough to chat with him in that attire. He had even encountered her without any clothes on some warmer evenings, and she was equally pleased to wave or greet him like that, at least from afar. He was sure that her exhibitions were for his benefit and that her flirting expressed more than everyday familiarity.

They had become friendly since the neighbouring couple moved in three years before, especially since Tommi began working later and Petra was at home more often.

After chatting over the fence one afternoon, Petra invited Stefan to join her for coffee on the terrace. He secretly hoped this would become a regular habit.

In the evenings, she was usually together with her husband, so he didn't attempt to engage her in conversation and instead just waved.

However, no such diversion was visible on the terrace tonight, so he withdrew from the fence and plumped down on a wooden chair by his small garden table on the deck. He cast his eyes upward again; It was a perfect night, clear enough to see far into space. As he observed, he tried to make out some of the more well-known star clusters and was thoroughly satisfied when he found 'The Plough'.

After this diversion, he picked up his drinks can and took a long sip of what was indeed now an ice-cold drink. It felt so refreshing as it bit the back of his throat.

Just right for washing the dust away.

After a few minutes outside, Stefan began to feel cold. He decided he'd imbibed enough fresh air and returned to the relative warmth of the wet room to drench himself with water, after which he returned to the sauna's heat.

That evening, he repeated the process several times: sauna,

beer, terrace, shower; sauna, beer, terrace, shower; and so on. As Tommi had been unsociable, he didn't bother casting his eyes in that direction again.

After his sauna routine, Stefan patted himself with a towel, wrapped it around his waist, and entered the living room.

Quite a mess, he observed as he wandered through the cluttered space. *Well, it's a 'project'*, he reminded himself.

Not wishing to stare at the chaos for long, Stefan retired to his bedroom and switched on the television. He flipped through the channels aimlessly with the remote control, eventually settling on an action movie just beginning. Stefan had seen it a few times before but was happy to watch it again. It felt appropriate not to tax the brain too much right now.

He removed his towel and threw it over the door to dry, selecting and pulling on a clean pair of white boxer shorts.

I think I'll have a drink and some chips with the movie. I deserve it, Stefan decided and headed back to the fridge.

After settling down again, he watched the film, propped up by a couple of pillows.

Despite feeling drowsy halfway through, he struggled through it until the final credits, even though he knew what happened in it anyway.

After that and the inevitable draining of another long drink, he found no trouble falling asleep.

SHOCK

Stefan awoke abruptly.

What was that noise?

Oh. I left the television on.

He took the remote control and switched it off. As a result, the bedroom went black.

Stefan looked at the clock: 2.32 am. He resisted his usual urge to check his mobile phone and decided to try and go back to sleep straight away.

He was just sinking his head into his pillow once more when he heard something: it was someone knocking at the door.

That's what woke me. Who's knocking at the door at this time? Stefan wondered as he rose from his bed, feeling decidedly groggy.

He walked through the living area to the front door, trying to move quickly but not succeeding. He banged into a temporarily-relocated table, giving him a painful jolt back to reality.

"Damn!" he cursed.

Stefan valiantly continued towards the door, hopping with pain as he did so, the sound of a fist still knocking. Repeatedly. Desperately.

"Alright, Alright. I'm coming. I'm coming," he yelled.

Stefan opened the door. Standing there was a young woman in pyjamas. It took him a moment to recognise her, partly due to his current demeanour and partly because he'd never seen Petra in her pyjamas. Neither of them said anything for a few moments. Then, he realised, somewhat embarrassingly, that he was standing in front of her wearing only his boxer shorts. However, the urgency of her expression shocked him into consciousness. What he wore didn't matter now. Something more important was at hand. Something was wrong.

"Petra? Is everything okay?" he asked.

"No. No, it isn't. It's Tommi. I think he's dead," she stammered, tears streaming down her face.

Stefan was momentarily shocked into silence, but the sight of his neighbour's wife in that condition, combined with the cold air now enveloping him, brought him to his senses. He wondered if he should call the police, go to his neighbour's house with her, or do something else?

He briefly questioned her, but she didn't provide any helpful information. She just stood there trembling and crying.

Stefan decided to find out for himself what had happened.

He grabbed a fleece jacket hanging by the door, pulled it on, and slipped his feet into a waiting pair of crocs. He took Petra gently by the arm to accompany him but immediately felt resistance—one look at her face told him that his visit to her house would be alone. Instead, he beckoned her inside, into his hallway, and sat her on the bench.

"Okay, you stay here. I'll go and check what's happened." Adding: "I'll be back soon, okay?"

Petra sat uncomfortably on the narrow bench, legs together and hands clasped in front of her. She was visibly trembling in her pyjamas. Stefan had never seen anyone like this before.

"Here, put this on," he instructed, draping one of his winter coats around her shoulders.

Setting his front door's latch to open and taking a last worrying look at Petra, Stefan closed the door softly and trudged across the lawn through the snow, making for his neighbours' house.

The snowflakes were falling, and the temperature had dropped. Stefan immediately regretted not layering up as he would've typically done, and he especially regretted not putting on socks. It just hadn't seemed the right thing to do at that moment—to calmly dress in warm clothes while that poor woman was so grief-stricken. Also, although it didn't bear thinking about, Tommi might be lying dead somewhere.

Dead, though? No, she must be mistaken. Maybe she's just had a nightmare, or they've had an argument, and Tommi has stormed out. Or perhaps he's lying down completely drunk.

Unsure of what lay ahead, Stefan gritted his teeth and approached the open front door of the couple's house. He hesitated for a few moments. This was mainly due to the resulting embarrassment if Tommi were standing there, wondering what Stefan was doing half-naked in his living room. Aside from that, it wasn't his own house, so it would feel like trespassing. Adding to this, Petra was currently sitting in her pyjamas in his hallway.

I'm not sure I want to get involved in all of this.

Notwithstanding his concerns, the hall light was on and somehow beckoned him inward. Stefan decided he didn't have much choice; he must go and see for himself. Besides, a severe accident could have befallen his neighbour—Tommi might be lying somewhere, bleeding.

Alright. Get on with it, Stefan. Just do it.

He pushed himself onward and opened the door. Seeing the other interior lights on, he entered the hallway, slipped off his footwear out of habit, and left them on the mat before proceeding into the open-plan living area.

He called out, just in case Tommi was there.

"Tommi! Tommi? Are you there?"

There was no reply. Stefan had no choice but to continue.

Walking through the house alone caused him to feel distinctly uneasy. He wondered why the living area felt colder than it had outside; his feet were now absolutely freezing, almost numb.

Looking around, he quickly identified the reason. With the front and back doors both open, a powerful, through-draught of freezing-cold air permeated the house.

Trying to ignore the temperature, Stefan began to search for Tommi. As he did so, he realised he hadn't asked Petra where her husband actually was. He cursed himself for not doing so, as this fact would have made his task much easier, especially as he couldn't find any sign of him anywhere.

Stefan scanned the open-plan living area and inspected the bedroom, bathroom, and kitchen area.

Where is he? Was she mistaken? Drunk? Dreaming? On drugs?

Now, Stefan was certainly regretting his involvement.

Why did I come here in the first place? What a stupid thing to do. I should have just phoned the police and told them I had a hysterical woman on my doorstep, saying her husband was dead.

He opened the door to the shower room and checked the sauna: still no one to be seen.

Well, he wouldn't be taking a sauna at 2.30 am in the morning, would he? The house is empty. What's she talking about? What am I supposed to do now?

Finally, almost as an afterthought, he leaned out of the doorway to the terrace, where he'd seen Tommi earlier that evening, and called out again.

"Tommi? Are you there, Tommi?"

Stefan felt stupid as if he were searching for a non-existent dog and calling its name.

He found the light switch, as it was in the same place as his own at home. He flicked it on, and a yellow light shone across the wooden deck, partly cleared of snow nearer the door but still covered towards its end by the fence.

After a few seconds, the whole area appeared in view.

Stefan hadn't expected to see anything and was about to turn and close the door when the sight ahead caused him to stop in his tracks. There was what looked like a body hunched over the rear fence. A chill ran right through him, and he trembled slightly.

Is that him? Why is he still there? Is there something wrong with him? It can't be.

"Tommi?"

Stefan moved closer to investigate, discerning by the longer hair that the body might really be that of Tommi's. He could see the figure was naked, ashen – almost white, more so with snow on its head and shoulders. Worst of all, it was perfectly still.

As Stefan neared the ghostly figure, he saw something on the ground. He peered down at the wooden deck and noted a pool of something dark on the bed of white snow, now congealed and frozen. He knelt down to take a closer look.

Oh my god.

He sprang back up.

"Tommi?" he asked again, although he knew his question was pointless as soon as he asked it.

The figure didn't stir.

Collecting his thoughts, Stefan was in no doubt that he was looking at a dead body. And apparently, that body belonged to Tommi.

That was enough for him. As Petra had done earlier, Stefan hastily retraced his steps through the house toward the front door. He exited the building and walked directly forward to the street, where he stopped and looked around for a few moments.

Stefan asked himself why he was doing that? Perhaps he was looking for some assistance with his predicament? But there was no one around to help at that hour. The snow was falling heavily now, and he decided he needed the warmth and security of home.

Upon opening his front door, he became more concerned for Petra than himself. She was sitting in exactly the same position as he'd left her, violently shaking, despite the relative warmth of the house. Stefan put his arm around her shoulder to gently lead her into the living area, and carefully onto the sofa.

Next, he went to his bedroom, collected his mobile phone and tapped 112 into the keypad—the police emergency number.

INVESTIGATION

Detective Superintendent Topias Torikka lay his head down on the soft pillow.

"Ahh. Finally,"

It had been a challenging day due to an unnecessarily lengthy meeting plus several overtime hours spent trying to batten down his caseload. The long days seemed to be becoming a habit, only made tolerable by an after-work steaming sauna, a decent bottle of wine and a few hours of slumber.

Unfortunately, much to his disappointment, his sleep was to elude him again, with his mobile phone ringing after just a few minutes of rest.

"Torikka," he answered, more impatiently than usual.

The caller imparted important news, and Topias jolted himself awake. He switched on the light—there was no risk of waking anyone else in the house as he lived alone.

Dressing quickly in the same clothes he'd been wearing that day, he made for the door.

On the way out, he collected his necessities, which he'd left by the entrance in a large pewter tray: his keys, a mobile phone, and service weapon in its holster. He realised he'd been lax in not placing his gun securely inside its safe that night, but he'd been exhausted.

Before leaving, he stopped to put on a thick, black overcoat, grey scarf and black leather gloves, and opened the door to greet the freezing night. Topias drew breath but instinctively coughed as the cold, dry air grabbed him by the throat.

Outside was bitter: the snow blew directly toward him, whipped up and intensified by vicious, unpredictable gusts of wind. He bravely battled towards his car, which was sat on the driveway from its arrival a mere forty-five minutes earlier. There had been no time for a sauna that night.

Turning the car's ignition key, it leapt into life. Topias reversed onto the road, changing gear to accelerate towards the address he'd received by text.

At least it's not like a freezer in here yet, he thought, giving himself some small comfort.

How much heat remained in the car from the previous trip was debatable, but at least, without the wind, it felt better than the outside world.

As he drove, Topias tapped the address into the GPS, which plotted the direction after a few seconds of deliberation. At least the place was close, and it would take only sixteen minutes to reach his destination.

Thankfully, despite the treacherous weather, the highway itself was clear, due to the efforts of the heroic snow-clearers in their trucks and tractors.

Topias pulled off the main road and noted the more minor roads remained challenging, with snow flurrying across the ice. Taking more care, he sped along the empty streets, wondering hopefully if hot coffee would be available at his destination.

He drew up outside the house in question. As his GPS had predicted, precisely sixteen minutes had elapsed since his departure.

As he alighted from his car, a door opened nearby, shining light out onto the street. A uniformed police officer approached from the gloom, whom he instantly recognised as from his precinct.

"Matti. How're things?"

"Evening, Detective Superintendent. Things are a bit gruesome. We've got a nasty murder here."

Topias noticed another man standing nearby, whom he didn't recognise, smoking a cigarette.

"And you are?"

"Me? Oh. I'm Stefan. Stefan Paikkala. Err. I reported this," he answered, making a meaningless gesture with his right hand.

Topias nodded in acknowledgement.

"That must have been quite a shock. Where did you find the victim?"

"On the terrace of the house, next door. That one," Stefan replied, pointing in its general direction. "He's my neighbour, Tommi. His wife knocked at my door and woke me up about an hour ago."

The man looked visibly shaken, so Topias asked him to return to his own house to keep warm and informed him they would talk later.

Topias turned around to the uniformed police officer.

"Is it just you at the moment?" he asked Matti.

"And Virpi. She's over at the neighbour's house, looking after the victim's wife, whose badly shaken."

"Any other potential witnesses other than those two?"

"No, just the wife and neighbour at this stage. We'll check the surrounding area when more officers arrive."

"Okay. I'm going to check around."

Matti nodded while Topias walked purposefully to the neighbouring house, number 19. He pushed the partially open door and peered in. The Crime Scene Unit had not yet arrived. Therefore, he knew he must be careful not to disturb anything.

He cautiously walked around the apartment just as Stefan had done a little earlier, checking each room in turn.

On reaching the sauna and shower area, he pushed open the already-ajar outside door with his foot.

The same discovery awaited him - a body draped over the rear fence of the terrace. It looked like the victim had died while clutching a can of beer. Topias glanced at the ground.

That's a lot of blood. He must have been here a while.

He checked his phone and noted no reports of anything reported by local people, at least none that had found their way to the police message board. Also, the man he now knew as Stefan Paikkala had been awoken by his neighbour's wife banging on the door, not a gunshot.

Topias moved closer, and as he examined the body, blue lights began to flash on the white snow around him, and he realised reinforcements had arrived.

Walking back into the house and through the living area, he met a forensic investigator whom he knew well coming through the doorway: Ina Stenvall.

"Topias," she greeted him enthusiastically.

She was one of the few permitted to address him by his first name publicly.

"Ina," he nodded respectfully.

"How does it look?" she asked.

"Not good. The victim is on the back terrace, and it looks like a shot or stabbing to the chest after his sauna session. There's an awful lot of blood."

"Not a pleasant end to a sauna."

"No, not at all. Well, I'll leave you to do your thing while I go and talk to the wife and neighbour. Let's catch up later."

"Sounds good. Are you okay, by the way?" she asked, eyeing him with concern.

"Yes, I'm fine. Thanks," Topias replied, wondering if he looked as tired as he felt.

It's a shame I only meet Ina in these circumstances when I usually look like crap, he lamented.

Topias crossed the lawn, wading through patches of deep snow, wishing he'd taken the path around it. On his way, he kept a keen eye out for footprints, noticing another set, which he deduced was probably the neighbour's shoes—he would check. Whatever getaway the perpetrator had made, it wouldn't have been over the front lawn where it was exposed. Despite the wintry weather, he was sure there must be signs of an intruder at the rear.

Reaching the neighbouring house, he rang the bell. Mr Paikkala, the neighbour he'd already met, answered, explaining the door was unlocked, so he could come and go as needed. Topias nodded and followed him into the living area, removing his shoes in the hallway. He was relieved that it was warmer inside. It had been like a morgue at the other house in more ways than one.

He went over to the young woman sitting on the sofa, introduced by Virpi, the other officer, as Petra Heikkinen, the victim's wife.

Topias was immediately struck by her skin colour, which was virtually white. He surmised that her natural complexion was porcelain-pale, but the blood now seemed to have left her face entirely. She looked ashen, just like the corpse he'd just seen. Notwithstanding this, she was distinctly beautiful. Incredibly beautiful. Not in the style of a poster girl, but instead, she resembled a perfectly-made statue.

Another distinctive feature was her lengthy, feathered hair, dyed lighter in the Nordic blonde style, which fell all around her shoulders and cut back to reveal her delicate ears. In addition, when she shook her hair away from her face at that moment, her piercing blue eyes immediately grasped and held his attention.

Topias introduced himself and asked a few basic questions to confirm the woman's identity. As he began, he noticed the neighbour perched on the sofa on the other side of the room, listening intently. Topias rebuked himself for starting an interview with a potential suspect in earshot. He deduced that he must be tired; he would never usually make that mistake. From previous experience, he always deemed it better to interview suspects individually at the police station rather than in the same room as anyone else.

You never know who has done what and to whom; in cases like these.

Topias stopped talking and informed Stefan Paikkala that they would need to speak at the station. He retraced his steps outside until he met another officer. There were several police cars on the driveway now, plus an ambulance. Murder was not an everyday event in Helsinki, and the emergency services had arrived in force.

"Evening Samuli," he greeted another officer he knew. "Would you arrange for the victim's wife and the neighbour who lives here to be taken to the station and placed in interview rooms? We need to separate them as soon as possible, as we don't know what's happened here yet. Better to take them in different cars too."

Samuli nodded and obediently left to perform this task.

Topias strolled back along the driveway to the victim's residence, searching for anything unusual. He reached the doorway and moved slowly through the house, a hub of activity.

He made his way to where Ina was painstakingly working on the terrace, assisted by a young man he didn't recognise. Both were wrapped in thick padded coats and wore hats and gloves.

"Ina, can I have a moment?" he called.

"Yes, Topias. I'm busy right now, but just for you, I can make some time. One second."

The woman in question carefully backtracked her steps from the corpse. She drew a cold breath to fuel her interim summary.

"Right. The victim is a roughly thirty-five-year-old male who recently spent time in the sauna. It seems he walked onto the terrace and was shot by someone standing just beyond the fence. The bullet hit him in the heart—a perfect shot, as it were. The victim probably didn't notice anything until it was too late. He wouldn't stand a chance at that range and likely died immediately where he stood. Subsequently, he froze, so I can't tell you exactly the cause of death until later, but you can assume at this stage that it was the bullet. The time of death was between three and five hours ago. You can undoubtedly consider this crime an unlawful death of some description. Of course, I need a few more hours before I can confirm this as murder and provide more factual information."

The report delivered by Ina was clear and concise, despite the challenging weather conditions and the short time she had spent with the victim to establish her findings.

"Kiitos Ina," Topias thanked her.

He left her to get on with it, and took himself on another inspection of the house, asking questions of other officers along the way. There didn't seem much to go on at that stage, at least from the evidence presented to him. He hoped that the crime scene officers would come forward with something interesting. However, it was now time to interview the victims while the events were fresh in their minds.

He returned to his car, manoeuvred it past the parade of vehicles parked along the verge, and headed to the station.

Back on the terrace at number nineteen, Ina stood up straight. She stretched, raising her eyebrows at her current working conditions as she did so.

"Who was that, by the way?" asked a man named Antero, Ina's new assistant, who was referring to Topias.

Ina replied while stooping down again, inspecting the victim's beer can for prints.

"Detective Superintendent Topias Torikka – everyone calls him Torikka. And don't worry. He's usually brighter and in considerably better humour. Actually, he looks like he needs a good night's sleep and a strong coffee; he looks exhausted."

"Is he a detective?"

"Yes. I'll introduce you another time. It's good that you get to know Torikka, as you may come across him in the future. He's been with the police force forever and solved more cases than I care to mention. He's now in charge of murder investigations, and he's a nice guy, but as you no doubt observed, he can get grumpy when tired."

Ina considered Topias for a moment. He still looked

handsome after all these years and had a distinguished edge with a hint of a beard together with salt and pepper hair. She always thought he looked like a dashing but ageing actor and had the theatrical aura to go with it. On the negative side, since his wife, Helene, had left him, his appearance could be unkempt at times, probably because she'd been the organised one in the relationship. Ina looked wistfully at where he'd been standing and then re-focused on the job at hand.

As he drove, Topias cranked up the heating in his car. At least it hadn't got that cold again since he wasn't parked at the victim's house for long. He popped a mint from a packet inside his glove box to help keep him awake. Then, taking the dual-carriageway and facing the winter weather head-on, he drove through it and pulled into the police station half an hour later.

COFFEE

Topias entered the station, nodding to the desk officer on duty, and swiped his card in the identity card reader. He walked into the main open-plan office, almost empty due to the late hour, and made a beeline for the kitchen.

He was pleased to find an almost-full jug of coffee on the hotplate and proceeded to fill a cup to the brim.

"Ahhh, that's better," he breathed with relief as he took a long sip.

In reality, the station coffee wasn't that tasty for him as it was weak and bitter, but at this point, some hot, dark liquid containing caffeine was enough.

He leaned against the counter, took another gulp, and refilled it. Then, he left the room, taking his cup to his desk.

Topias sat down, picked up an old biro, and began to chew it. It was a well-used pen, one he kept at his desk. This habit helped him think and was a substitute for cigarette smoking, which he had finally kicked the year before. However, the biro didn't lift his mood when he was tired.

"Moi Torikka, you're in early?" one of the officers joked, walking down the central aisle of the open-plan office.

Topias waved his hand as if in a royal gesture, in the general direction of the man's voice. He was thinking, and most officers knew it was better to avoid disturbing him during that process.

Something was bothering Topias. He took a piece of paper and set to work on it. He'd never been that proficient at using a computer and always preferred to map things out manually, much to the amusement of some of his more technologically-adept fellow officers, especially the younger ones. With great care, he drew the murder scene and, after a few minutes, surveyed his somewhat crude attempt at portraying it.

Topias began to list questions as they occurred to him, which helped his thought process.

Why was he killed on the terrace?

How did the murderer know he would be on the terrace at that moment? The house has solid doors and effective locks. Did someone intend to break in through the back door if the victim hadn't been using their sauna? It seems very convenient that he was there, or perhaps it was just lucky, or unlucky, that he was? I wonder if the killer had been watching the house for a while?

There had been few homicides in Helsinki over the past year, as was usually the case across Finland. Ordinarily, with this type of incident, Topias' thoughts would have headed towards a jealous husband or boyfriend or perhaps a drunken fight—more crimes of passion than anything else. But assuming this one didn't involve a passing maniac in the forest, which was unheard of, the incident felt much too well-orchestrated.

He drained his coffee mug, set down the pen, and went to the kitchen again.

It was still deserted, and he poured himself a refill and took a sip.

"Ugh,"

Surprisingly, the coffee tasted even worse now. Nevertheless, Topias took a full cup and returned to his desk. He had neither time nor energy to make a fresh brew.

He booted up his computer to use one of the few programs he'd learned: maps.

When the website had loaded, he entered the address of the incident and zoomed in on the street in question. He clicked the button to show a photograph of the road, then closed in further to view the street and inspected it.

There were three buildings in a row, each comprised of four residences, with an additional section at right angles to either side. The two neighbouring houses he had been inside that night formed the right-hand wing and backed directly onto a forest. No other neighbours overlooked those two rear terraces.

Rubbing his eyes with tiredness, he reached for his reading glasses, a well-used pair that he kept at his desk specifically for the computer. Topias didn't use them all the time as he felt it showed his age, but he had to use them more and more as time went on.

He studied the screen, eyes following the cursor, peering at the rear of the building complex to inspect each residence in turn. There was nothing unusual to see. Each garden couldn't have been more uniform: almost perfect rectangles. At the end of the forest behind the houses was a walking track running parallel to it.

So, the killer could have used the forest trail to approach the area and arrived unnoticed at the rear, waiting to take the shot. Although, if they used a pistol from that range, they would need to be a crack shot. Especially as, according to Ina, it was pitch-dark when the murder took place. Perhaps he came much nearer to the house? But then he would risk being noticed or leaving footprints.

Topias resolved to return to the house at first light and check the surrounding forest for clues.

As he took another sip of coffee, his eyes tracked to the neighbour's house. Looking at the angle of the windows and the victim's position.

Although the neighbour, Stefan Paikkala, had a good view of the rear of the terrace while standing up, it was unlikely he would've been doing that at the exact moment the victim was shot. Of course, he may have seen Tommi's figure if it had been slumped there for some time, and it was also dim in that area. In addition, Paikkala's terrace and his house weren't that far away not to have heard a shot, meaning the shooter may have used a silencer attachment.

There was also the possibility of Paikkala's story being fake.

"Mmm," he murmured, deep in thought, fumbling for his half-chewed pen once more.

No, this doesn't seem like a snap decision made in anger. Too accurate and undoubtedly pre-meditated.

Topias entered some details into the police database. In a couple of seconds, Stefan Paikkala's record appeared on the screen, and he scanned the information in front of him.

He has a passport but only travels occasionally. There are a few minor speeding convictions, now expired. There's a reasonable monthly salary. No obvious criminal or financial issues, it seems.

Topias made a note to have his team contact the relevant bank to obtain a strip list of transactions over the past couple of years, together with his credit history.

He repeated the process for Petra Heikkinen and found she had a clean record and nothing worthy of note in her file. He would wait for more details from his team when they arrived and began working.

Gulping down the last remnants of coffee, Topias headed to

the section of the police station containing the interview rooms. It was time to talk to the victim's wife if she was in any condition to do so.

Suddenly realising, he turned back to his desk; he needed a pen, at least to twirl, if not to chew, for this task.

PETRA

Topias took the stairs to the upper floor, where a line of grey doors with Venetian blinds provided access to the interview rooms. They were the spaces used to talk privately with suspects and witnesses, away from prying eyes.

He approached one of the illuminated rooms, glanced through the window blinds, and recognised his first subject: Petra Heikkinen. She was seated upright at a table, staring straight ahead, clasping a cardboard cup.

Topias entered the room, where a female officer, Saana Koskinen, was seated in the corner. By the looks of things, she had exhausted the usual small talk, and the room was silent. He thought that any conversation would doubtless be challenging in this case anyway, with the woman in question only recently, and violently, losing her husband to murder.

He disliked these interviews because the victims' relatives would be upset, and he needed to use kid gloves to question them. Topias always tried his best but wasn't that comfortable sympathising with grieving widows or other relatives. Somehow, he was looking forward to meeting this particular woman again, though. There was something different, even exceptional, about her.

Nodding at Saana, he pulled a chair from the opposite side of the table and observed the woman for a few moments. She appeared to look straight through him.

Now he had a second opportunity to study her; he found her even more attractive than before. She exhibited a distinctly delicate demeanour, like a thin, bone-China cup that one would treat with the greatest care.

She certainly had the appearance of a grieving widow, that's for sure. There was a redness, staining her blue eyes, a tissue in one hand and a cup clasped tightly in the other, long since drained. He knew he would need to tread sensitively.

Time to begin, he decided and drew a breath.

"Hello, Mrs Heikkinen. My name is Detective Superintendent Torikka. We met earlier at your neighbour's house."

"Yes, I remember you."

"How are you feeling?"

"I don't know. I feel so numb. I can't believe what's happened."

"I'm not surprised. You've been through a terrible ordeal. I'm very sorry for your loss."

He waited a moment to allow time for his sentiment to be appropriately received.

"I'm afraid I need to ask you some more questions. Is that alright, Mrs Heikkinen?"

"Yes. It's fine. And, please call me Petra."

Although lucid, the young woman's voice was distant. Topias surmised that she must still be dazed, in shock, and probably exhausted. Not surprising, as she had scarcely slept. She would probably just go through the motions, answering his questions, but in a detached, monotonic way.

Her fragility was more pronounced due to the previously flowing long hair tied tightly back from her face. Topias thought it might cascade to her waist if loosened.

He sympathised strongly with her condition; still, he needed to get answers to his questions. In this situation, it was better to obtain them while everything was fresh in her mind rather than dragging things out later, with facts possibly adjusted for hindsight. So, the interview continued.

"Would you like some coffee or water?"

Topias had noticed her grip on the cup had become noticeably tighter since they started talking, and it was now buckling under the pressure.

"No. I'm fine, thank you," Petra responded.

"I realise this is difficult and painful for you, but please, talk me through yesterday evening's events, up to and including the moment you found your husband's body on the terrace."

Petra proceeded to outline what had been a pleasant winter's Saturday: walking in downtown Helsinki, getting coffee, browsing in boutiques, having lunch, and then later: cross-country skiing in Nuuksio park, eating pizza, and finally, a sauna. She added that it had been a busy but enjoyable day, the best in some time.

Petra volunteered that it was customary for them to take a sauna together most evenings, especially since her husband had lovingly created their perfect sanctuary.

On this occasion, she explained that although a sauna was planned, she hadn't felt like spending long there and had gone to bed shortly afterwards. This wasn't unusual, as she didn't share her husband's passion for the practice quite as much as he did.

Once comfortable in bed, she had spent an hour reading a book, and after that, with no sign of Tommi, she had fallen asleep.

"Did you find it unusual that your husband didn't come to

bed last night?" Topias asked.

"Well, yes, and no. I was expecting Tommi to come to bed, but it wouldn't be the first time he spent two hours in the sauna and then came to bed later, sometimes much later if he had a few beers. Sometimes he would wake me up, and sometimes not."

"Why would he wake you up?"

"Well, you know, to be close to me," she squirmed slightly in her chair.

Topias detected a faint smile, quickly disappearing when she remembered the current circumstances.

"So, you went to sleep and woke up early in the morning. What caused you to awaken?"

"I don't know. I remember it was ice-cold in the room."

Petra shook her head and shuddered, apparently trying to recall why the temperature had been so low.

"So, no noise? No shouting? Just the feeling of cold?"

"Yes, that's all."

Topias asked what happened next and after that. He gradually established a precise story sufficient for a statement. As was his habit, he absent-mindedly chewed his pen while preparing his notes, which would be typed up for her to read and sign later.

"Did you used to smoke?" Petra inquired.

"Oh, yes." The question surprised Topias, and he put the pen down for a moment. "Sorry. An annoying habit, I know."

He detected another fleeting smile and proceeded down other avenues of enquiry.

"Do you or Tommi own a gun?"

"No. He wasn't a hunter or anything, so we didn't need one. Of course, he knew how to use one due to his national service." Then, her voice grew more urgent, "Why? Is that what happened to him? Was he shot?"

Tears began to roll down her already tear-stained cheeks, and she visibly tensed in front of him.

"Our initial inspection revealed that he was shot with a firearm, but we haven't confirmed it was the actual cause of death. It does seem probable, though. I'm sorry."

Petra's gaze dropped to the floor, having run out of words.

Topias offered her a tissue, which she accepted with a glimmer of appreciation.

"You didn't hear a shot?"

"No."

Topias left a space for her to breathe and then continued.

"How long have you been married?"

"Almost three years now."

"Happily?"

"Yes. Like most couples, we have, rather we had…"

Topias noticed that Petra corrected herself to the past tense.

"…our ups and downs, but everything was fine. We did okay."

The last sentence was spoken like a statement. It was a kind of reinforcement about the status of the couple's relationship.

"Did you or your husband have any enemies, or has he ever been in trouble with the police or any other authority?"

"No, and no."

"Do you know if anything has been taken from the house?"

"No, there hasn't. At least, I don't think so."

"How well do you know your neighbour? The one who helped you: Stefan Paikkala."

"Not very well. Only to say 'Hello'. Sometimes we chat when Stefan is on the terrace; we both like being outside, you see."

"Did your husband know him?"

"In the same way, I think."

"Did he visit your house much?"

"Never. Well, maybe only to drop over a parcel delivered to the wrong house, that kind of thing. We were just neighbours, and we talked a few times, but that was an over-the-fence thing, nothing else."

Topias found it encouraging that she was now opening up and volunteering extra information. He found her apparent denial about a relationship between her and the neighbour interesting. Knowing how to interview people, he temporarily switched his line of questioning. He could return to the topic later.

"What did your husband do for a living?"

"He worked on building projects, buying materials and arranging transport, and that sort of thing. Tommi worked mainly on apartment blocks, but sometimes other things too."

"How long had he been doing that?"

"About ten years. Before that, he worked as a carpenter; at least, that was his trade."

"Who did he work for?"

"The company's name is...?"

She pondered this for a moment.

"…Advantage Asunto. They're based in Helsinki."

"And you, Petra? What do you do?"

"I was a Human Resources Coordinator in Helsinki but was made redundant last year when the company had some problems. I couldn't get another job in the same field, so I decided to return to university to change my career. Now, I study law."

"An interesting area," commented Topias.

Petra nodded.

He asked a few more questions and then, deciding to let her take a break, made for the door.

"Detective Superintendent?"

"Yes," answered Topias.

"I'm afraid. Am I safe here?"

"Completely, Petra. Don't worry; we'll look after you. And by the way, please call me Topias."

"Kiitos," Petra thanked him meekly.

On his way out, he asked Saana to bring her fresh coffee, water and a sandwich; he hadn't finished with Petra yet.

STEFAN

Topias strode up the corridor and checked the window of the adjacent interview room. There sat the neighbour he'd met: Stefan Paikkala.

He walked in, re-introduced himself, established some basic facts for the voice recorder, and then proceeded to the areas of most interest.

"What time did you see Tommi out on the deck?"

"It was about half-past ten, I suppose. He was leaning over the back fence, and I assumed he'd just been in the sauna, as Tommi often did. He had a can of beer, which also wasn't unusual. I was doing the same thing myself at the time."

"Was he actually holding the can of beer?"

"It was in his hand. So, I guess so."

"Did he say anything to you?"

"No, I greeted him, but he ignored me."

"Was that normal?"

"Well, not really; I mean, he could be a bit moody sometimes and wasn't the most sociable person in the world."

"Was he moving when you saw him?"

"Moving? I don't think so. He was simply leaning there."

"Was his position the same as when you found him early this morning?"

"I really couldn't say. It may have been about the same. Perhaps the angle looked different, but I suppose it would from my terrace."

"Is that a 'yes' or a 'no'?"

"Well, he wasn't dead then, so maybe he was more upright or alive-looking. It was hard to tell."

"How do you know Tommi wasn't dead then?"

"Oh. I don't. I just assume he wasn't. Everything seemed okay, I mean, it was a normal Saturday night, and I was getting some air on the terrace when I saw him. I often saw him there."

"Did he usually speak to you?"

"Usually, yes."

"Usually, or always?"

Stefan blew out through his teeth.

"Okay, almost always, but as I said, he wasn't that sociable. He had ignored me before, and if he spoke, 'Moi' was as far as it usually went."

"So, just to confirm, he didn't say anything to you that evening, not even a 'Moi'?"

Topias pressed him on this.

"No. As I said before, I called over, but there was no reply." Stefan lowered his voice as if someone were listening, "As I said, he could be a bit miserable sometimes, so I just let it slide."

"Okay. Thank you."

Topias made some notes, more to unsettle his interviewee

than anything else.

"What was your relationship with his wife, Petra?"

"I don't know. We didn't have much of a relationship. Friendly neighbours, I suppose. She was sociable, talked a lot, and spent much more time outside than Tommi, so we chatted sometimes."

"What did you talk about?"

"This and that. Nothing special, to pass the time of day, you know. She had a friendly smile, and it was always a pleasure to see or talk to her. I don't feel that Tommi talked to her much about the wider world, so we enjoyed each other's company. I also felt that his obsession with the sauna bothered her a bit. Everyone likes a sauna, but to just do work and then stay in the sauna every evening? That was probably boring for Petra."

"Do you find her attractive?"

"Well, yes. Don't you?"

Topias ignored the question.

"Did you visit each other?"

"No, we weren't that close. We weren't even friends; we just talked across the fence."

"So, this friendship never went any further?"

"How do you mean?"

Topias raised his eyebrows.

"Oh no. We didn't have that kind of relationship, and not like 'that', anyway. Petra was married, and I'm recently divorced and not looking to get into anything complicated, that's for sure."

The last words were emphatic.

Suddenly, something else entered Stefan's mind.

"I'm not a suspect, am I?"

"This is all standard police procedure in these types of cases. We must talk to everyone involved and establish their relationship with the victim. No one is a suspect at this point."

Stefan seemed to relax a little.

Topias continued a similar line of questioning as with Petra. It didn't reveal anything new, so he thanked Stefan for his cooperation, promised to return shortly, and adjourned to the kitchen.

The conversation had been straightforward, and determined that Stefan probably hadn't witnessed the murder, that's if he was telling the truth. The questions relating to Petra received similar answers to those she had given. However, the interview left him with an odd feeling that there was something there, perhaps some chemistry between them. Still, he couldn't pinpoint whether anything more than being neighbours had taken place. It could raise the possibility of motive and establish Stefan as a suspect if it did.

Topias was considering this while standing in the kitchen when in walked the accompanying officer, Saana.

"Same for me, please."

Topias obliged and filled the mug held in her outstretched hand.

"What do you think of Petra?" he asked, keen to get a second opinion, as he'd noticed Saana observing her intently.

"She seems genuine enough, and her story concurs with the evidence we've found to date. Not sure if she's holding something back, though. I don't know if it's just me, but her answers seem quite carefully measured."

"Hmm. Yes, I agree. Petra's story matches the neighbour's

version. Maybe it is too close. I want to have a clearer idea of the time of death before I make any conclusions. Stefan seems to think Tommi was alive earlier when leaning against the back fence, but that may not have been so. He may have already been dead when Petra was in bed reading. She probably thought her husband was alive and enjoying the sauna and the terrace. I'm also not sure how well Petra and Stefan knew each other. There's something there. Let's see."

"Do you suspect her or the neighbour? Or both?"

"It certainly wouldn't be the first time two people have had an affair, and the partner finds out, resulting in some violent act. Perhaps even one or both plotted to rid themselves of the husband, so they could be together. Let's keep an open mind for now. In the meantime, we'll hang onto them here until the on-site forensic investigation is complete. I want to know if anything interesting shows up. Perhaps they were frequently in each other's houses, or someone has traces of blood or gun residue on them."

Saana nodded.

"I'll ask Ina when their clothes will be tested. Should I release them when we've finished?"

"Provided it all comes up negative, yes. I need to get some sleep now; otherwise, I won't function for the rest of the day. If anything arises that looks suspicious, you'll call me on my mobile, yes?"

"Count on it. I hope you get some rest. See you later."

Saana smiled at him and left the room.

Topias drained his coffee, returned to his desk to pick up his bag, and walked to the carpark.

During his car journey, he called Saana to request an inventory of the house contents to be cross-checked with Petra to see if anything was missing. It hadn't looked like a burglary, but it was a possibility.

Driving home, he pushed on through the snow. It had been a long day, yet again, and he was looking forward to feeling the heat of his own sauna.

SALONEN

Immo Salonen stood up from the desk in his office and stretched. His back was bothering him as he'd been sitting upright since early that morning. However, much was to be done that day, and the papers on his desk wouldn't wait.

While taking a break, he surveyed his modest office and wondered how impressive an office should be sought for the future.

His current facility sat within a large rectangular edifice, typical of those surrounding it. Like many of that era, it had been constructed with concrete blocks during the post-war period. It emitted a sanitary feel with an accompanying whiff of mould from its structure. Immo felt the building was soviet in its design and didn't care for it, but the lease met his budget.

Things would change in future. He planned to work somewhere very different from his current location. His place of business would make people gasp when they walked into its grand foyer, knowing they were in the presence of someone important. It would be the type of place that oozed success and guaranteed future business.

And successful it would be, thanks to a deal of a lifetime that was just about to be confirmed. Salonen was currently engaged in its details and was reviewing a contract before attending the lawyer's office later that day.

The terms of the agreement would enable his company to

develop large swathes of land on the outskirts of Helsinki. This was not just an opportunity for him to build another small apartment block or office building, as he was used to. No, this area was destined to become an entirely new residential area of the city, with access via a grand suspension bridge to a campus of new corporate offices.

The site would have entertainment, shopping and travel facilities, all within a short distance. It was to be the perfect site for up-scaling technology companies and those working there.

It was named 'Uusi Satama' (New Harbour). Undoubtedly, the development would grow to be one of the most popular places in the city. What was even better, it would be his company, Advantage Asunto, that would build it.

Salonen sighed with satisfaction as he looked out of the window at his current project, a rapidly ascending apartment block containing twenty-four apartments. Together with the adjacent building, it was the saviour of his company and the stepping stone to his dream. He had been fortunate to have met his benefactors, although he now regarded them with disdain.

The process had been a long and costly one. It had also involved more people than he was comfortable with; too many mouths that might chat openly after a few glasses of wine. The journey hadn't just been about polite lunches with politicians and council employees; there had been some greasing of the palms of critical decision-makers too.

Construction was a competitive market, and gaining a contract in Helsinki was often more about who you knew than anything else. If you didn't have connections, the only way to cut through this was to provide a sufficient incentive. Thanks to hard work and promises of wealth, he had secured the right connections - those who could influence one of the most significant contracts in Helsinki to land in his lap.

From one point of view, Salonen was elated about the

deal. From another perspective, it annoyed him to pay such large bribes to those who were already wealthy and influential people. Those who were so high and mighty, lunching in the best restaurants and living in fine houses, with fine boats languishing in the harbour for use on fine Sundays. Still, he tried to put this to the back of his mind and focus on himself. Such costs were necessary in his business, just like the purchase of bricks or cement.

For a change, he couldn't wait to celebrate with his new 'friends' that evening. Immo Salonen would finally be one of them instead of trying to ingratiate himself with handouts.

He smiled as he made more coffee before returning to his task.

◆ ◆ ◆

Topias awoke that morning to an ear-splitting sound from outside.

Is that drilling? he wondered, his head still cloudy with sleep.

He sat upright. The noise stopped. Then it started again.

"Argh, come on. Really?"

The sound rose and fell, from loud to extremely loud. He made his way over to the window and peeked through the blinds. A team of orange-jacketed workers were outside, having cleared the snow, apparently drilling a hole in the road.

Shaking his head, baffled, Topias walked down the stairs from his bedroom into the living area and opened the blinds to see better.

The scene in his small backyard and the space beyond was one of deepest winter. It was March, but it had been snowing since early November and was the whitest season he could recall. Everywhere was carpeted in at least twenty centimetres of snow that morning.

Why, then, was there drilling in the road outside? This activity usually waited until at least the first signs of spring, so maybe there was some urgent problem they were fixing.

These days there was always construction of some kind going on around every corner of the city. Yet, its population didn't seem to change much. Topias could never understand who lived in all the new apartment blocks or drove on the new roads.

The drilling began again. Topias resolved to find out what was happening, but later on.

First, he needed breakfast, especially coffee. After putting slices of bread in the toaster, Topias took some cheese from the fridge while he added a few heaped spoons of coffee into the machine, added water and switched it on.

With his breakfast in progress, accompanied by the satisfying blub-blubbing of the coffee machine, Topias went to the bathroom.

He switched on the light and winced at his reflection in the mirror: it was that of a tired middle-aged man. He was sure he didn't usually look like this, but the current work schedule had taken its toll. The previously tidy, brown hair, streaked with maturity, had evolved into an untidy mop of greyness. He also had two days of stubble, okay for a weekend but not for the police station. In addition, his ordinarily bright eyes looked lifeless, apparently having used all their energy to hold up the heavy bags beneath. Topias decided he looked and felt much older than his age of forty-six.

"God help me," he muttered, staring at himself with a forlorn expression.

At least he'd slept a few hours of unbroken sleep; that

was something. He had also stopped smoking some months back, which had been no mean feat. And his diet had slightly improved, except for the quantity of wine.

Clearly, he needed to do some self-renovation this morning: a shower, a shave, go for a haircut and get some more sleep later. He had plenty of hours banked, so why not use them to recover instead of cashing in the overtime?

But first, coffee.

Topias returned to the kitchen, poured himself a mug, and sat on a high stool at the island in the centre to check his phone messages. His wife had insisted on this feature when the kitchen was remodelled, which cost him a small fortune. He had been reluctant to splash out at the time, but bizarrely, this place had become his favourite perch.

Checking his watch, it was 8.10 am, and the day shift had begun. There were already several messages on his phone relating to the previous night's suspected murder. The first one he read was a text message from Saana.

Hei Torikka, Results from the tests were clear for Stefan Paikkala and Petra Heikkinen. Nothing unusual at either residence. Traces of both were in each other's houses. Still, as that could have just happened, we've released them: Paikkala to home and Heikkinen to her sister's apartment in Vantaa (I have the address). The victim's body has been removed, but his wife (understandably) doesn't want to return home. I hope you slept some, Saana.

Topias nodded; nothing unexpected there. It would have been conceivable for there to be a relationship between the neighbour and the wife next door, but the suspicion seemed unlikely after their interviews. He wasn't going to dismiss it yet, though. They would both remain suspects until proven otherwise.

Noting the text's signatory, he thought about Saana for a

moment. Topias had worked with her a few times before and was always impressed. She was keen and optimistic. He had already earmarked her to work for him again, either on a case or in a permanent position. He would certainly keep her in mind: good people were hard to find these days.

A second text message was from his bank: it seemed he'd forgotten to pay an invoice from his electricity company. He cast an eye over the pile of papers and envelopes on the kitchen counter and resolved to go through them at the weekend.

Next, he checked his emails. The first was from Ina, from the forensics team.

Topias. Info as requested: Cause of death—a gunshot wound from the front penetrated the victim's heart from around five metres. A standard bullet from a 9mm calibre pistol—no other notable findings. More detailed info to follow from the post-mortem exam. Ina

Topias looked across the backyard, pondering this update.

Just five metres away? Could Tommi have known his killer due to the close proximity of the shot? On the other hand, it would've been dark further toward the forest, as the light didn't reach so far. But he was leaning against the fence, and the shot came from the front.

Topias made a mental note to check how far the light shone from the terrace beyond the fence and how much cover the trees provided. He reasoned it must be enough to make out if someone was there or not, even at night, as the person would have to stand there and take aim for at least a couple of seconds. There may also have been accompanying sounds.

Perhaps it was someone who had a justifiable reason to be there. Maybe someone who the victim knew more intimately, for example? That certainly keeps his wife and neighbour in the frame.

Topias scrolled through a few other updates and bulletins.

He came across another message sent by Petri Karlsson, another member of his team, who had picked up his request to check the victim's phone and financial details. It seemed he'd already been hard at work.

Torikka. Regarding mobile and financial records. Principal calls to Tommi's mobile were from his wife, his bank: Nordic Savings, and suppliers of building materials (currently following up). Additionally, random calls were from withheld numbers, although these may have been sales calls. His bank account was healthy—2500-3500€/month deposited into his account monthly (awaiting account records as it's a Swedish bank). More info later.

PS. Heikkinen had a criminal record. A robbery (without violence) charge imprisoned him for two years (released three years ago). Also, an accusation of handling stolen goods arose but was dropped due to insufficient evidence.

Topias read through the email twice and pondered the sender and its contents. He liked Petri; he was always efficient and an excellent asset to his team: sharp as a blade. He considered the new information carefully.

So, the victim had a record, but his wife said he'd never been in trouble. Maybe she didn't know? After all, it happened before they were married, perhaps before they even met each other, at least the prison sentence anyway. Hmm. No financial issues there either, although I'll be interested to hear if anything arises from Tommi or Petra's banking records.

He replied briefly to several more messages about other cases, deleted others, and began his planned bathroom schedule.

◆ ◆ ◆

Immo Salonen left his car in the underground carpark near the Central Helsinki Railway Station. He jogged up the stairs with a spring in his step; this was a good day.

As daylight appeared, he left the exit and looked upward at the iconic stone men on the station's edifice, carved from granite, holding their lanterns and seemingly guarding the centre of Helsinki.

Something like that would be perfect to distinguish my new development from everything else. It should be much more than another cookie-cutter set of office and apartment blocks. I want to leave a legacy for the city. I'll have to put some thought into it.

Striding across the square, Salonen turned left. He made his way up an inclining street to the offices of Happonen & Aarnio, the project's lawyers, housed in a grand pale-yellow building that stood adjacent to a hotel.

On arrival, Salonen pressed the buzzer for entry.

After announcing himself, there was a 'ping', signalling the door was now unlocked. He entered and strode to a mahogany reception desk to be greeted by a young woman in a dark grey suit with blonde hair in plaits.

"Welcome, Mr Salonen. It's nice to see you again. Please take a seat in our waiting area. Mr Happonen will be here presently."

Salonen nodded and recognised his own lawyer, seated in a suitably expensive-looking distressed leather armchair and poring over an armful of documents.

"Everything in order, Marko?" he asked.

"Oh, Good Morning, Immo. Yes, everything seems fine to me. Just a matter of putting pen to paper and signing it now."

"Excellent," Salonen replied, making himself comfortable in a coordinating green leather sofa. Almost as soon as he did so, the receptionist arrived and beckoned them to follow.

They entered an old lift that creaked laboriously upward to

the top floor. Salonen secretly approved of the law firm's offices, although he would never mention it.

The building was traditional, in the Byzantine-Russian style, and had been tastefully improved with high-quality furniture and lighting. It was a perfect blend of new meets old, a mode Salonen aspired to in his own life. Although, he begrudged the law firm for having it.

Typical lawyers. Never short of money. Salonen complained inwardly, recalling how much this transaction had cost in legal fees to date.

Eventually, the lift reached the appropriate floor and groaned to a halt, where the two men were shown into a lobby.

Here, another equally polished receptionist was waiting for them. She immediately rose and took them through to a conference room, where she poured coffee, offered pastries and assured them that Mr Happonen would arrive momentarily.

Salonen didn't take a seat; he had something on his mind. Now it was time to sign the final papers. This caused him to be apprehensive of anything that might go wrong at the last minute. Instead, he occupied himself, taking in the view over the city's rooftops.

"They are nice offices, aren't they? I wouldn't mind an upgrade to something like this myself," commented Salonen's lawyer.

He regarded Marko, nodded and smiled but didn't comment. Marko also had superior offices to Salonen.

A few minutes later, Mr Frederik Happonen himself entered the room with a flourish, flanked by two more lawyers, one male and one female, in matching expensive suits together with yet another receptionist or personal assistant trailing behind.

She must be the assistant to the personal assistant, Salonen mused to himself.

It was the first time he had actually met one of the lawyers that the law firm was named after, having only dealt with one of the two lawyers who sat on either side of Happonen: him being his primary contact, an Englishman named Peter Oliver.

They sat down at the table where coffee and cinnamon buns were served, during which the representatives of the City of Helsinki arrived.

A round of hand-shaking and pleasantries followed, with some bland small talk focused on the wintry conditions.

After the informalities were completed, it was time for business. The group reviewed the contract, page by page, clause by clause. This task confirmed that nothing new had been surreptitiously or unknowingly added to the document since the previous exhaustive review.

The agreement summarised that Advantage Asunto would become the sole developer of the area known as Uusi Satama (New Harbour). It would initially receive the sum of forty million euros from the council to prepare the ground. Salonen's company would then appoint sub-contractors to enable them to develop the approved infrastructure and buildings.

The first phase would consist of a hotel and leisure area with ten office blocks and thirteen apartment blocks. A shopping centre and transport facilities would follow as part of phase two.

At a conservative estimate, the sale and lease of the buildings and apartments would exceed six hundred and thirty million euros. Advantage Asunto's profits were expected to be fourteen per cent for the six-year project—over 88 million euros. After distribution to his new investors and payment of relevant taxes, Salonen expected a net gain to his bank account of at least 20 million euros.

Salonen thought of the costs already incurred to reach this point, including some expensive bribes that totalled five million euros. He begrudged this; however, it now seemed outstanding value for money on balance.

He accepted the proffered pen, signed at the appropriate place, and then painstakingly initialled each page. As he did so, the document was circulated among the people at the table. It took some time; however, after fifteen minutes, the deal was done, and everyone shook hands. All those seated around the table smiled in appreciation at each party's beneficial financial return on 'Uusi Satama', not least Immo Salonen.

With the pressing business done, the next stop for Salonen was to drive to Haaga, where he had pressing construction matters to handle. He had to get his other work out of the way as quickly as possible before focusing his energies on his prize project.

MEETING

A refreshed and considerably better-presented detective arrived at the address where the murder victim's wife, Petra Heikkinen, was temporarily staying. He had showered, shaved and freshly dressed in chinos, a white collared shirt, and a comfortable blue jacket. He felt much better now, perhaps even a few years younger.

Topias rang the bell and straightened up to his full height, ready to greet whoever might answer the door. He was looking forward to meeting Petra and asking questions that would hopefully lead him in the right direction.

The door opened, and he was surprised to find the woman herself in the doorway.

"Good morning, Petra." he greeted her, trying to find the right balance between sympathy and pleasantry in his tone.

"Good morning."

Petra uttered the greeting hoarsely with the meekest of smiles.

Topias couldn't help but notice she had applied some subtle makeup. Whether it was the shock subsiding, the applied cosmetics, or both, she looked decidedly healthier and, if possible, even easier on the eye. He felt a sudden pang of guilt at thinking of her like that in her current situation and state of mind, mentally chiding himself for being unprofessional.

"May I come in? I have a couple of questions, if that's alright?"

"Yes, of course. I'm alone, and no one else is here; my sister and brother-in-law are at work."

Petra invited him in, and they made their way into the living room, a comfortable and cosy space. It was the kind of place where one felt immediately at home, although probably in better circumstances. She bade him take a seat and offered coffee, which he gratefully accepted.

While she was pouring the drinks, Topias took in the room around him, first noticing a wooden cabinet lined with photographs in silver frames. One was of Petra and another woman about the same age, probably taken a few years ago. They were smiling gleefully into the camera while holding up glasses of a blue cocktail. It looked as if it had been taken abroad, judging by the range of exotic-looking flowers in the background.

At that moment, Petra arrived with the coffee and handed Topias a mug. As she did so, she noticed him looking at the photograph.

"That was taken in Rhodes, during a holiday in Greece. That's my sister, Terhi. This apartment is her place, and those were happier times."

"Was it taken long ago?"

"A little over three years, I think, just before I met my husband."

Topias noticed that there were no photographs of Tommi on display. Still, not everyone displayed pictures of relatives in their living room, especially those not blood-related. They may even have been removed after his demise, although the reverse was usually true in bereaved families.

"Thank you for seeing me, and please accept my deepest

sympathies once again," Topias expressed solemnly.

"Kiitos, Detective Superintendent," she replied. "I appreciate that."

"Topias," he reminded her.

He studied her expression for a moment. The upset from the night before had evolved into a distant melancholy, some improvement from before. The shock had been replaced by sadness. The eye contact was also different this time—she hadn't wanted to look at anyone directly for too long the last time he had seen her. Now, her eyes were locked straight into his.

"Let's begin, shall we? Firstly, may I ask if you know anything about your husband's criminal record?"

Topias thought he'd chosen his words and tone as delicately as possible, but they didn't achieve the desired effect.

"His criminal record? He doesn't have one. To my knowledge, he's never been in trouble with the police; why would he? Maybe a speeding fine or two, like most people, but that's about it."

Treading carefully now, Topias continued.

"I think I'd better explain. A few years before your husband met you, he robbed a house. There was no one there at the time, and he didn't steal much; however, he was arrested, convicted and sentenced to three years imprisonment, from which he was released slightly earlier. Mr Heikkinen was suspected of another crime shortly after his release, but that wasn't proven. Petra, all this happened a few years before you were married."

Topias let her process this for a minute before continuing, but Petra interrupted him before he could speak again.

"Are you sure? I wasn't aware of anything, and certainly not that he'd been in prison. He just wasn't the type. No, I don't believe it; you're mistaken."

She was becoming indignant. Topias noticed the eye contact had dropped, and the rug on the floor was now her primary object of interest. He'd seen her do that before. He also noted that she now talked about Tommi in the past tense. His job was to notice things like that, details that could give someone away and point the finger at a potentially guilty party.

To calm her down, he changed his line of questioning.

"When did you meet your husband, Petra?"

"About three years ago, as I mentioned. A year later, we were married. Everything happened quickly. We were both quite similar, and everything was easy; things just fell into place."

She paused for a few seconds. Topias could tell she was still thinking about the previous question, so he gave her some space. He knew that silence was one of the most valuable techniques in such interviews; people would often fill an uncomfortable gap with helpful information.

Petra continued, referring back to his previous point.

"I don't understand. Why wouldn't Tommi tell me that he had a prison record?"

"I don't know why he didn't. But from experience, it's not usually something people are proud of or volunteer information about. He may have thought it might damage your relationship somehow, and as his crime had been in the past, and duly paid for, maybe he thought it wasn't relevant to mention it."

Topias waited a few more moments before asking his question.

"Would it have affected your relationship, Petra?"

He wasn't sure about that last question, but they seemed to be getting on well, and it would be interesting to hear the response.

"I don't know. Maybe, but I may also have understood if it was something in the past. Anyone can make a mistake, especially when they're younger. I still find it extremely difficult to believe, making me wonder what else Tommi was hiding?"

"Yes, of course. I understand it's a shock, especially so soon after your husband's death."

He paused.

"Have you ever been in trouble with the law yourself?"

"No, and I'm sure you can check that."

He nodded. He knew this anyway but was interested in how the woman might react. He took a sip of his coffee and waited a few moments again. He knew he couldn't rush these types of conversations.

"I'm sorry I have to ask these questions. It's just procedure. We want to find out who did this to your husband and punish them for it."

Petra nodded.

Topias continued to probe gently, one step at a time, asking about friends, family and associates. As he talked, Petra mentioned the occasional name, and he compiled a shortlist of people to speak to, hoping to uncover something that might identify a motive for the murder of the woman's husband.

After completing the questioning, at least for the moment, Petra raised her head and looked him in the eyes again. Topias could tell she had reached a tipping point, and it was time to conclude.

"Do you have any more questions, Topias?"

He could see her eyes welling up, but she bravely resisted shedding tears.

"No, not for the moment. Will you be staying here with your sister for a while?"

"I don't know. I think so. I can't go back home."

Topias nodded in agreement.

"Here's my card with my mobile number, just in case you remember something. Don't worry; I'll see myself out. I appreciate your cooperation."

Topias bowed out of the room and left through the front entrance, where he walked into the chilly air, carefully closing the door behind him. He drew a deep breath, exhaled slowly, and shook his head at the young woman's plight.

As he drove away from the house, he continued to think about Petra Heikkinen.

Having met her three times, clearly, she had made progress since that fateful night. She seemed strong enough to cope with such a blow as the violent death of her husband or at least outwardly so.

Petra was somewhat disarming due to her doll-like beauty, but he couldn't let that interfere with his judgement; things were not always as they seemed. Until she was eliminated from his list, she was a suspect. The perpetrator was sometimes the spouse in these situations. However, at this stage, he was inclined to believe her.

Topias dismissed her from his thoughts as he would be fully occupied the rest of the day. The next job was to visit Tommi's employer and the list of contacts provided by Petra.

INTERVIEW

Tommi's employer, and the Director of Advantage Asunto, was Immo Salonen.

When Topias called him, he agreed to meet that day. He advised that he wasn't in the main office at the moment but out on-site; hence the meeting would take place at a construction site in the Haaga area of Helsinki.

Topias drove through what was pleasantly light traffic for the time of day. As he did so, the sun broke through the clouds and provided a welcome respite from the continuous snowfall of recent days. Blue sky appeared in patches between the clouds, and the week began to look promising, making him feel more upbeat. He turned on the radio to listen to music.

At that moment, the phone rang through the car's loudspeakers, and he pressed the button to receive the call.

"Hei Petri," Topias greeted the caller enthusiastically, noticing the name on the phone's display.

"Hei Topias, how's your day going?"

"Good enough. I've just met the murder victim's wife and am now on my way to Haaga to visit his ex-employer."

"Ah, good. I hope it'll be a productive trip. I have an update for you on the case."

"Go ahead."

"The bullet casing was found a few metres from the fence. It was from the type of gun already identified, wih nothing unusual about it. Just the one bullet, used at close range. The snow was deep where it was found, so it had to be gently scraped away in case something else was underneath, hence the delay."

"Kiitos. Was there anything else found?"

"Just some impressions from what looks like a boot under the top layer of fresh snow. Quite a common print, though. I don't think it'll help us much, but they'll try and get a match for it in forensics."

"Okay, you never know. Anything else?"

"I have an appointment at the bank this afternoon, so I should have more information on the detail of the victim's accounts. I was thinking of going back seven years, as the criminal conviction was six years ago, just in case there's some history, and that should more than cover it."

"Sounds good. Do the same with the wife's account as well. Call me when you've retrieved and analysed the information, would you? I'll probably be out all day, talking to people."

"Will do. Enjoy."

Petri rang off.

Topias consulted his GPS and noted he was a few minutes away from the site. He pulled off the highway and marvelled at the number of newly-constructed apartment blocks in the area. Each was quite similar, with the occasional splash of colour or additional glass decoration to differentiate one from the other. The city was growing, and the commuter belt was expanding ever deeper into the forest.

After a short drive, he approached one particular construction site with an enormous billboard outside, promising 'modern, bright apartments with excellent transport connections'. He pulled up in a small carpark, roughly hewn from the surrounding rock, and exited the car, cursing as he stepped straight into deep snow.

No wonder the parking space was available, he thought, as he shook his leg to shake off the offending material.

Topias waded out of the small snowdrift and walked to a pre-fabricated rectangular mobile office across the carpark. Assuming this was the place, he knocked on the door, simultaneously opening it. This didn't seem the kind of place where anyone would stand on ceremony.

Inside, the temporary office was divided in two. The first part contained a large trestle table covered in plans and papers, while two desks at right angles sat at the far side. Both desks were currently occupied. One by a younger man, concentrating intensely on his computer screen. At the other sat an older man wearing a smart grey suit, who Topias thought seemed a bit overdressed for a building site. The man looked up from his papers and watched his approach with interest. As Topias neared, he couldn't help noticing the sizeable expensive-looking gold watch loosely attached to his wrist.

The man raised his eyebrows to query the visitor's name and purpose, so Topias introduced himself.

"Ah, yes. Just give me a moment, please," the man replied.

After tapping his keyboard for a few moments, he swivelled to face the detective.

"Nice to meet you. My name's Immo Salonen, and I assume you are the police officer who called? And a detective, no less. What can I do for Helsinki's finest today?" he asked.

"Thank you for making time for me today. Is there somewhere we can talk in private?" Topias asked, eyeing the younger man nearby. "My questions relate to one of your employees and are of a rather sensitive nature."

"Of course. But here in the office is fine. Take a seat." Then, he said to the younger man, "Ilkka, please give us a few minutes."

The younger man rose from his desk, wrapped himself in his coat and scarf, and departed the hut as soon as his shoes could carry him.

After he left, Topias began his questions.

"Do you have an employee named Tommi Heikkinen?"

"I may have. You understand I have quite many employees, some permanent and some flexible. Give me a moment, and I'll check on the list."

A few seconds of tapping and scrolling on his keyboard followed, combined with the hum of an unrecognisable melody.

"Ah yes, here we are. Yes, Heikkinen. He's a contract worker and has been with us for three years. According to the system, he hasn't checked in for work today as planned, but it might not be updated yet. What's this all about, by the way? Do you know where he is?"

"I have some bad news. I'm afraid Tommi Heikkinen is dead."

"Oh, dear. I'm sorry to hear that. When did this happen?"

"We believe between Saturday night and early Sunday morning."

"How unfortunate. Now I think about it, I do know of him. I didn't know the man well, but I recall meeting him a few times. He did some buying for the company when we needed him and other jobs around the construction sites, too, I think. What happened to him?"

"He was murdered while at home."

"Oh my god. That's terrible. Did he have a family?"

"Yes, a wife, no children."

"I'll have my assistant organise some flowers and send them to his widow."

"I'm sure that'll be appreciated. May I ask you a few more questions?"

"Yes, of course. I'm not sure if I can be of any help, but go ahead."

Topias asked his questions and confirmed Tommi's dates of employment. He also checked if the man had any close colleagues or people he didn't get on with.

"Not that I know about, but as I said, I didn't really know him. From memory, he was an average employee. You know, a good worker, friendly enough to be social when needed, but like most people here, just here for the money, wanting to get home to their homes or families at the end of the day. Construction isn't a calling for most people. It's usually just a way of making money to live."

They discussed Tommi's working location. It appeared he was mobile, working between building sites, visiting suppliers and contractors, and helping with carpentry and general duties. He seemed anonymous to all intents and purposes, just doing what was required and then disappearing.

"Is there someone I can talk to who might have known Mr Heikkinen better?" Topias asked.

"Yes, I believe Arto may be able to help you. He's the Foreman here, and he's worked at some of our other sites over the years. He may have known Heikkinen better or know someone who does. You'll find him around here somewhere."

"This seems a good business these days. I passed many

apartment blocks on the way. All yours?" Topias asked casually.

"Unfortunately, not, but this one is, and the one next to it. Construction has its moments when the risks work out, but it doesn't always go that way."

Topias nodded.

"Well, thanks for your time," and he left.

Salonen nodded in return and went back to his laptop.

As Topias was leaving the building, he met the young man who had obediently left them alone, named Ilkka, waiting patiently outside.

Topias introduced himself and explained he was looking for Arto.

"Please, take this," he said as he offered Topias his white hard hat. "I think he's over there by the cement truck."

Topias made his way over to the building and found Arto quickly. He was a man visibly in authority, holding a clipboard, pointing to things that needed attention and directing workers from place to place.

"Excuse me. Arto?"

"Yes, that's me. Who's asking?"

"I'm Detective Superintendent Torikka. Do you have a few minutes to answer some questions?"

"Sure. Things are quite busy around here, but I can spare you five. What's it about?"

"The death of Tommi Heikkinen."

As Topias stated the fact, a nearby digger started up and ploughed into a massive pile of sand.

"What?"

"The death of Tommi Heikkinen," Topias said in a raised voice.

"Oh, that's terrible. I had no idea. Listen, it's too noisy to talk here. You'd better come this way."

He led Topias into the apartment building's entrance and onwards into what would likely be the lobby.

"That's better; it's quieter in here," he said as he closed a temporary door.

"Yes, thanks. Look, I'll get straight to the point. I can see things are busy here. How well did you know Mr Heikkinen?"

"Tommi? I knew him a little, the same as most other guys here. We spoke when we needed to and occasionally drank coffee together. I also spoke to him during occasional after-work sessions at the local bar over a few beers."

"Did you meet up recently?"

"Yeh. Just last week. At another construction site, in Vantaa, where we'd been subcontracted to help another company for two days. We discussed a late delivery of bricks he was trying to resolve. It stuck in my mind because Mr Salonen was going nuts about it, or something else. That was it."

"And did you notice anything unusual about Tommi? Was he agitated, angry or distressed at all?"

"No, just the same as usual, which was pretty calm. But we only talked about the bricks, that's all."

Topias explored the existence of co-workers who might know him well, but these were few and far between. In summary, Tommi Heikkinen appeared to be a model employee: he was on time, did his job and went home.

"Just one more thing," Topias added as the interview drew to a close.

"Yes?"

"Mr Salonen. How is he to work for?"

"Fine. Well, he calls a spade, a spade, you know. You have to do what he asks, and he doesn't take bad news well. But he's okay, I guess. He's certainly a smart guy but sails close to the wind sometimes. I've had creditors on the phone a few times saying they haven't been paid, but we seem to survive. I've heard he has some important connections. Maybe that's why things are always alright in the end."

Topias thanked him, returned to his car and retrieved his notebook, listing a few more names Arto had mentioned that probably wouldn't be followed up.

He also read another update from his mobile, this time from an officer in his team named Katja Sivonen. She informed him that Tommi was part of a small family, even smaller since his parents had passed away some years before. The only remaining relative was a sister who lived an hour away in Lohja, so he called the number he'd been given, and a woman answered.

Helle Virtanen was a single woman who lived on her own. The local police had already informed her about her brother's death, so he was thankful he wouldn't be the bearer of that particular bad news. Treading as sensitively as he could, Topias asked to meet with her. However, the interview would have to wait. Miss Virtanen was currently further north in Finland at a sales meeting in Seinajoki, so he arranged to see her the following day.

A couple of Tommi's friends were also on the list, so he tried to call them. One didn't answer; the other worked in the city centre and could meet him within the hour.

Topias jumped at the chance of crossing off another contact

from his list and left the construction site to meet him.

AIMO

Topias was driving towards the city when his stomach growled to announce it was empty. His nourishment was sporadic these days, and he tended to eat when hungry rather than at any particular time. However, after noting his reflection in the mirror that morning, he realised his diet hadn't been the best recently, and decided to make an effort.

Noticing a service station, he pulled in, fuelled the car and entered the small shop. There wasn't much selection available, but instead of the usual junk food, he opted for a rye sandwich with cheese, ham, egg and salad, with fresh orange juice. Satisfied this was a positive contribution to his well-being, he ate lunch in the car while pondering the progress of the case.

By the end of the following day, he planned to have talked to the critical people in Tommi's life and compiled a reasonably clear idea of the kind of man he was. The list of the victim's contacts had been decidedly short of friends and acquaintances. Heikkinen didn't seem the type to have attracted any enemies either. He appeared to be a quiet man who went about his business and enjoyed a simple life with his partner. Nothing yet had challenged that.

Who shot Tommi, then? And what did they have to gain by killing him?

Although his wife hadn't realised it at the time, Topias was informed that two laptops were stolen: his and hers. With

Petra asleep, the perpetrator would have had plenty of time to take more items if so inclined. Initial inspection had revealed it unlikely that other items were removed. This would be confirmed later by a detailed inventory.

Surely a couple of laptops are not worth killing for, especially when the murder was probably carried out in advance of the robbery?

That seemed to rule out theft as a primary motive. There appeared to be three remaining options. Either Tommi was shot deliberately with intent for some specific reason, as yet unknown, and he wasn't ruling out a jealous lover at this point. Or, he had been the accidental victim of a disturbed person with a gun who just happened to be on a killing spree. Finally, the laptops could have been the target or something contained within them. The two latter of these theories seemed unlikely but not entirely impossible. He was inclined to think the former. However, in that case, why then were the laptops taken?

Incriminating photographs or emails, perhaps?

Time would tell.

After completing the forthcoming interview with Tommi's friend, he planned to return to the station to see if his colleagues had uncovered anything beneficial to the case. He was particularly interested in reviewing similar crimes over the past five years or if a likely suspect had recently been released from prison.

Topias drove to downtown Helsinki. He enjoyed going to the city centre, appreciating the architecture and ocean views along the way. The area looked even more spectacular that day, with sunshine shining off the frozen sea. Today, many people were visible walking across the ice.

Turning the corner, he passed the president's palace, looking resplendent in its blanket of snow. After which, he negotiated the busy streets and headed to park under one of the department stores.

On arrival, he left his vehicle in an underground carpark and took the lift to the shopping area. It was busy that afternoon, so, head down, he ploughed through the bustling shoppers with their yellow bags and exited the entrance nearest where the man had arranged to meet.

Topias strolled down one of his favourite streets in Helsinki, the grand boulevard of Esplanadi, and reached the well-known café halfway down it.

Inside it was heaving. Glancing around at the clientele, he spotted a likely individual perched in the corner at a small table with two seats, apparently defending the other one from all who asked for it. Topias ordered a cappuccino and went to introduce himself.

He'd been correct in his assumption, and the man was the subject of his meeting. He looked in his thirties, with a trim beard and round glasses. Topias took him for an artistic type. He was smart-casually dressed in a brown checked jacket and matching trousers and thoroughly engrossed in a book.

"Aimo?" Topias enquired.

"Yes, that's me. You must be Detective Superintendent Torikka."

They settled down to talk, and after expressing his sympathies for the death of the man's friend, Topias asked a similar set of questions as he had other interviewees.

During the conversation, he couldn't help thinking that the friendship between Aimo and Tommi seemed a bit mismatched, but he didn't judge. He wanted to determine how close Aimo had been to the victim and if he'd noticed any behavioural changes.

"I knew him from playing squash over the past ten years, as

we went to the same club. Although, there was a gap in contact when he went away to prison. Did you know about that?"

Aimo asked that question at a lower volume.

Topias nodded.

"Well, after that, and no one was more surprised than me about it, we didn't see each other so often. I did visit Tommi a few times in prison, every few months or so. I wanted to support him, but prison isn't somewhere I feel comfortable if you understand."

Topias nodded in agreement and let him continue.

"When he came out of prison, as I'd known Tommi for some years, I thought it might help him if we continued our squash games. Maybe to also have some after-game drinks, like we used to. Mainly, I wanted to help a friend and prevent him from reoffending. As it turned out, things went much better for Tommi as time went on. He got himself some work, not the best in the world, but something that paid the bills and kept him on the straight and narrow. Then, he met a girl, and they even bought a house together. I met Petra a couple of times; she's lovely. I was happy for him and thought he would be set for life, and now this."

The man's head dropped in regret.

Topias didn't mention Heikkinen's subsequent charge of handling stolen goods, which had been dropped.

"And his behaviour, his mood?"

"Tommi was not the most gregarious person at the best of times, but he was pleasant enough, the same as many other people. We always got on well, anyway. The last time we played was about a month ago. It was strange, as he seemed very withdrawn and reflective. I asked him if anything was the matter, and he brushed it off. He wasn't the type to talk about his feelings, not even in the sauna, but I was concerned. I was worried that something might go wrong again. You know, in the criminal direction. Anyway, the next appointment we made was cancelled by text, at short notice and without reason. I should have called him back. I should have known something strange was going on."

"Do you know where this mood might have come from or what caused it? Could it have been his wife, work, finances, or did he mention a problem with someone?"

"No, he didn't. Sorry, he didn't mention anything or anyone, just stood or sat there, brooding."

Topias continued this line of questioning to ascertain if they knew anyone in common, but this, not surprisingly, wasn't the case. He wondered whether to visit the sports centre where the two friends played but decided, for now, it probably wasn't worth the time, although he noted its details.

With the interview over, at least for now, he thanked Aimo, who mentioned his next destination was the bookshop, and promptly left the café.

Topias thought Aimo seemed a well-meaning and caring person who enjoyed Tommi's company and supported him through difficult times. He appeared to be a good friend but still not close enough to know him well.

Topias remained in the café for a while, ordering another coffee, and called the other friend on the list. There was no answer this time, so he left a message, asking him to call at his earliest convenience. He also noted a missed call from Petri, so he called him back.

Petri answered immediately. He had just visited the bank branch where Tommi and Petra had their individual and joint accounts and proceeded to pass on relevant information regarding their finances. He explained he had met the branch manager and, following her approval, viewed the detail behind the couple's financial affairs.

Petri explained that despite being a contractor, Tommi received a regular salary, which varied between 1,200 and 2,000€ per month. Petra received a subsidy paid by the government for her law studies of about 500€ monthly. Her income was much less than Tommi's but guaranteed. The information revealed that at one point, Petra earned 2800€ per month, which Petri pointed out was during her time in regular employment before being made redundant. Still, with their combined average income, they could pay their home loan and manage. In addition, Petra had savings of some 4000€, although this was slowly dwindling. There were no debts apparent.

Not wealthy, but they were surviving, Topias thought.

Petri made one revelation that surprised him regarding Tommi's personal account. One month before Tommi's death, and on two further occasions during the previous months, there had been a payment of exactly 25,000€. These credits had resulted in a fairly substantial balance in his deposit account. Combined with a small monthly savings contribution, the current balance in his account amounted to 81,000€.

Interesting. That's quite a nest egg Tommi built up in a short time. Now, where did that come from?

Further investigations by the bank informed that the large payments emanated from an overseas bank account in Riga, Latvia. They only had the payment reference: Lat1 SIA, which didn't reference anything useful. Further research would be necessary to determine the original source.

Armed with the most intriguing piece of evidence so far, Topias drained his coffee and left.

◆ ◆ ◆

The afternoon found Topias, Petri and Ina mustered together in a meeting room with a colleague who worked with Topias on the more complex cases. His name was Detective Sergeant Olli Nieminen, and he was also a friend. Topias had also requested the addition of Saana Koskinen, the uniformed officer he had worked with on several occasions. There was another officer whom he didn't know but had been the response to a secondment request: Lasse Korhonen. These two extra resources were now available to assist with what was turning out to be a challenging case.

The meeting room they were currently in was named 'The Incident Room'. This title also heralded the construction of Topias' infamous case boards.

Preferring to visualise things on a grand scale to avoid missing an important detail, he plotted developments with photographs, newspaper clippings, and snippets of information. This display could sometimes take the form of a giant corkboard. It was supplemented by multiple whiteboards to either side in more complex cases.

Before the meeting, as usual, the team was invited to add important information about the case. More information would follow later, but now was the time to discuss where each person was with their line of inquiry. Also, the additions to the investigative team had to be updated and given their tasks.

Topias usually delegated everything except the essential interviews and inspections. His skills, except for overall leadership, lay in recognising suspicious behaviours, unintentional words or lapsed facial expressions. He was a master of human behaviour. The other responsibilities were divided amongst those with different but equally talented abilities and experience.

Petri began the afternoon's update by reporting that he was

working through similar crimes and possible suspects from the criminal world but hadn't pinpointed anyone worthy of further investigation as yet. Topias asked him to continue on that path, stating there was a probability that the shooter had been involved in something before. The accuracy was compelling evidence for this.

Following Petri's update, the murder investigation team's longest-serving member, Katja Sivonen, arrived. She apologised for her tardiness due to an extended phone call.

She began, and as usual, had completed her tasks efficiently. She proceeded to update the group on the inventory of contents at the Heikkinen home. Katja confirmed that aside from the two laptops being stolen, one belonging to each of the inhabitants, definitely nothing else had been taken.

"Thinking back, when we first met Petra early Sunday morning, didn't she state that nothing had been stolen?" Topias asked, puzzled.

"She did, but she was probably in shock," answered Saana.

"Hmm. So, Tommi was shot from beyond the fence, and the shooter came into the house to steal their computers?"

"Or he had an accomplice?"

"Odd. Did the killer know the computers were there? Why not just steal them when the couple were out in Helsinki centre that day? Why shoot him?"

Topias removed the pen he was currently chewing and made some notes on some A4 paper about this. When he'd finished, he pinned it to the cork noticeboard.

During the continuing discussion, the mysterious payments into Tommi's bank account became a focus of attention and debate. Nothing else of any significance had shown up regarding this money.

As the meeting drew to its close. Tommi's mobile phone records appeared, much to the interest of the assembled group. Immo Salonen's number appeared on it, not once or twice, but five times within two weeks.

"And he said he didn't really know him," Topias remarked. "Let me ask Mr Salonen about this at an appropriate time."

After the updates had concluded, Topias handed out the next steps to the assembled participants.

Saana took the job of investigating the Latvian company from where the payments had emanated. Petri would continue the analysis of existing criminals, cases and potential suspects. Lasse would cover general desktop research on Tommi and his background, including his time in prison and any known associates there. Due to Katja's organisational skills, she was the coordinator to ensure everything was compiled and adequately recorded. As Olli had just joined the case after supporting the fraud office with an investigation, he would spend time familiarising himself with it, later partnering with Topias in the field.

At the end of the meeting, Topias decided enough was enough, and those who were due to end their shift should do so. As for himself, his evening would be free to relax and catch up on sleep. Tomorrow was another day, and he would spend it visiting Tommi's sister, other known contacts, and anyone else who might pop up on the radar.

Satisfied he could do no more, he unusually left the station before five o'clock and headed homeward.

DISCOVERY

That evening found Topias cooking.

Despite usually dining alone, he liked to concoct various cuisines at home in the evenings when time was available. As a result of a recent separation from his wife, his newfound cooking skills were developing considerably. This had been out of necessity at first and, later, enjoyment.

Tonight, the dish in progress was chicken curry. To this end, the kitchen was covered in an array of pots, pans, and spice jars. Fresh herbs were draped lovingly over the cutting board, and the smell of spices was pungent with an in-built sweetness from brown sugar and lashings of coconut milk.

With soft jazz playing over the radio, he was currently busy stirring a large pot while sipping a glass of tasty Rioja. As cooking evenings were few and far between, Topias had decided to make food for several days to make life easier. He'd concluded that it was just as simple to make a big pot as a small one. After the first fresh tasting this evening, the remainder would be easily microwavable for consumption after coming long days. It would also be healthier for him, recognising that his belt had become a little tighter of late.

Placing the spoon in his mouth, he tasted the curry sauce. A burst of chilli, coriander, ginger and garlic assaulted his senses, but in a good way.

"Hmmm, now that is excellent," he remarked, nodding

approvingly.

Topias placed the lid back onto the pan, turned on his quirky chicken-shaped egg timer to forty-five minutes, and switched the hob to its lowest setting. Taking his glass of red wine, he took a long sip and smiled with satisfaction.

It wasn't easy for Topias to sit and relax, and he decided to check his phone messages during this interval. Not immediately locating it, he looked around the kitchen. He remembered he'd left it in the bedroom, so he walked upstairs and found it on the nightstand. Picking it up, he walked out of the bedroom just as the delicious aroma began to float upstairs, invading the whole house.

At that moment, the phone rang in his hand.

"Hello, Torikka," he answered.

"Have you heard?"

It was Olli Nieminen on the other end of the phone.

"What's that? Something new?" asked Topias, walking down the stairs.

"Yes, you might call it that. There's been another murder."

"Two murders within twenty-four hours; that's something new. Tell me more."

Nieminen proceeded to describe the incident in as much detail as possible.

"And the other victim, Tommi Heikkinen? You were trying to track down and interview one of his friends. His surname was Hämäläinen, I think."

"And Jari-Pekka was his first name. That's him. He's the victim. He's been shot, like the other one, and fairly recently too. His body has just appeared, dumped by the side of a bridge in

Vuosaari."

"What? That's too much of a coincidence. There has to be a connection."

"It certainly looks like it. Listen, I just wanted to let you know. Why don't you get back to your dinner? I can handle things here and fill you in with the facts tomorrow morning. You've been working flat-out."

"It's okay. Give me time to turn my pans off, and send me the directions. I'll meet you at the scene as soon as possible."

Topias swiftly turned off the cooker and reluctantly set everything to one side.

It looks like a late dinner; after all, Topias decided, sighing.

He took off the apron he'd been using and briefly rechecked his phone, noting an unopened text message.

"Sorry, you'll have to wait. I'm busy," Topias muttered to his phone and switched the device off.

❖ ❖ ❖

That evening, Topias found himself staring at another dead body.

The male victim was probably about the same age and build as Tommi and had been shot in approximately the same place. The single well-placed shot to the chest, would have cut him down immediately; no time for either struggle or escape. From what Topias could tell, the shooting was carried out at close range, just as before, but the experts would confirm that later.

Olli and Topias looked at each other, heads shaking.

"Where are we, Mexico City?" Topias grimaced.

There were few murders in Helsinki and even fewer that

anyone could classify as potentially professional hits. But this was the second in just two consecutive nights.

"Do we know anything?" Topias asked Olli, noting Ina's approach as he spoke.

Olli replied, "Well, he wasn't killed here, that's for sure. He seems to have been shot and subsequently dumped. The murderer presumably didn't want the body found where it fell."

"And just one shot, like the other one," Ina interjected as the detectives nodded, acknowledging her presence.

Olli continued, "I don't know if anything has been taken. He had a wallet with a credit card and cash, although no mobile phone was there. We don't know whether it was removed or if he didn't have it with him at the time."

"Who found the body?" asked Topias.

"It was a young lady jogging back from the park. Apparently, she almost fell over it and called 112 right away. The poor thing's beside herself. As a rough guess, I think she must have found the corpse soon after it was dumped."

"Any other witnesses?"

"No one. It's a quiet area with the nearest building three hundred meters away. The young woman said that nobody else uses this path except a few other joggers and an occasional dog-walker."

Topias walked over to the track and began strolling forward as it rose back up to the road, hoping he might notice something unusual on the way.

As he was doing so, his phone buzzed.

It was another text message. Topias noted a second message. Like the previous one, it was from his ex-wife.

"What does she want now?" he grumbled as he opened the text.

Topias, Will you take the dog next week as I'm away on a business trip?

At least that was a simple request from her. They weren't always that straightforward.

On this occasion, it was more than acceptable. Topias was always happy to take Otso, their dog. His wife had 'custody' of him due to the demands of him being a detective, but when she occasionally travelled, the dog would stay with him.

Otso was a retired police dog and had won awards for his service. He was an Alsatian, much larger than most, christened with that name due to his size. Otso, a common name for a bear in Finland, fitted him perfectly.

Topias hadn't known him when he was younger and in active service, but how he had performed his duty was beyond imagination. Otso wasn't exactly the most energetic of dogs unless he heard the sound of his lead jangling or his dinner being made.

Returning to the matter of murder, Topias strolled further along the path bordering the road. He looked up and down and walked over to where the route met a bridge connecting two of the islands in the area, collectively named Vuosaari. The mist had settled over the bridge, and snow gently fell around it in large flakes, picked out by the streetlights lining it.

Topias shuddered as the cold invaded his coat.

"There's no need to track this one down now, anyway", he commented to Olli in an unusually unsympathetic manner.

Olli wondered if he'd been dragged away from something important to cause that reaction.

Topias continued, "Come on, let's find a coffee somewhere and talk. Uniform has got this all wrapped up, and it doesn't look like there's much for us to learn here until forensics have got some news."

Olli nodded.

They left the scene in their separate cars, with Olli tailing Topias until they came upon a brightly-lit service station. They pulled up outside and went in.

Olli headed directly to the gents' toilets as Topias went to the counter and ordered two black coffees with pulla buns. He was starving now, and all thoughts of a diet were temporarily forgotten. He retired to a table in the corner by the side of the window as Olli returned.

"There you go—enjoy," he said, offering the refreshments as Olli sat down.

They both fell silent for a few moments, taking desperately-needed gulps of coffee together with bites of the cinnamon buns before continuing.

"So, any idea what the connection might be?" Olli enquired.

"Well, they were known to each other; that's a start. We need to find out where the two victims knew each other from and trace back in time to see if anything they were involved in came back to bite them. Given what we found in Tommi's bank account, I'm curious about this latest victim's financials. It could be that they were both into something they shouldn't have been. Whenever I see large regular payments like that, my first thoughts are blackmail."

"Yeah, we already took a quick look at this guy, well, when we thought he was alive, that is. He had a strangely similar profile to Tommi. About the same time, he did a spell in prison for burglary, but since he came out, he's been straight, and nothing has cropped up on the computer since; not even a speeding fine."

"What did he do for a living, do you remember?"

"I don't think Petri got that far at the time. I'm sure he'll be back on it tomorrow morning, now the priority's changed somewhat."

The two detectives chatted further about the case. At the same time, they finished their refreshments but didn't get any further with their deliberations. They were both tired.

Topias glanced at his watch – it was 9.30 pm, and he still had time to enjoy his dinner with a couple of glasses of wine.

"Okay, you're right. There's plenty of people at the scene. We can't do much else tonight, so I'm heading home to be fresh for tomorrow morning. You?"

"Ditto. Minna is cooking tonight, and I had to leave when it was almost ready, so whatever it is, it should still be warm, hopefully. And you?"

"I'm making an effort and cooking up a curry from scratch, even if it's just for me tonight. I'm fed up with eating the usual crap. Enjoy your evening."

They said their goodbyes and parted in different directions toward either side of Helsinki.

◆ ◆ ◆

After his short drive to Kauniainen, where he lived, Topias pulled up at his house, now covered in more snow and illuminated by street lights.

Looking around, he noted there was something unavoidable he had to do now: snow work. He had allowed it to build up over the past few days.

As a consequence of keeping the streets open, the snow-clearer had caused large banks of snow to pile up at the end of his driveway. Therefore, he resigned to the task, took a shovel and spent half an hour transferring snow to the growing mountain of what was formerly known as his front lawn.

After the task was complete, Topias entered the house, a little worse for wear and sweating profusely. Despite this, and deciding a shower could wait, he immediately changed into grey sweatpants and a white t-shirt and started preparing dinner again.

He poured a generous glass of red wine before he set about slicing and chopping once more. Topias fully intended to be unavailable for whatever else happened that evening.

He enjoyed making the dinner and sipped his way through another couple of glasses of wine before settling down to eat at the table. It was probable that the bottle of wine would be empty by the end of the meal.

◆ ◆ ◆

After dining with some satisfaction, Topias left the dishes to do later and plumped down on the sofa. He proceeded to scroll through the list of unopened messages, unusually ignoring work correspondence and focusing on personal emails and texts instead.

One message was from a woman with whom he'd had dinner the previous week. She was keen to see him again, but he didn't share this feeling.

He had met her at a cooking class he attended in an attempt to improve his pasta dishes and, at the same time, meet some new people. The woman was nice enough but a little odd at the same time, he'd determined. She was also a little too serious.

Having survived a barrage of questions from her that evening, he had felt lucky to escape intact. He wasn't in the mood for anyone serious or desperate. Topias had just got out of one relationship and had no appetite for sailing into another.

He deleted the text, deciding that was the preferable option, and turned off his phone.

Topias checked his watch and decided the sauna must now be pre-heated.

After undressing, he took a cold beer and placed it on the shelf outside, and went to relax on the wooden bench. He threw water onto the hot stones and felt the relaxation from the steam. Even though he was tired, Topias felt much better now and sighed with satisfaction.

After half an hour, he slipped outside and took a long drink.

Thank God for saunas, he reflected.

Following a quick shower, he retired to bed and picked up the book he was sporadically reading from his table. It was an old Agatha Christie novel he enjoyed, knowing it would send him off to sleep after a few pages.

It worked its magic, and it wasn't long before Topias drifted off, with the book lying on the bed, waiting for the next time he was so inclined.

COURAGE

Topias awoke feeling fresh after a peaceful sleep. Recent nights had not been so pleasant.

It had snowed again during the night, but not so much as to be inconvenient. And the temperature of one degree was uncharacteristically warm for the time of year.

When Topias checked his front yard, it was with some relief that he noted he could skip the snow work, as the light new dusting of snow would doubtless soon melt.

After a hot shower and breakfast, Topias left the house and walked to his car, parked on the driveway. His phone vibrated just as he was about to start the engine.

Don't forget to collect Otso before 6 pm today, the message stated.

Topias smiled to himself. He was happy to have some company for the evening and must remember to pick up dog food from the store. With luck, he could avoid talking with his ex-wife, Helene, when he picked up Otso, as their conversations had been draining recently.

On his way to work, Topias' mind wandered back to the current case. He wondered how well Tommi's wife, Petra, might have known the latest murder victim. He thought about calling her and driving there immediately but had second thoughts about it. There were other priorities to consider. Although, he couldn't help thinking that another visit to Petra would be a treat rather than a chore. On balance, he decided to head straight for the police station.

◆ ◆ ◆

On arrival at the station, Topias received a summons to the boss' office. He'd expected this invitation as he hadn't seen her in over a week. With two murders within days, no doubt she would now take a keener interest in his diary.

He headed to the kitchen first, as usual, nodding his head to acknowledge various people on his way— it seemed the office was busy that day. He poured himself half a cup of coffee, which he drank before continuing to the floor above.

These moments in the kitchen were not just about ingesting caffeine for him, they provided time to create a structure in his mind for the day ahead, and now he needed a plan. Much as he enjoyed his boss's company, she didn't like murder cases hanging around for long and would be keen to see early progress.

Topias arrived at the upper floor and entered what was termed: 'The Executive Suite'. As he did so, he waved to the chief's assistant, an officer named Davina, fresh from the academy, who flashed him a welcoming smile as he passed her.

She's undoubtedly an improvement on the last one, he thought, remembering the stoic expression of her predecessor.

Known for her efficiency, his boss, Heidi, didn't suffer fools gladly, and her assistants tended to change more frequently than most.

As he knocked on the closed door of his superior, a voice boomed from beyond.

"Enter. Ah, Topias, Good to see you," greeted Chief Superintendent Heidi Anttila as he walked in.

"Likewise, Heidi," he replied with a smile.

"Please," she gestured towards one of the four armchairs surrounding a low coffee table at the other side of the room.

Topias obliged and made himself comfortable.

Chief Superintendent Anttila cut a striking figure, smartly dressed in a black suit and white blouse. Topias had known her for years, and she'd been his superior for five of those.

Because of this time and her trust in him, Topias was afforded considerable freedom to perform his duties. His boss knew he usually managed to track down the culprits of whatever crime was his focus. If he didn't, then doubtless, no one else could. Topias maintained a reputation as one of the best-performing detectives in the force, an opinion his superior shared.

He had equal respect for Chief Superintendent Anttila, or Heidi, as he called her privately. She had risen through the ranks via an unblemished career, entirely focused on the most senior jobs available. This was unlike Topias, who had found his niche early on. He was happy to remain in his current position, which entirely fulfilled his needs and wishes, probably until the end of his career.

Unbeknown to anyone, the pair had been involved in a brief relationship beyond police work, but nothing serious. It resulted from excessive time spent together on a case, including late nights, hotels, dinner and drinks together, and an obvious attraction between them. There had been many stolen moments within a short time, but this had passed without any ill feelings. Both of them accepted it was history, but Heidi remained a member of the select club that addressed him by his Christian name, as did he with her, but only in private.

Today, Heidi had pressing matters on her mind. She was concerned about him and the recent murders, which had been the catalyst for arranging this particular conversation.

"How are you?" she asked, taking a seat on one of the other armchairs.

"I'm okay, thanks. Busy at the moment, but what else is new?"

She smiled.

"Let's get to that in a moment. I want to know how you are doing now that your wife is out of the picture."

"Well, she isn't entirely out of the picture. We have shared custody of Otso, you know."

Heidi smiled again, knowing he was referring to his beloved canine companion.

"And aside from that?"

"Yes, things are okay. We still have occasional arguments about what belongs to whom, who pays for what, and when. I've come across that before, though, and I'm much more flexible than I used to be."

"You, flexible?" she laughed.

"You can laugh, but I'm a changed man now."

"Hmm. I'll bet, or maybe you're just resigned to the situation. You do look tired, though."

"I'm not surprised. Some of my cases have really tested me, recently. Often, they take all the hours I can give and more."

"I'm not surprised. Perhaps there could be some leisure time on your horizon; what do you think about that?"

Topias tilted his head to the side, smiling. He searched his jacket pocket for a pen to fiddle with but was unsuccessful.

Heidi continued and changed the subject.

"What's the latest on the murders?"

Topias explained where they were with the first case. After this, he updated Heidi on the second killing. Knowing she would need more details: he told her about the substantial deposits into Tommi's account, apparently unknown to his wife; the method and accuracy of the shots; and the relationship between the two victims.

"I agree the two incidents must be connected; that's obvious. How will you progress?"

"I need to know more about the latest victim, his connections and finances. The team will dig that out for me while I get back on the road and keep talking to people. I'll take Olli with me; two minds are better than one."

"I agree. You two work well together. A larger case always justifies more resources. Just watch your team's overtime, not just because of the budget, but more for your health."

Topias nodded.

"Will do."

"Oh, and after we've wrapped this up. I want to see your application for annual leave on my desk. At least two weeks, understand?"

"Loud and clear."

With that, Topias took his leave and headed for the door.

Heidi eyed him up and down wistfully until he closed the door.

No, that relationship wouldn't have been easy, she reminded herself and returned to her desk and computer.

◆ ◆ ◆

It was time to pull the team together for a detailed review and push the investigation forward. After this, Topias intended to do some interviews.

They met in the incident room, and he greeted Olli, Petri, Katja, Saana and Lasse, who took their seats. In addition, Ina, from forensics, joined the meeting to update everyone on the previous evening's events.

"Welcome, everyone. All got coffee?" Topias began. "Okay, let's begin. Ina, perhaps you'll begin by updating us on last night's victim."

"Yes. Well, quite simply, it looks like a carbon copy of the previous one. The victim was shot at close range in the heart with either a similar or the same gun. I still need to check that. One difference is that the shooting occurred elsewhere, and he was taken to where he was found. We don't know where the incident occurred; however, we did find what looked like some sand on his shoes, just like in the first case. It could have been from a path or beach. We're analysing it. The mobile phone is missing and isn't at his home address, but his other possessions were left untouched."

"Thanks, Ina. I'm guessing the phone was missing because it could have stored incriminating messages or pinpointed his previous location. We'll need that number to see if that can still be done. Petri, do you have any more background on victim number two?"

"Yes. His full name: Jari-Pekka Hämäläinen or J-P as he was known as. He was born in Hyvinkää but lived in Vantaa for some years and was single. We're learning more about his lifestyle, and we'll access his apartment soon. It's fairly unremarkable so far. Apparently, he lived in a small place with occasional work that paid the bills and probably nothing more."

"Hmm. Thanks for that, Petri. Katja, anything from J-P's

past?"

"We don't know much except that he was in prison for a while, doing time for breaking and entering. Notably, this was in the same prison as Tommi Heikkinen, and their prison terms coincided. This may have been from where they knew each other."

"There are several similarities here. Can we officially link these two murders and move them into the same case file?" asked Katja.

Topias nodded.

"No doubt about that now. It looks like we need to come up with a third party who knew them both and presumably didn't like them very much."

They continued the discussion for another hour, with Topias allocating responsibilities and making notes across the whiteboards as they went.

After the meeting finished, it was time to get on the road.

PRISON

Topias and Olli headed to the police station garage. Olli would drive his car to the prison so his colleague could have time to catch up on the increasing number of updates heading his way. Anything helpful would then be verbally relayed to Olli en route, so they were kept simultaneously informed.

During the trip, Topias reached for his phone and dialled Immo Salonen. He'd been holding onto the mobile phone statement in his pocket, which stated Salonen received five calls from the first murder victim, Tommi Heikkinen, across two weeks.

The call was answered immediately.

"Yes?"

Topias recognised the voice and tone and introduced himself. Without warning, he went directly to the topic.

"I want to ask you about your relationship with Tommi Heikkinen once again."

"Yes?"

"You said you didn't know him very well?"

"No, I didn't."

"Can you please account for receiving five telephone calls from him within two weeks?"

Topias proceeded to give him the dates and details of the calls.

"You'll find other phone calls I receive from employees on my bills, Detective Superintendent."

"Not so many, it seems."

"I think you know he sometimes made purchases for us. Sometimes I was directly involved as such expenses can be substantial."

Salonen spoke confidently as if it were true or he'd already carefully considered his response. Topias also detected some annoyance and arrogance in the man's voice.

"Thank you. Just following up on our enquiries."

After the call ended, Topias mulled the conversation in his mind as they approached the Vantaa prison where the murder victims, Tommi and J-P, had spent time as inmates.

The detectives wanted to talk to the warden and any officers or inmates who might know something about the murders. Perhaps there had been an incident behind bars? Maybe the men had been known to associate with a third party in a close group?

Reports were helpful, but Topias valued nothing greater than face-to-face conversations. After many years of experience, he could tell by someone's eyes, body language, voice, and sometimes just intuition if they were hiding something or being intimidated.

The car pulled into the prison carpark, and they got out and walked to the main gate. The prison facility was constructed of plain grey concrete and looked a forbidding place from its exterior; a perfect building for its purpose, made grimmer by the wintry weather.

Topias had already made a courtesy call to expect their

visit, so they entered without ceremony. A guard escorted the detectives to the warden's office, who greeted them warmly on arrival. His name was Antti Leino. He was older than the detectives, nearing retirement, with a distinct military manner. Topias wondered if he had spent much of his career in the military service. He carried an air of efficiency that one would expect only from someone of experience and rank.

The two detectives were served coffee while they waited; everyone took it black without sugar. Antti asked what he could do for them, and Topias explained the situation regarding the two murder victims. The warden nodded gravely and made a short phone call.

Interestingly, his answer confirmed what Topias had suspected: that the two victims had known each other and were seen frequently in each other's company.

A short while later, Topias and Olli were drinking more coffee in a small anteroom when the warden reappeared.

"Alright, I might have something interesting for you. After speaking to some of my officers, I found two inmates worth talking with. One of them shared a cell with Tommi for a couple of years before he moved to join J-P Hämäläinen, your second victim. The other was Tommi's second cellmate, who was later regularly seen in J-Ps company."

The warden explained he would arrange for the two inmates in question to be taken to separate interview rooms, and wished the detectives, good luck.

One of the corrections officers took Topias and Olli down a level in a lift to a secure area, where several interview rooms stretched the length of a soul-less, grey corridor.

Firstly, they interviewed Tommi's first cellmate, who, before his incarceration, had been a serial car thief. He had no factual information but no reason to decline the meeting either. For him, this was an excellent excuse to relieve the monotony of another day inside.

Topias ran through several questions, but it soon became apparent that the man had nothing of value to impart.

The second interview was with an inmate named Karl Sommers, Tommi's second cellmate who had been close to J-P after Tommi was released. This interview was more revealing.

According to the file, Sommers had been convicted of serious online fraud and sentenced to five years in prison, of which he had served four.

His crime was enticing people to enter their details into cunningly-designed web links so he could steal their bank information and account contents. He'd been successful up to a point but was caught when the police cyber-crime division had been alerted.

Topias proceeded as before, asking the same questions again.

At one point, Sommers breathed a long sigh and summarised what he thought of Tommi Heikkinen.

"Tommi was a strange one. He visited me a few times after his release and called me too. However, I haven't heard from him for a couple of months. He was always on about leaving the country and going to live on a beach in some exotic place. He offered to get me involved and said he needed my help. But I often hear about so-called big jobs here, and I have no intention of ending up in prison again. I said, 'What can I do from in here, anyway?' I've only got twelve months to serve, less with good behaviour. Maybe when I get out of here, I'll look him up and see if he made it to his beach."

"I'm afraid that's not going to happen; He's dead," Topias told him, carefully watching the man.

Topias thought he noticed a split-second reaction in

Sommers. However, this disappeared, and he shrugged his shoulders in silence as if to convey it was an occupational hazard and not entirely unexpected. He still asked how it happened.

When Topias explained the circumstances, Sommers changed his stance and refused to say anything else. Olli mentioned the subsequent murder of J-P and tried to coax more information from him, but this just made him more agitated.

Clearly, the inmate wasn't going to cooperate further in this state, so he was returned to his cell. The detectives thanked the warden with nothing further to discuss and left the prison.

"What do you think of that?" Topias asked Olli when they were back in the car.

"I suppose it's pretty natural for someone in prison to clam up about something if they find out someone has been murdered. Or more than one in this case. Sommers was laughing about Tommi at one point, but after we mentioned he was shot, that was it. Maybe he was involved in something big after all. Maybe Sommers was in on it too?"

"Could be. Possibly Sommers knew more about things than he was letting on and got scared."

"Agree. It does seem that Tommi was not planning a life on the straight and narrow, that is if his boasts to Sommers are to be believed. Tommi and J-P could have been planning something together, and if others found out about it, that something could have been big enough to kill them. It could well have been all about that money."

"His story sounded rehearsed, don't you think?" asked Olli.

Topias nodded.

"It was odd for him to make that speech."

"So, what next?"

"J-P's friends and family."

They turned the car towards Hyvinkää, a town about an hour from Helsinki. It was almost noon, and lunch looked like the delights of a service station grill once again.

◆ ◆ ◆

At the station, Petri was scanning the pages on his open laptop. His regular tasks included finding critical information that would either confirm, deny or lead an investigation in a particular direction. He was a young officer who was incredibly astute at spotting a needle in a haystack. The force had been lucky to recruit someone like him. Otherwise, a technology company might have snatched him up and locked him away on a high salary.

Petri was currently searching for interesting facts about the second murder victim.

Something he came upon by accident made him look twice, so he made a call. The result of the phone conversation was also interesting, so he called Topias with the new information, who put him on speakerphone for Olli to hear.

"According to the tax office, J-P sometimes worked as a casual employee at the same company as Tommi Heikkinen. That's the same one you visited, Topias. I contacted their HR person, and it seems Tommi helped J-P get a job there when he was released. He was contracted hourly, as and when they needed him. This shows that the two victims were close and kept in touch after their release."

"But what caused them to be murdered? Both shot within such a short time." Topias asked no one in particular.

"It does look like a hit," replied Olli. "There was a reason they both needed to be out of the picture quickly. Possibly something ongoing from their prison stretch. Maybe drugs?"

◆ ◆ ◆

The detectives arrived in Hyvinkää, a small town which served partly as a dormitory for those commuting to Helsinki and Vantaa, easily accessible by road and rail. Here, they met with J-P's family and friends, such as they were, who lived in apartments in a cluster of ubiquitous 1970s tower blocks.

The meetings proved to be more of a tick-box exercise rather than being of any real value.

After a fruitless round of interviews, they drove back empty-handed to Helsinki later that afternoon.

On their way, they received another call from an officer who had attended the residence of J-P, the most recent victim. To their disappointment, nothing had been found. He'd lived in a small studio apartment in a cheaper part of town, the kind of place an ex-con might typically rent to commence life after prison. A check with the landlord indicated the victim had lived there for a year. He'd been quiet and always paid his rent on time.

The weather was kind, and the Helsinki city limit sign soon appeared on the highway. With nothing further to gain by spending more time on the case that evening, Olli dropped Topias off at the station, where he collected his own car.

Instead of driving home, Topias headed west to his ex-wife's house, a small place on the outskirts of Kirkkonummi, a wealthy Helsinki suburb.

"Here we are; look who's here. It's Daddy!" Topias' ex-wife, Helene, told Otso.

The dog was inside, waiting for 'Daddy', with his head resting on the window-sill, eyes alert and tail wagging expectantly.

Topias got out of the car as the hound bounded down the driveway to meet him. A few moments of frantic greeting followed before Otso calmed down. Topias opened the back door, and he jumped in to make himself comfortable.

"Otso is yours for the week, then," Helene shouted.

He waved in acknowledgement; that was about all possible between them or advisable. Their communication was better restricted to hand signals or texts. That seemed to work well enough, and both were content with the arrangement.

Topias glanced once more at the already-closed front door of the couple's old house, indicated, and reversed out of the drive. Otso was wagging his tail with his chin resting on the seatback, sending his hot breath onto Topias' right ear, despite his owner's protests. He drove to a supermarket to purchase dog food and snacks and soon arrived home.

Otso was delighted to arrive at Topias' house and thoroughly investigated it, as was his usual habit. This intensive review promptly ended when dinner time was announced: dog food for Otso and microwaved curry for Topias, with a glass of red wine.

After eating, he took Otso for a walk, covering three kilometres along a track around a local lake. After which, they returned home, and one man and his dog were content for the evening.

Topias felt better from the exercise and skipped the sauna routine that evening, deciding to spend time with Otso instead.

SEARCH

Topias awoke the following morning to find that nothing eventful had occurred during the night. As a Detective Superintendent, he was to be contacted if any incident related to his cases occurred. This communication would generally happen by email if non-urgent or by phone call if viewed as serious. He was content that morning to have enjoyed a good night's sleep.

Feeling something oddly heavy on his legs, he sat upright and smiled at what was a familiar sight when his dog visited.

Otso was sprawled across the central part of the bed. Having forsaken his basket, he had cunningly opened the bedroom door and made himself comfortable.

Topias gradually extracted himself without waking Otso's dead weight and made for the bathroom. He knew the dog would immediately awaken when he heard his breakfast bowl being filled; Otso had a sixth sense where food was concerned.

He stepped into the shower cubicle and turned on the taps. The blast of initially cold water woke him with a start, and it was a relief when it became warmer. After that, it was a quick shave, and when this was done, he wrapped himself in a towel.

Exiting the bathroom, Topias was immediately set upon by an excited Otso, waiting for his breakfast and morning walk.

He went to the kitchen and prepared breakfast, which the

hound immediately wolfed down as Topias dressed hurriedly.

Otso needed his exercise before Topias left for work at the station. He planned to return early that afternoon for the dog's sake too.

◆ ◆ ◆

The night had not been as restful for Petra Heikkinen. She struggled to sleep, and her intermittent snoozes meant she awoke at her sister's house after its occupants had already left.

This was no hardship for her, as she didn't feel like talking much these days and deliberately avoided the necessity whenever possible. Also, she was beginning to feel it was time to go home. However, the prospect of returning to the place of her husband's death unnerved her somewhat, not least because of her distinctive memory of him hunched and frozen over the fence—dead.

There was the added fear of a stranger being in her house. That person could have been a murderer. She kept telling herself that it was pointless worrying; it was just a house, and the whole awful episode was likely at an end.

Petra got ready after a quick shower and dressed. Her brother-in-law had already returned to her house. He had brought clothes and other belongings in a pair of large suitcases. At least she could dress with some style again.

She checked the luggage contents and put on a pair of distressed blue jeans, a black top, and a white jumper. She combined this outfit with black leather boots and a long, quilted grey coat: the type that wraps people entirely down to their footwear. She played with her hair for a few moments in the mirror but quickly lost patience and tied it back with a hairband. After a touch-up of make-up, she was ready to leave.

Petra didn't have a car as she'd been in such a state that fateful night, also, the police had wanted to examine it. Therefore, this morning, she reluctantly trudged her way through the snow to the bus stop, and after a few minutes, one appeared.

It took about forty-five minutes for her to arrive at the house, with the bus making multiple stops on the way.

As her home came into view, she approached it with mixed feelings. She wanted to get back inside familiar surroundings but, at the same time, was nervous about entering. She looked at her neighbour's door and wondered if Stefan might be available to go with her but dismissed this as unwise. She'd felt uncomfortable when the police asked questions about their potential relationship; they'd seemed very suspicious about that, so she preferred not to be seen with him.

Petra took a deep breath, stepped forward, and strode purposefully to the house entrance, inserting her key in the lock and pushing the door open.

Inside, it was chilly, despite the underfloor heating being on. Although the temperature hadn't dropped, there was an odd, cold, clammy feeling in the air. As if no one lived there or something terrible had happened, which, of course, it had.

She slipped off her boots but retained her coat. The first task was to adjust the thermostat controls, assuming her brother-in-law had turned the heat down in her absence.

She gasped as she entered the open-plan space—it was a wreck. It had been destroyed. Smashed photographs lay on the floor, and furniture was overturned and ripped apart. Floorboards had been taken up, and the ceiling had a gaping hole. The sofa the couple had chosen and bought together lay in pieces, with its cushions ripped open and contents spilling out. Their remaining possessions were strewn across the floor.

Petra felt dizzy and steadied herself by placing a hand on a cabinet by the door. She felt sick and suddenly panicked.

What if whoever did this is still here?

She rose and returned to the hallway, quickly pulling on her boots. Despite her previous misgivings, she returned to where she'd gone for help on an earlier occasion: Stefan's house.

Why didn't I ask him to go with me in the first place? She asked herself, wiping away tears and rapping on his door for the second time that week.

There was no sound from inside, so she knocked on the door again, this time harder, but to no avail.

As Stefan was clearly absent, she pulled out her phone to call for help. She dialled 112 and somehow explained her situation to the emergency operator.

◆ ◆ ◆

Petra was still rooted to that same spot, in front of her neighbour's door, when a police car arrived ten minutes later, just as it had done a couple of days before.

While driving, Topias was surprised to learn that one of the murder victims' houses had been ransacked.

Tommi Heikkinen's wife, who he now knew as Petra, had entered the building and been greeted by an over-turned house, reported as a break-in. Puzzled, he turned his car back in the same direction he had driven and selected the destination from his GPS list of recent addresses.

◆ ◆ ◆

What he found was mind-boggling. It made him gasp. He

hadn't seen anything like this for a long time, if ever.

It hadn't just been a break-in. The house had been searched within an inch of its life. It looked more like the beginning of a renovation than anything else—even flooring had been removed. Also, the ceiling had been opened, wallpaper peeled back in places, and furniture prised or ripped open.

Walking into the couple's beloved sauna, which he had admired only days earlier, he found wood ripped off the walls. The fantastically star-lit ceiling was now partially hanging down.

Topias went over to a female police officer who had been comforting Petra, the victim's wife. He had a strong sense of déjà vu as she looked remarkably similar to how she'd done at the murder scene.

Petra noticed him approach, and her soft blue eyes opened visibly wider. Topias could see tears welling up in them and waved the officer away as he took her place on the sofa next to Petra. She pushed her head into his shoulder, and he put his arm around her as she sobbed. This happened quite naturally, and it was no time for questions, so he let her continue until the weeping subsided.

"I'm so sorry," he said. "Have you any idea why someone would want to do this?"

"No," she whispered, barely audibly.

"It seems they've been searching for something. It's not normal for thieves to spend so much time in a place they're burgling, nor to look as thoroughly..." Topias surveyed the scene as he spoke, "...as this. When did you arrive?"

"About an hour ago. I phoned the police as soon as I saw it. Can I go now? I need to get away from here."

"I think that's the best idea given the circumstances. We'll need a statement, but that's a formality if you didn't see anyone here. May I just ask one thing? Sorry, I have to ask you questions now, but they're important."

"Okay."

"Did you know anything about any large payments made into Tommi's bank account?"

"No. What payments?"

"There were three deposits of 25,000 euros each, and he had over 80,000 euros in his deposit account."

"What? No, sorry, I don't know anything about that. I don't understand. He didn't have that kind of money."

"Alright, thank you. Let's talk about this another time."

Topias gestured to the female officer, who had been waiting a short distance away.

"Would you please take this lady to her sister's apartment?"

"No. Please," Petra pleaded with Topias, clinging onto his jacket. "I don't trust anyone else. Would you take me there?"

He looked at her, thinking it was an odd request, but didn't have the heart to say 'no', especially with her being in the state she was in.

"Yes. Yes, of course, I will. I'll just be a few minutes."

Although Topias would have wanted to remain at the scene, he decided he would take in the general picture now and return later. Perhaps Petra might mention something in the car that could help the whole investigation, as there seemed to be a bond of trust developing between them.

At that moment, Olli arrived, and he and Topias inspected the mess together. The police crime scene photographer came a few moments later and promised to furnish them with a complete set of crime scene images.

Topias asked Olli to remain and see if he could find any clue that might help and then left with a supporting arm around Petra. She seemed unsteady on her feet and in a daze from the shock of her discovery. It took a couple of minutes for her to walk the short distance to his car.

When seated, Topias switched on the ignition and turned the car toward Petra's temporary residence. He couldn't help thinking that it might be some time before she returned to this house, after everything that had happened there, if ever.

◆ ◆ ◆

On the journey to her sister's apartment, Petra was quiet. She was aware of answering the detective's questions, mainly with a yes or no. However, she was apparently confused and wasn't engaging in the conversation. Not surprisingly, Topias didn't glean any new facts during the journey. He was relieved when he drew up outside the apartment block.

After ensuring Petra had her key, he offered to escort her to the door, but she advised him that it wasn't necessary.

Before she left the car, she whispered, "Thank you," and leaned over, nuzzling her face into his neck.

Topias thought he felt the warmth and moisture of Petra's lips on his skin unless it was his imagination. He smiled and asked her to take care of herself as she left the car and walked toward the main door of the apartment block. He waited there to ensure she had entered safely. Then, he finally drove to the police station.

Inside the building, Petra let herself into the apartment, closed the door, locked it, and slid the chain across. She would open it later when her sister arrived. For now, she just wanted to feel safe.

◆ ◆ ◆

"What d'you reckon then?" asked Olli as he approached Topias' desk.

Topias held his head in his hands for a few moments, then looked up.

"You tell me, Olli. This situation is getting weirder and weirder."

"Curiouser and curiouser, don't you mean?"

"What?"

"Alice in Wonderland,"

"Now you've completely lost me," Topias replied. Realising the meaning of Olli's comment, he shook his head in sympathy: "Oh, yes, now I've got it. And I thought I was the older one in this duo."

"Did you see that place? It was less of a search and more like a demolition. What exactly would someone hide behind wallpaper, for god's sake?"

"I've no idea, but clearly, someone thought there was something to find. The big question is—did they find it? Or are they still looking? We can deduce that Tommi or J-P knew something about it, given the recent events. But they either refused to give it up or knew too much about what or where it was. They were probably viewed as a high risk. That's why Tommi and Petra's apartments were searched as well. I've just sent a couple of uniforms to J-P's address. It won't surprise me if his residence has received the same intensive treatment. At least, that's one thing I can forecast in this case. Unless, of course, they've already found what they're looking for. In which case, there would be no point."

"Let's wait and see. We'll know soon enough," remarked Olli.

As Topias predicted, he received a call from the officers at J-P's apartment shortly after.

Apparently, despite it being so sparsely furnished, it had been ransacked in precisely the same manner. He was informed that forensics were already on their way, but the team at the station weren't holding out much hope; there would probably be nothing to find once again.

After he put down the phone, Topias spent time at the noticeboards in the incident room, adding the latest updates, namely both homes being searched and their resulting conditions.

He wrote in large letters with a whiteboard marker in red: *What are they looking for?*

◆ ◆ ◆

In a forest, an hour away from Helsinki, a log cottage lay at the end of a narrow country lane. It was secluded yet accessible to the highway in a matter of minutes. It had been chosen for a specific purpose, rented for three months, and paid in advance.

In the living room, the blinds were drawn. Two pistols, one with a silencer, sat on a table with a box of ammunition.

Some disposable overalls were piled on the floor in the corner. A toolbox lay adjacent, containing everything necessary to conduct a detailed search, even if that search required the removal of wallpaper or the creation of a hole in a ceiling.

There was a click as the door was closed and locked as someone left the cottage. The sound of a car driving away signalled the departure of its occupant.

ATTRACTION

When Topias came home that afternoon to take his dog for a walk, Otso was as excited as usual.

After quickly changing into casual clothes, they headed to their usual destination: the track around the lake. The plan was to do a circuit, or possibly two, by the look of Otso's energy levels.

Topias noted the ground had become notably icier after the snow melting and refreezing. Negotiating the path was challenging, but Otso was determined to enjoy its slipperiness, with his paws skating and skidding across its surface.

Despite the conditions, the intrepid pair completed the first circuit and pushed on for a second. It was midway through that jaunt when Topias' phone vibrated in his pocket as he received a text message.

It was from Petra and stated quite simply: *Can we talk?*

He looked at his watch: it was approaching 7 pm. After walking Otso, he planned to pick up his guitar again. This was a lapsed hobby that cropped up from time to time whenever he had free space in his diary and the energy to do so. Such spare time was few and far between, and he wanted to make the most of it.

All the same, he was curious about the message and, as he walked, wondered what Petra might have to say to him. Besides, it wouldn't bother him to be in her company for a while.

She was a uniquely attractive woman and the kind of person who naturally lent themselves to being looked after; he didn't mind being the one to do it. On the other hand, he was a busy man, she was connected to the case, and he wasn't sure if he wanted to become the person responsible for her wellbeing.

After fighting with these feelings, he stopped for a moment. Otso gave him a considered look as if wondering what was going on. Topias nodded and decided he would visit her after all.

Perhaps she'll reveal everything she knows to me?

He was still suspicious that she was keeping something back about the case. Maybe she knew all along what had caused the two men's murders and subsequent ransacking of their homes?

At this point in their walk, Otso became bored and began investigating a nearby tree with great interest, so Topias took the opportunity to reply to Petra's text.

Hi Petra. When and where? Is everything alright?

The reply arrived a few seconds afterwards.

I'm okay. My sister's place. 9 pm.

Topias pocketed his mobile phone, and the two friends made their way around the remainder of the lake path, this time at a faster pace, and returned to the house.

❖ ❖ ❖

Petra left the shower and dried herself with an oversized towel. She entered the apartment's smaller second bedroom that had become her temporary haven and closed the door.

After selecting what she decided was an appropriate outfit for her meeting with Topias, Petra slipped it on. She blow-dried her hair until satisfied with how it looked and carefully applied subtle makeup.

She used considerable time to prepare herself and decided the final result was well worth it. Eyeing herself in the mirror, she added lip gloss as a final touch and then smoothed down her hair, padded to the living room barefoot, and prepared a jug of fresh coffee.

◆ ◆ ◆

Topias' car drew up outside the apartment block where Petra currently resided.

The weather was changing for the worst again. Although he enjoyed the winter and usually didn't mind driving in it, he preferred to be inside when the snow was so heavy that you could hardly see the road ahead. He wasn't looking forward to the return journey much either; the forecast was for conditions to worsen.

After locating the correct apartment number, he pressed the button on the call panel, and a buzzer sounded to signal the door was unlocking, so he opened it and went inside. The temperature was pleasantly warmer in the lobby.

When he entered the lift, he removed his gloves, opened his scarf and unbuttoned his coat. Then, he walked to the now-familiar apartment and pressed the bell.

The door opened almost immediately and took Topias by surprise.

She must have been waiting for me, Topias thought. *Lucky for me, I'm punctual.*

He was struck dumb for a few moments when the door opened. There was Petra. She was wearing a clinging white lace dress, her hair loose and falling over her shoulders. Her face was pretty as a picture, the most beautiful he'd seen her yet.

"Detective Superintendent," she greeted him with his full title.

"Topias, please," he reminded her firmly as she invited him in.

"Please have a seat, Topias. I'll bring some coffee."

He sat on one part of a white angular sofa and made himself comfortable. There didn't seem to be anywhere else in the apartment to sit down.

"Is your sister or her husband home?" he inquired.

"No, they've gone to their cottage for a few days. It's winter-liveable. They wanted me to accompany them, but I felt they needed some space. I've been hovering around them for almost a week already, and as I don't think I'm leaving anytime soon, I thought they could use the time together."

"Understandable and thoughtful," Topias commented.

Petra moved to the kitchen area and returned with two coffees and a plate containing aromatic cinnamon pulla buns.

"They look delicious."

"You have to try them. I don't have much to do here, and when I'm bored, I bake. I'm not too bad at it; one of my many talents."

"Kiitos," Topias thanked her.

Petra smiled the broadest smile he had yet seen.

She sat next to him on the sofa, leaning on a cushion. Topias couldn't help but notice that she brought her legs upward, the short dress revealing just the right amount of thigh.

Realising he was staring, he quickly lifted his eyes upward, but the glimmer of a smile told him she'd noticed his glance.

"It's good to see you're looking better," he remarked.

"Yes, it's all been a terrible shock, but life continues, I suppose. I don't think Tommi would want me to be miserable forever."

Topias thought she had bounced back remarkably well, considering recent events and the short time that had elapsed since her husband's passing. Still, he didn't comment and instead just nodded gently.

"Was there something, in particular, you wanted to talk to me about, Petra?"

"Yes, there was."

"I wondered if you'd found out where that money was coming from: those large payments you mentioned that were deposited into Tommi's personal account?"

"Well, we found the source. It was an overseas bank. But that's as far as we've been able to go. They won't release any details without the account-holders permission. We'll ask you to sign some papers soon to help us to do so, as you're the next of kin."

"Of course. Hopefully, it will tell us something about all of this. Any news yet about what happened to Tommi or our house being destroyed like that?"

As she asked this, she stood up from the sofa and walked to the window. Topias' eyes followed her intently.

"Not yet. We're still pursuing our enquiries, and I'm happy to update you on our progress periodically. You can call me anytime, especially if you think of something that might be useful."

Topias took a sip of his coffee and replaced the cup on the table.

"Thank you. I appreciate that, and if it's okay, I will," Petra replied.

She turned away from the window, returning to the sofa, sitting noticeably closer to him than before, and placed her hand on his arm.

"I'm so pleased you're the one handling all this. I don't know what I would do if it were someone who didn't care."

Topias coughed anxiously, feeling that Petra was closer than she should be. She detected this and obligingly removed her hand.

"Rest assured, I'll do everything possible to bring your husband's murderer to justice, as will everyone else on my team. You need have no worries on that score."

She looked directly at him for a few moments. Her blue eyes sparkled, enhanced by the eye shadow surrounding them. He returned the smile, and she placed her hand on his arm again, squeezing it slightly, her eyes not breaking contact with his own for a second.

Suddenly feeling awkward about this extended gaze, he looked downward, his eyes dropping unintentionally to her breasts, evident through the revealing dress.

Topias quickly searched for something more appropriate to look at and decided on the pullas on the table. He also needed to say something quickly; he was getting warm in his jacket.

"Was there something else you wanted to ask? Something connected with the case?" he stammered uncomfortably.

He looked back up at her and noticed her smile had grown wider. Topias couldn't help wondering if Petra was fully aware of the situation she was creating and was enjoying the control.

"Just something I wondered," she answered softly.

"What's that?"

"It was odd. Tommi received a call on his mobile a couple of days before, you know, it happened. I asked him what it was about, but he didn't answer. He seemed to panic and then left the house for a couple of hours. When he returned, everything seemed fine. I teased him that he had another woman, but he didn't see the humour. He said it was something to do with an important delivery that hadn't arrived at the construction site, but I knew different. I'd never seen him like that before. I saw something in his eyes. The call startled him, and it was not about bricks."

Pleased to find a more business-related topic of discussion, Topias asked her about the time of the call and if there were any more details. He noted them carefully, but as she hadn't heard any part of the call, and her husband hadn't revealed the content, that was that.

Feeling their conversation had run its course, at least on a professional basis, he feigned checking his watch.

"Thank you for the information and the coffee, Petra. I should be going now, as I have another appointment. Please keep in touch, and don't hesitate to contact me if you have any more information or concerns."

"Oh, I shall do, Topias." She added wistfully, "Isn't Topias a nice name?"

He smiled, feeling the colour in his cheeks once again as Petra rearranged herself attractively on the sofa.

At this, Topias decided to take his leave, hurriedly making his way to the door, slipping on his shoes, and bidding her farewell.

When he was gone, Petra stretched her legs across the sofa, nestled into its cushions, and chuckled.

◆ ◆ ◆

Outside, the weather had deteriorated. Powerful wind gusts blew into Topias' car on his return journey, buffeting it from side to side, seemingly determined to throw him off the road. He fought onwards bravely, coming across few other vehicles on such a stormy night, and finally made his way home.

Closing the front door to the howling wind, he went to the kitchen.

"I need a drink," he told an invisible Otso, who was sulking somewhere because of his master's absence. However, the thud of his heavy tail could be clearly heard from behind the sofa.

Topias poured himself a generous glass of red wine from the bottle he had opened the day before and sat in an armchair.

After his unnerving experience with Petra and the dreadful weather, the warmth of the wine going down his throat was a pleasant feeling.

He moved to the sofa and switched on the television, planning to do nothing in particular for the next couple of hours.

As he did so, Otso finally forgave him and lumbered from behind the sofa to the rug in front, stretching out flat to occupy most of its surface.

◆ ◆ ◆

The following day brought a spectacular winter scene. A heavy snowfall had released more snow from the night sky. It had finally stopped in the early morning hours, resulting in the picturesque landscape now visible through Topias' window.

As he looked out, one thing was clear: he would need to do the snow work before doing anything else. An app on his phone told him the temperature would drop that night, as much as minus 19, so he had to do it now. It would only be more difficult later.

Topias spent a good hour clearing the snow from his drive. He moved it away from the bin and cleared a path to his front door.

Otso joined in playfully, delighted about the whole process. He was almost nine years old but always regressed to a puppy-like state in such situations, pouncing on the snow as Topias cleared it with an outsize snow shovel. He would dive straight into it on purpose, shaking the white powder everywhere, ideally within the vicinity of his owner.

Even though he wasn't much help in the snow-clearing process, Topias appreciated Otso's antics; it made the task fun instead of tedious.

As a result of his toil, he would arrive at work later than planned. Still, he decided there was no rush, considering how high his overtime balance remained.

Topias couldn't help thinking about Petra all the time he was working.

I could easily have stayed longer at the apartment yesterday evening, but what might have happened?

It felt as if Petra had prepared herself for his arrival, or was that her usual attire while relaxing at home? He thought not.

And how can she recover from her husband's death so quickly?

Topias decided it was probably just as well he left when he did.

◆ ◆ ◆

Ismo Kantola, an inmate at Vantaa Correctional Centre, put the telephone receiver down and stood up. He ambled to the door, where a Prison guard buzzed him out of the room.

After nodding to the guard, Kantola continued down the corridor that led to the main recreational area. Humming to himself, he made for a table where a fellow inmate was reading a book.

Pekka Antilla raised his chin from a book and nodded to his right as an invitation for Kantola to take the vacant seat adjacent to him.

"You look like the cat who just got the cream," Antilla remarked as Kantola stretched himself out and released a satisfied sigh.

"We have a job. And it pays well."

"Oh, really. Tell me more."

Kantola explained the content of the telephone call and the generous offer that had been made, after which the lunch bell sounded.

❖ ❖ ❖

After eating a good meal of potatoes and sausages, Kantola and Antilla clambered up the steps, taking the walkway to the west wing.

Antilla took up position outside the cell of one Karl Sommers while Kantola strode in purposefully.

Sommers was relaxing on his bunk and barely noticed Kantola's presence.

In one swift move, Kantola slipped on gloves, doubled up to minimise the risk of DNA, and plunged a concealed shard of metal into Sommers' heart while clamping his mouth firmly shut.

Their victim didn't stand a chance, and he faded from life without knowing what was happening. Kantola and Antilla walked swiftly away, having dropped the murder weapon inside.

Following this act, they split up, and Kantola headed straight for the refuse area, where he dropped the outer set of gloves. After this, a visit to the bathroom saw him stuff the remaining gloves down a sink, followed by a generous measure of cleaning fluid.

Kantola returned to his cell, where he picked up a puzzle and was soon engrossed, satisfied with the money that would soon be deposited in his bank account.

In the hour that followed, several visitors attended Sommer's cell, this traffic being designed to confuse any witnesses or CCTV evidence. All would be paid in cash or drugs for their participation and silence.

UNEXPECTED

The shocking news about the prison murder reached Topias that afternoon.

As it was a local issue, the Vantaa police force took the lead, so the information took longer to get to him. It would have taken even longer had the prison warden not recalled the victim's conversation with the detectives just before the incident and made a call.

Topias was disturbed by the news. He couldn't help wondering about their visit to the prison the day before.

Could our interview with Karl Sommers be the reason for his death?

This was the third murder within days. It seemed as if those connected with the first victim were being picked off one by one, despite the latest victim being secured in what might be considered a place of relative safety.

Topias' subsequent thoughts were of Petra. He was more concerned about her than anything else. He was worried that if her husband, friend and ex-cellmate had been targeted—why not Petra herself? Whoever was doing this must know she was closer to Tommi than anyone else. Being in that privileged relationship, she might be privy to his deepest secrets.

The incident also signalled that the murderer hadn't found what they were searching for, if that was indeed the rational explanation for the crimes.

Considering Petra's situation, Topias decided to arrange a meeting with the Witness Protection Team.

Due to the low level of serious or organised crime in Finland, this was a small team. There weren't many individuals under its protection. However, from time to time, the need arose.

Liaising with Topias' superior, the team arranged for a car to be stationed outside the apartment block where Petra was staying, twenty-four hours a day, for one week. Not everyone had been entirely convinced of the threat and some considered that Petra would have been attacked before, if others had thought her directly involved. However, Topias worked to change their minds and negotiated adequate protection for her.

The situation would be reviewed the following week, after which a decision would be made to either cease or elevate the security level. The latter would mean transferring her to a safe house. It was also agreed that one of Topias' team would remain with her, someone that she knew and trusted; that officer was Saana Koskinen.

Topias decided to call Petra personally with this news so she would feel safer.

During their phone call, he advised her to remain inside the apartment for the time being until they picked her up the following day. From that point onwards, she would be under the direct protection of the police, and he could concentrate on the case once again.

◆ ◆ ◆

The murder investigation team sat in the incident room that afternoon.

Two additional detectives had been drafted in and swelled

the team's ranks further, with other resources at their disposal if needed. The directive had come down from above: find the perpetrators, and do it quickly.

They had already updated the noticeboards. Other files associated with the case sat around in labelled boxes and folders, ready for reference when required.

The team were somewhat perplexed as they considered the range of evidence in front of them. Only the time spent in prison was the common link between the three murder victims. What had they been involved in that would be enough to get them all killed?

After some brainstorming that led nowhere, Topias stood up to list some next steps.

"Let's find out more about this prisoner, Sommers. Something in his past could lead us to a fourth known associate or organisation. Next, we have to learn more about any past convictions and connections between previous crimes. Let's also squeeze our informants. Is there a big job being planned? Or is some precious item or information being sought? Come on, three dead in a week in the Helsinki area. I can't remember the last time this kind of thing happened. There has to be someone out there on the streets who knows something."

Everyone set to work with renewed energy. Calls were made, and computers were searched. However, at the end of the day, only a little tangible progress was made.

Notable was that no connection was found between the victims' historically-committed crimes. Some information on the prisoner, Sommers, had arisen concerning dubious involvement in receiving stolen goods, but that led them nowhere. There was no other connection between him and Tommi Heikkinen aside from prison time. Research would continue until the next team meeting the day after.

Topias left the station discouraged but, at the same time, relieved to be outside in the fresh air. The atmosphere inside the station had felt stifling that day: too much heat and not enough oxygen. He was looking forward to taking Otso for his evening walk. Something was also bothering him, and continued to do so until he pulled into his driveway.

The first victim was shot where he stood, naked and draped over the fence. The third victim was stabbed in his cell and left to die. Why was the second victim moved?

The only explanation he could think of was that the killer of the second victim didn't want him to be found where it had happened.

Was it because it was a place that could be associated with the killer?

Topias' remembered the sand found on the first two victims' shoes, something that Ina had promised to come back to him about. He expected an answer by now and resolved to contact her the following morning and check on her progress.

Exiting the car, he walked to the mailbox to pick up his post. Inside was the usual collection of adverts, bills and complimentary newspapers, which he put under his arm. A white envelope caught his eye, and he opened it while walking to the house. The contents caused him to smile: it was a birthday card.

"Surely not that time of year already?" he mumbled as he opened the front door.

The card was not just a greeting but a forewarning that his sister would descend on him that weekend, as she had every year for as long as he could remember. Sometimes she came with her husband or the whole family, but always, at least herself. She never allowed him to forego his birthday without celebration.

Was it just a signpost to visit him once a year? He didn't know, but as much as her presence swept in like a whirlwind, he still looked forward to her arrival. Due to the past few days' events, his birthday had completely gone out of his mind.

Topias opened the door, and before he could close it, a strong draught grabbed it and slammed it shut.

"Whoa, what's that?"

He placed his keys on the shelf, put his bag down and slipped his shoes off. It was cold in the house.

Brrr. I know it's gone colder, but not that much, Topias wondered as he strode through the house. *What's happened to the heating? And where's Otso?*

He looked around the living area but couldn't find any sign of his faithful friend.

As he walked to the rear of the house, he noticed the utility room door was closed. He opened it, and Otso bounded in, with the back door flapping open behind him.

Topias was confused about the door. He didn't recall leaving it open; the dog was in the living room the last time he looked. With his talent for opening doors, it would be easy for Otso to access the utility room but not open the back door, surely?

His mind flashed back to the break-ins at the other apartments, and he suddenly became concerned he'd received the same treatment.

He walked around the house, checking everything of value, including his small floor safe. Fortunately, everything was secure, and there were no apparent signs of unlawful entry.

His mobile phone rang.

"Hey, Topias!" the voice greeted him enthusiastically.

"Terhi? Is that you?"

"Hello, little brother. How are you?"

"I'm fine, thanks. Just in the middle of something, though."

"Anything I can do to help?"

"Not really."

"That's a shame because I'm right here."

Much to his amazement, the lock turned, the door opened, and there stood Terhi, his sister, clutching a bag of groceries in one hand and a bottle of wine in the other.

"Many Happy Returns!"

"Oh, wow. I didn't expect you until this weekend."

"I decided to come earlier. Hello, again, Otso."

The dog welcomed her for the second time that day, but only in a slightly less manic state than before.

Then the penny dropped for Topias.

"Have you been here already today, by any chance?"

"Yes, I have. How clever of you? No wonder you're a detective. I arrived a couple of hours ago and let Otso out. You didn't have much food in the fridge, so I went shopping for dinner."

"Thank goodness for that. I thought someone had broken in. Hang on, so did you leave the door open?"

"Oh. Did I? Probably, yes. Sorry about that. Otso seemed happy playing outside, and I didn't want to leave him inside."

"Hmm. Now, this place is freezing."

"Stop complaining, you," Terhi came over and hugged him, giving him a quick peck on the cheek.

Topias was relieved no one had broken into his apartment. At the same time, the unexpected early arrival of his sister surprised him. He didn't like surprises much, but this one was tolerable.

"How long are you staying for?" he asked.

"Why, fed up with me already?"

"I just don't want to catch a chill," he gestured at the back door as he increased the temperature using the remote control for the heat pump on the wall.

"Ho-ho." she laughed deliberately. "I'm here today because I have to be home at the weekend. Well, not home; my new guy is taking me for a weekend away. So, sorry, tonight will have to be our official celebration of your birthday."

"Okay. We can do that. By the way, have I met this new guy? I want to ask him what his intentions are towards my sister."

Terhi gave him a sad look.

"Don't hold your breath yet. Let's see how it goes. Now, where's your casserole dish? Come on; we're cooking together tonight."

The siblings prepared a meal together with the assistance of a bottle of white wine provided by Terhi. It was a Chablis, her favourite. They chatted about bygone and more recent times as they chopped and cooked.

When it was dinner time, Topias raided his wine cabinet for a fine red wine to go with the stew containing beef, onions, and carrots. It was flavoured with plenty of rosemary and thyme, giving rise to a profoundly fragrant smell that obliterated any lingering curry scent from Topias' previous cooking efforts.

"I hope you don't mind eating at home. I was pretty tired by the time I got here, so I thought it would be just nice to spend some time here with you."

"It's perfect. My schedule has been crazy recently, so right now, with this food, wine and company, home is the best restaurant in town."

Topias poured more wine. It looked like he would waive his sauna again that evening, albeit for a good cause.

BIRTHDAY

Topias enjoyed the evening thoroughly.

He often rued the fact that he saw his sister so little these days. There was no particular reason, it was just that life got in the way. He was busy, she was busy, and it was challenging to put dates in the diary for which they would both be available.

Terhi was a buyer for a sizeable Finnish fashion retail chain and often travelled. His job as a detective was even more erratic. However, their birthdays were sacrosanct, so he was surprised that she had moved it forward for the first time in their history and that the reason was a man.

After partaking in their main course, he broached the topic as they put down their knives and forks.

"So, go on, tell me about this new guy. Something tells me you're hiding something."

Terhi smiled coyly, not something his sister often did. It was clear that Topias would need to do some digging. However, his phone rang just as she opened her mouth to answer.

"Excuse me. This call might be from work. We'll come back to this topic in a moment."

He took his phone to the other side of the living room and answered the call.

"Hello?"

"Hello, Topias."

It was Petra. For some reason, he wasn't surprised.

"Is everything okay, Petra?"

"Yes, everything's fine. Well, kind of."

"Sorry, just a moment. Terhi, the oven!"

Terhi looked up from her phone that she'd been scanning to realise it was past the time to take the dessert meringues out of the oven. She sprang across the room like a cat and removed them hastily, just at the right moment.

Topias was impressed and made a face to convey it.

"Sorry, is this a bad time?" Petra asked.

"No, no, it's fine. I'm just having dinner with someone."

"Ah. I'm sorry if I've interrupted something with your, err... lady-friend."

"No worries, I don't have one—just my sister."

There was a pause.

"I was wondering if you would like some company? I'm all alone again, and I wondered if you were too. You seem busy now, so perhaps later this evening?"

"It's probably not the best time to talk at the moment. Nothing's happened, has it?"

"No, don't worry. It would just be good to speak to you. Just to chat. I know the police officers are around, but it's not the same as knowing you are available should anything happen."

"And I am available. Rest assured of that, Petra. Listen, I'll call you later when I have time to talk. Is that okay?"

"Yes. Let's talk later."

Petra rang off.

Topias stood for a moment, wondering about the call. It hadn't sounded like a work call this time. It sounded much more personal.

Wondering if I would like some company, he repeated her words in his mind.

It made him feel good that such an attractive and younger woman could be interested in him, but at the same time, he felt torn. Fraternising with someone involved in an ongoing investigation would certainly be frowned upon by his superiors and his team. Theoretically, it could also compromise part of the investigation.

Topias dismissed these thoughts; he had company right now. He would deal with anything else later, so he walked back to the table and topped up his sister's wine, avoiding his own glass in case he needed to drive later. Then, realising he was probably over the limit to get in his car anyway, he poured more generously.

"And who, by the way, is Petra?" Terhi inquired suspiciously.

Topias shook his head and changed the subject immediately while she maintained a knowing smile.

"Let's agree not to talk about anything incriminating, shall we?"

They finished dinner and talked for a couple of hours afterwards. Both made covert attempts to dig into respective potential partners, but neither successfully uncovered any more details.

After Terhi went to bed in the spare bedroom, Topias offered Otso a late-night walk. This offer was gratefully accepted, and the lead was dropped seconds later at his feet.

They left the house and began their usual walk while Topias retrieved his phone and made a return call to Petra.

"Hello, Topias," the voice answered in Petra's signature soft tones.

"Petra. Everything okay?"

"Yes, still fine. It's nice of you to call me back to check on me."

"It's the least I could do. I've been tied up this evening and drunk way too much to drive, but I could drop around tomorrow if you're free."

"That would be nice. It would be even nicer if you could drop around tonight, though," Petra suggested tantalisingly.

"Maybe that's not such a good idea, Petra. It's been a long day, I'm tired, and some might think it's not the proper thing to do. As I mentioned, I've had a few glasses of wine too."

"I'm not worried about what it looks like to others. I'm only interested in what it looks like to you. And as I'm lying down on my bed, alone, in only my underwear, I would be willing to bet that I look pretty good right now."

Topias no longer believed that Petra needed someone to comfort her or was flirting with him. It was now clear to him that she was in active pursuit.

"I'm sure you look amazing, but trust me, it's not a good idea. I'll check on you tomorrow. Goodnight, Petra."

Topias closed the phone and breathed a long sigh, with Osto giving him a curious look. He shook his head wryly as they continued their walk.

MONEY

Olli was driving to work midway through his first service station coffee of the day when he received a call from Petri.

"Hei Petri, you're up early."

"Yeh, I just bumped into Ina, and she said she has something for you and Torikka. Can you be at the station later? It's something about a gun."

"Sure. Has Ina mentioned anything about it to you already?" Olli asked, keen to know more.

"No, I thought it better that she explained to you both."

"Okay. Anything else while you're on the phone?"

Petri proceeded to impart some information about the case. There was something about Tommi's telephone records concurring with Salonen's. Olli dismissed it; he was much more interested in the gun.

"We'll be there at 8 am. Please pass that on to Ina. Thanks."

◆ ◆ ◆

8 am. Ina stood in front of the two detectives in her office. She picked up a large handgun from her desk and artfully displayed it. Topias knew a presentation was forthcoming.

"Gentlemen, this is a Maxim 9. It's a relatively recent model with a silencer built-in to the gun itself. The weapon leaves a unique signature on its bullets. Therefore, we know this type of gun was used in both murders. We have also confirmed that the recovered bullets came from the same weapon: single shots to the heart. Furthermore, I have tested the bullets retrieved from each body, and I'm convinced they match another shooting from three years ago."

Topias' ears pricked up at this news, the first sign of a possible new lead.

Ina continued, "The markings on the bullet are identical in each case, and I re-checked them using all the available tests. The same gun, wherever it may be now, shot and killed a woman called Tarja Kangas. In addition, she was shot in approximately the same place, in the heart's left ventricle. Although the gun could have exchanged hands since the incident, everything suggests we are dealing with the same killer."

"Was the perpetrator of that murder ever found?" asked Olli.

"No, and neither was the gun. And now, it has reappeared again in a new, or the same, assassin's hands."

Ina handed Topias a folder, which he accepted with a nod, and carefully leafed through its contents.

"It states here that no one was ever charged with the woman's murder, and there doesn't even seem to have been a credible suspect."

He continued scanning the papers for the key facts.

"It seems the husband benefited from a fairly hefty insurance windfall at the time —almost a quarter of a million euros."

"Wow! Was he ever a suspect?"

"No. The husband was investigated early on but had a cast iron alibi." Topias shook his head. "It states here that none of the suspects even had a police record."

"We did check Tommi's insurance policies, didn't we?"

"Yes. The house was covered, but there was nothing else. The property's estimated value is one hundred and twenty-five thousand euros. Taking away the bank loan for the property and an additional loan they took out for their new sauna leaves barely ten thousand euros remaining."

"Do we know if any financial arrangement links all three victims?"

"I'll check on it," said Olli, and he disappeared into the depths of the building to commence his research.

"Thanks, Ina," remarked Topias as he nodded at her. "This is great work that could help a lot."

"Well, thank you, Mr T. Please keep me informed."

Topias smiled and left, thinking Olli's research could be interesting if there were just one clear connection.

He returned to his desk with a refreshed coffee. He checked his emails, noting first that Terhi, his sister, thanked him for a lovely evening and wished him: a 'Happy Birthday'. She also told him that she'd left the house, advising that after walking Otso, she had closed and remembered to lock the back door, signed with an 'X'.

Later the morning, Topias received a further text message from Petra, more pressing in its tone this time.

I have to see you urgently. Please come to the apartment as soon as you can.

Topias sighed and hoped this was a genuine call for help or some essential information on her part. He didn't want to risk any complicated entanglements. However, she was a vital person in this case, and a lead was a lead. He wasn't getting anywhere in any other direction except perhaps with Ina's latest revelation.

Resigned to the meeting with her, he finished up his inbox and clicked off his laptop. As most of his colleagues had left for lunch, the office was quiet, so he went unnoticed downstairs to his car.

◆ ◆ ◆

Topias arrived at the destination within thirty minutes, despite heavier lunchtime traffic. He strode to the door, waving at an unmarked police car across the street. As he did so, its occupant immediately sat up straighter and acknowledged him.

Before he was able to ring the bell, the door opened. A sad young woman appeared before him. He could immediately tell she'd been crying.

Petra wore a short pink t-shirt revealing her trim waist and fashionably ripped jeans cropped above the ankles. Her feet were on display as usual. She meekly welcomed him into the apartment.

"Are you okay?" Topias asked with concern.

"No. I'm not, really. Things have been tough in the last days, and they're not getting any easier."

She led the way into the living room and offered coffee. Topias gratefully accepted it and set about determining if any new reason or event had caused this mood change.

Petra brought two cups back from the kitchen and took a sip from one, placing his on a mat on the coffee table. Then, she sat next to him and waited for his questions.

"Is there anything you'd like to tell me?" he questioned.

Petra looked at him, opening her eyes wide.

"I'm sorry, Topias. I just needed you last night. I woke up this morning thinking you didn't care about me anymore. I don't feel safe. I need you."

Much to Topias' amazement, Petra got up from where she was sitting and promptly sat on his lap. She leaned in, closer to him, taking his hands and placing them on her body. They naturally moved closer, and clothes were discarded.

◆ ◆ ◆

Topias awoke with a start.

He looked around, wondering where he was. He was in bed. Then, he remembered. He checked his watch: it was almost 1 pm.

Damn, I must have fallen asleep.

Topias looked down and saw Petra fast asleep, her long blonde hair half-covering her face. He felt her warm face on his chest. She looked so peaceful there, gently breathing in time to his own. He shook his head, partly happy with the pleasant experience while simultaneously berating himself for the act. He told himself it had not been the most sensible thing to do.

No. Not at all.

He carefully transferred her head to a pillow, silently slipped out of bed, and dressed.

At one point, Petra moved onto her other side, and Topias froze, not knowing what to say if she should wake. However, she continued sleeping, and he crept out of the room to the front door, where he slipped on his shoes and closed the apartment door.

Outside, he noted the unmarked police car had changed to a different one and breathed a sigh of relief. There had probably been a change in shifts. He wouldn't have wanted to explain such a lengthy 'interview' to anyone.

Topias got into his car and made his way to the station.

On arrival, he avoided eye contact with anyone. He poured a coffee and submerged himself in the laptop at his desk.

He didn't come up for air for the rest of the afternoon and spent the time reading emails, reports and research. Other officers left him to his own devices, knowing it was better not to interrupt the Detective Superintendent when he was concentrating.

By the end of that day, he had caught up with everything. It was time to go home and look forward to a soothing sauna to calm his nerves.

◆ ◆ ◆

After returning to his house and taking Otso on their constitutional walk, Topias sat down and contemplated Petra again. He felt guilty about sneaking away.

Do I call her? Do I meet her? Do I say this was just a mistake?

His instincts told him he should do the latter. Yet, their previous meeting had been so passionate that he was reluctant to lose the opportunity of a reoccurrence. His current interest in Petra was growing into stronger feelings. In addition, he didn't want to upset her in the middle of a delicate situation. He wondered if he had taken advantage of her because she'd been vulnerable. But the controlling influence had very much felt like the other way around to him.

After much thought, he decided to call her.

No answer.

Topias tried again but to no avail. He decided not to leave a message as Petra would see and return the call anyway.

Despite two more attempts at phoning Petra that evening, she didn't answer. Topias was now concerned that she didn't want to speak to him. They had crossed a boundary, and her apparent reaction to this didn't look good.

Well, there isn't much I can do it now. I'll try and call Petra tomorrow, Topias decided.

MISSING

The next day brought sunshine to bear on Helsinki. The temperature began turning the snow into water, being over zero for the first time in months. Cars churned brown slush as they drove, depositing it at the roadside as they attempted to follow the two lines carved out in the centre of the ice road, similar to railway lines.

Topias noted a few minor accidents on his way to work, as drivers fell into the false sense of security that the sun brought out in them by driving faster than was sensible. He was used to the sight; the same thing happened every year. He noted several police cars engaged in various traffic management duties.

When he reached the office, he prepared for the morning meeting.

Despite his concerns about a certain young woman, he felt optimistic the team would make good progress that day and strode into the incident room with considerable energy and determination.

Topias greeted his team and sat down to open his laptop when he was interrupted by a voice carrying across the open-plan office.

"Detective Superintendent – I've just had a call from the officer stationed outside Petra Heikkinen's residence. It's been broken into, and she's disappeared."

"Damn! I don't believe it," Topias cursed under his breath, his thoughts in a whir.

He grabbed his coat and bag, left the room and made straight for his car, heading towards the apartment with blue lights flashing.

Topias made good time and joined several police cars parked outside the apartment. He nodded at an officer outside who recognised him.

After a brief discussion, Topias continued along the familiar path to the apartment. His mind was racing, wondering if he should have stayed with Petra. Perhaps he could have prevented the kidnapping if he had stayed with her or returned to her?

That's why she didn't answer her phone yesterday evening.

Topias entered the apartment and took in the scene in front of him. The place showed signs of being searched, but not as thoroughly as the previous break-ins, and not as aggressively either. A preliminary report stated that no one in the adjoining apartments had seen a woman leave. However, as this was effectively a dormitory area, most people hadn't noticed she'd been staying there in the first place.

As they did their work, Topias remained with the crime scene investigators, hoping they would discover some vital evidence of Petra's whereabouts.

After an hour, this seemed unlikely when one of the investigators turned around and waved at him.

"This is odd. There are four copies of the same book in Petra's bedroom, and there are no other books here, so she could have brought them with her. One has a slot carved out of the middle as if it was a place to hide something."

"I've seen that done before, but it's unusual for someone to have multiple copies of the same book. I wonder why?" asked Topias.

"No idea. The books were lined up on the shelf."

"Okay, it doesn't explain the woman's disappearance, but it may be something. We need to ascertain if she left or if she was taken? Let me know if you find anything else."

At that moment, Olli appeared at his side.

"Did you find her phone?" Topias asked.

"No sign of it here. I can't find a purse or keys either. Obviously, she left with the items, or they were stolen. I found this, though," Olli commented while holding up Topias' business card.

He ignored this, and Olli continued.

"We're getting hold of her phone records as we speak; they might tell us something. We're also trying to pinpoint her location if her phone is on. We can't tell if anything else has been taken unless it's the contents of that book. Her suitcase is here. She would have taken that together with her clothes if she'd left on her own accord."

Topias nodded absentmindedly. He was starting to think he would have to tell a believable story about why there'd been so many calls from her to him, and vice versa, when the phone statement arrived. He also wondered if he might have to explain why he'd spent those hours with Petra the day before. Dismissing these issues from his mind, he tried to focus on the matter at hand—her disappearance.

The two detectives loitered in the hallway to see if anything else arose. Nothing did. Petra's sister and her husband had already been contacted and would be interviewed on their return to Helsinki. Now, he had to return to the station and mobilise the team to consider possible locations where Petra may have been taken.

Topias and Olli decided to go their separate ways. However, just before he left to return to the station, Topias received a phone call from a number he had not expected to hear from.

"Topias?" a female voice asked.

"Petra, is that you?" he gasped in amazement.

"Yes. I've still got my phone. I've been kidnapped," she whispered, sobbing.

"Listen, I'm going to find you, don't worry. Do you have any idea where you are?"

"No. It's dark here, and I can't move. I'm scared. You have to find me," still sobbing.

"Petra, this is very important: how long were you driving before you reached your destination?"

"Not sure. Maybe half an hour?"

"Did you see or hear anything at all?"

"No, they blindfolded me, and I didn't hear much either."

Topias asked the obvious question.

"Why have they let you keep your phone?"

"While they were searching the apartment, I hid it on myself."

From his brief experience with Petra, Topias couldn't imagine she would be wearing enough clothes to hide a phone. And how would kidnappers not notice if it were concealed on her person? Still, experience had taught him that anything was possible.

"Right, this is very important. Keep your phone on, switch it to silent and hide it somewhere in the room. We're going to track your signal and find you."

"Okay."

"And Petra? Do you know what they want from you? Did they say anything at all?"

"No. Some men grabbed me and put a hood over my head. I'm terrified, Topias. Please."

"Don't worry. I'll find you as soon as I can."

Several officers had gathered around Topias by this point, who now sprang into action at his direction.

One of them arranged to pinpoint the phone's location, and one rallied a squad at headquarters to prepare to drive to her assistance. The others continued to inspect the crime scene with renewed energy.

"I need a couple of minutes to think," Topias told Olli.

He went outside and breathed in the cold air, starting along the building's path to the main pavement. The ground was sheet ice with surface water, so walking was perilously slippery. Still, he needed to pace to think in peace, so he walked with his feet flat-down and his eyes on the ground to avoid a painful accident.

His mobile phone rang again, and he answered it immediately.

"Yes?"

"Inspector, the missing person's phone has pinged some antennas, and we've triangulated the phone's signal. We have the following position."

"Yes! Hang on a second."

Topias hurried back to the apartment block, narrowly missing his step. He grabbed some paper and a pen and wrote down the address details.

"Let's go," he instructed Olli, telling another officer to send the squad patiently waiting at the central police station: three police cars and a van.

The detectives leapt into Topias' car, and he slammed his foot down on the accelerator. The tyres briefly spun on the ice before their tiny metal spikes dug into the road and propelled the car rapidly toward its destination.

The squad made good progress along the highway, but when they turned off, they found the route treacherous. Topias tried to strike a balance between pace and safety as he sped along the icy roads. Due to the urgency, he erred on the side of the former and narrowly avoided losing control at one point when he swerved around a hairpin bend. Fortunately, his car's winter tyres gripped onto the road surface to continue its mission.

After a few more minutes, he approached what his GPS informed him was the destination: old farm buildings with a grain storage barn and a few small outhouses. There were no lights nor activity apparent, so he skidded his car into the yard, coming to a stop near the old barn.

After briefly checking the area, Topias chose the barn as his primary target. He removed his pistol from the glove compartment, confirmed it was loaded and cocked it, ready to fire.

As there were no visible threats, he slid out of the car and kept low, half-running, half-walking to a group of empty oil barrels. Knowing other police vehicles were heading his way, he remained outside, watching and listening. All the time, his pistol levelled ahead, scanning the broader area from time to time.

Before long, a convoy of police cars swept into the yard, with the sound of tyres crunching on the ice as they abruptly halted.

Topias joined the uniformed officers to commence a search, assuring them someone may be armed inside one of the buildings. Two officers remained by the cars, blocking off a potential escape into the road. Although, no other vehicle was visible anywhere at that point. The other officers and Topias approached the old grain barn and stopped by its entrance.

Deciding it was better to warn first where firearms were involved, he shouted: "Police. Come out of the building with your hands in the air."

Silence. They waited for a minute, and Topias repeated his warning.

Nothing.

The door looked fragile, so with a nod from Topias, one of the officers aimed a gun at the door. At the same time, the other quietly lifted an external latch and aimed a small but powerful battering ram.

When the hit came, its strength splintered the door, falling into itself. The barn was dark, and their guns followed the pools of light dancing around the brick walls.

In one corner of the building, the torches settled on a lone figure, seated on the floor on a blanket, hands chained to a large metal pipe.

"Petra," gasped Topias.

SAFETY

Topias eyed Petra thoughtfully through the window of the interview room. She struck a pathetic figure at that moment: huddled in a blanket with both hands, clenching a mug of coffee as if her very life depended on its existence.

She hadn't said much in his car on the journey to the police station. This may have been due to an officer accompanying her in the back seat attempting to console her. It could also have been the shock effect of her traumatic ordeal. In any event, Topias had no idea about her thoughts and feelings at that moment.

He entered the interview room and tried to make her comfortable. It didn't go well.

After his unsuccessful efforts, he withdrew to discuss her condition with Saana, who had been sitting with her. Both expressed concern. They were worried something else might have befallen her during the ordeal, so a request was made for a doctor to examine her.

Half an hour later, the doctor arrived and declared everything was satisfactory. Except for mild bruising on her wrists where she had been chained to the pipe, there were no other physical signs of abuse. From another perspective, the doctor had diagnosed mild shock and asked that she relax and sleep as she wanted, for at least a few hours. After that, he would permit the police to hold a short interview, performed as delicately as possible, with the doctor in attendance.

Topias complied, even though it restricted his access to her. At that moment, all he wanted to do was to hold her in his arms. That was all he'd wanted to do since he found her chained to that cold, hard floor.

For the following few hours, Topias busied himself with paperwork at his desk. He eagerly awaited any clues from the farm building where Petra had been held. Early signs of evidence revealed nothing except a bottle of water she'd been given and the chains and padlock with which she'd been secured.

When he was notified of her improved condition and willingness to speak, Topias quickly made his way to the interview room, where he greeted her.

Petra's response was a meek smile and a muted greeting, still a promising sign of activity, given that she hadn't uttered a single word since her rescue.

"Petra, in your own time, do you feel able to explain what happened?" Topias asked.

"I don't know," she muttered almost inaudibly.

Tears rolled down her cheeks. Topias handed her a tissue and left the box on the table. He could see she had a slight purple bruise on the opposite side of her face, which he had previously not noticed.

"Take your time. It's okay. Do you feel up to answering some questions or would you like more time?"

She looked at him with her blue eyes, not sparkling now but at least calm, and nodded.

"It's okay. I can do it," Petra confirmed, although this answer escaped as a mere whisper from her lips.

He nodded and took a sip of his coffee. He suddenly felt guilty and offered Petra a top-up or water, but she declined. He knew this would be a challenging conversation for them both.

"In your own time, Petra. Please tell me what happened."

"I was at the apartment, just finishing off tidying the place. As my sister and her husband had been away, I didn't want them to arrive and find the place a mess. After that, I planned to relax and watch something on television."

She took a deep breath. Telling the story was visibly taking a lot of effort. Topias waited, catching the female police officer's eye, seated on the edge of her chair in the corner of the room. She was also listening in anticipation.

Petra continued, "...and the bell rang. It was the bell of the apartment, not the entry phone from downstairs. I supposed whoever it was had been let in by someone else or maybe a neighbour. Actually, at the first moment, I thought it was...."

She trailed off again, slightly turning, remembering someone else was in the room. Topias assumed she had been about to say his name and was grateful she'd checked herself and hadn't done so.

"Please continue. What happened then?" Topias urged her.

"I went to the door and opened it. I didn't think to use the entry phone to ask who it was. Two men were standing there, and they barged their way in and closed the door. They were aggressive and told me to be quiet, or I would end up like my husband. I felt faint, and one of them took me by the arm and sat me down.

"They both started searching the apartment as if they were looking for something specific. I said I could help if they needed something, but they ignored me. They didn't care about anything except what they came for—whatever that was."

She breathed deeply once more.

"Do you know what it could be?" asked Topias.

"I don't know what they wanted, and they wouldn't tell me."

Topias left his questioning for a minute, concerned that she was about to burst into tears.

At an appropriate moment, he continued.

"How long did they search the apartment for?"

"Probably fifteen minutes. During that time, they were so busy that I retrieved my mobile from the table in front of me, and I managed to put it in my sock. Thank God they were so busy they didn't notice. Apart from an occasional glance to check that I was still sitting there, they didn't seem to care about me, but I didn't dare to try and leave just in case they hurt me. I was too afraid."

Petra was becoming more lucid now, so he continued.

"Did they find or take anything?"

"I don't know. As far as I know, there was nothing to find, and I certainly didn't take anything there of great value. I don't think my sister or brother-in-law have anything worth a break-in, except maybe laptops, phones and wallets, but they'd taken them away with them."

"What happened then?"

"One of the men told me they had to take me with them."

"Did they harm you in any way?"

"No, they weren't aggressive, but straightforward. They said everything would be okay and I'd be released soon. Apparently, I was just their insurance policy. If I did as they said, one man told me that nothing would happen to me. I didn't know whether to scream or not. I was just so scared, so I didn't do anything."

Topias looked down at the table, trying to understand why they had taken Petra.

They knew she didn't have what they were looking for but took her anyway. Perhaps as a bargaining chip? Who did they hope to bargain with? Who had the item of interest and would be prepared to surrender it in return for Petra?

He studied her again. She was struggling, but he could leave her in peace if only she could get through a few more questions.

"So, what happened next when they took you away from the apartment?"

"Water, please," she pleaded.

Saana passed her a bottle, which Petra grasped and gulped before breathing deeply, apparently resetting herself before continuing.

"The same man told me I had to keep quiet or it would be all the worse for me, so I went down the stairs and out of the door with them. The other man never said a word the whole time. Unfortunately, we didn't meet anyone who could help me on the stairway, and they took me by the arm to a waiting car. The engine was running, and another man was in the driver's seat. We left immediately."

Topias asked her about the men: what did she remember about them? Voices, faces, height, clothes, shoes etc. She didn't remember much except for dark clothing and short hair. He decided to have her sit with a visual profiler and re-create their images later when she was feeling better."

"And then, after they put you in the car?"

"We drove out of the city to the place you found me. They pushed me down onto a blanket and chained me to a pipe, but not before throwing me a bottle of water. I was worried they might do something to me, but thankfully, they just drove away, and I didn't see them again. After that, the next person I saw was you. Luckily, they didn't think to search me for anything; otherwise, I wouldn't have been able to call you. Maybe they thought I was too frightened to do anything while they were in the apartment with me. I might still be in that awful place if I hadn't taken my phone."

"We would have found you, Petra, rest assured," Topias answered, reassuring her but not at all certain that they would have found her so quickly. "There are officers at the scene now, so we hope to apprehend these men if or when they return. At that stage, we'll need you to identify them. Will that be alright?"

"I'll try."

"Good. Your brother and sister-in-law are home now, so their apartment will be secure. You can return there sometime in the future. However, while these men might still be looking for you, as we'd planned, I'm placing you under protective custody. You can remain here for a while, and then we'll move you to a more comfortable but safe location."

"Will you be there?"

"I'll go with you to the address with Officer Saana Leinonen. You've met her before. She's nice, and I'm sure you'll get on with her. Officers from another division will remain outside to ensure you're alright. Those men won't be able to get to you now, and the police will protect you. Besides, they won't even know where you are. The more I think about it, the more I don't think they thought through what they were doing properly. I don't see how you could've been useful to them. I doubt they'll try anything again, and if they do, we'll be there."

Topias stopped, wondering if he'd spent so much time reassuring her that it might have the reverse effect. Petra looked him directly in the eyes again and expressed a faint smile. Topias thought he saw a suggestion of the same sparkle in her eyes that he recalled from their previous meeting.

"Thank you, Petra. Oh, just one more thing. Why did you have four copies of the same book in your room at the apartment?"

"Oh, those. I always keep a few at my sister's place, just in case an opportunity to sell one comes along. It's my book, you see. I wrote and published it independently under the pseudonym of Elina Huhta. I used to keep a memory stick with the book inside one of them in case I deleted it on my laptop by mistake. But I think I used it for something else."

"Ah, very talented. And that explains that. Thanks. We'll have a few more questions, but those can wait until later."

Topias smiled at her, nodding at Saana that he was finished. He'd already decided to concoct more excuses to check on Petra while she was in protective custody. He certainly felt more comfortable that she would be looked after at a safer location, especially with Saana, who he knew wouldn't leave her side.

When he returned to his desk, he called one of the officers at the old farm, where they had found Petra. They told him it was calm there. No one had even driven along the neighbouring road. He wished them luck and left them to it, where they would remain until the following day.

Topias considered how expensive this case was becoming: in addition to his team and its temporary, additional members, there would be officers guarding Petra and six more on location, waiting for the kidnappers. Anytime now, he thought to himself, there would be a meeting with his superior about overtime levels, but hopefully, that would happen after the case was solved. With a bit of luck, such success would outweigh the cost.

His next task was another additional expense, to arrange for a sketch artist to spend some time with Petra.

Perhaps some profile pictures will help us track them, whoever they are?

It was time for Topias to bring the investigating team together again.

When they convened, each officer reported on their research. As usual, he updated the noticeboards and discussed possible theories on the kidnapping.

"So, where do we go now?" Asked Olli. "Now that we know it wasn't Petra who did all this?"

"Not sure. At least we've eliminated one possibility, which makes other possibilities more probable. Let's go through everything and try and define what exactly they are."

At the end of the meeting, they went for lunch.

After this, Topias briefly visited Petra to ensure she was being taken care of. He found her playing with a salad in one of the station's kitchenettes. She looked slightly better.

At his arrival, Saana left to attend to something, so he took the opportunity to briefly take Petra in his arms and hug her tightly. She welcomed this, put her face against his and kissed him lightly.

That's enough for now, Topias decided.

Petra was safe, and he couldn't risk anyone walking in on them.

HAVEN

They were ready to go. Two officers joined Topias and Petra to drive to the safe house. It was snowing again, quite heavily this time. The previous milder days had seemed to signal an end to the harsher part of winter. However, it was a false ending to the season that had now returned with a vengeance. The team drove into the weather and headed to their destination, which wasn't far away, in Leppävaara.

The apartment wasn't the most pleasant of accommodations, having been well-used in the past without being updated, but it was serviceable and safe. Saana promised Petra pizza that evening, which lifted her spirits considerably.

After waiting until she'd settled in, Topias left the apartment in the mid-afternoon and drove back to the grain store where they'd found Petra.

A quick check-in with the officers informed him that nothing had happened since his previous phone call. He walked around the whole area, trying to find something that might provide a clue to the purpose of the abduction or the whereabouts of the kidnappers, but this was to no avail. Also, a fresh layer of snow now covered anything that may have been waiting to be discovered.

Time to go home, he decided and called off the operation.

At least Petra was safe now, and Otso would be waiting avidly on his return.

On his way back, he resolved to bring Otso on evening or night excursions. The trips would provide something to occupy him rather than simply sulking in the kitchen for his master's return. Their dog didn't usually stay with Topias for long periods, and he was considering talking to his wife to arrange more frequent and longer stays. Coming home at night was often a lonely experience. He found Otso made him finish work earlier, forced him to exercise, and was generally good company.

That evening, though, despite an enthusiastic welcome by Otso, Topias spent a problematic evening at home. He struggled to put Petra out of his mind. He put some effort into this, including a long walk, dinner, a movie, and half an hour's relaxation in his sauna. Ultimately, he resolved to visit her the next day at the safe house and ascertain how she was doing.

◆ ◆ ◆

Topias' decision to visit Petra the next day evolved into 'the earliest opportunity' by the following morning.

After a hurried shower, shave and breakfast-to-go, he dressed smartly in a grey suit with a blue shirt and headed to the safe house.

Although its outward appearance was plain, the safe house apartment boasted steel plates on the door and bullet-proof windows. It also had additional locks on the doors and windows.

Inside, the apartment was sparsely but comfortably decorated, mostly in beige and white, in the style of a budget hotel. It contained two bedrooms, one for the witness involved and one for a bodyguard. Although extra officers were sometimes brought in to protect the vulnerable, this was usually reduced to one, due to the additional security the premises boasted.

Topias rang the bell and, following a few moments, after checking the visitor through a peephole, Saana opened the door to let him in.

"Good morning," Topias greeted her. "I thought you might like these."

He handed her a cardboard cup tray with three coffees and a brown paper bag containing fresh croissants, newly purchased at a nearby bakery.

"Thank you, Torikka, you're a lifesaver. You would think someone could buy groceries for this place every so often to ensure there was always something here, but there isn't. And I didn't want to leave Petra alone for a moment."

She stepped away to allow Topias to enter and, guessing his primary purpose wasn't to visit her, gestured that Petra was in one of the bedrooms.

"I appreciate that, Saana. Let's have breakfast together, and then you can go and blow my expense account on suitable provisions."

"That sounds good. I'm going to need a few things. "Then, in a hushed tone, "How long do you think Petra needs to be here?"

"I have no idea. We need to keep Petra safe, but I'm not convinced she has told us everything. I think the threat remains very real."

Saana nodded as she took the cups from the tray and set the croissants on plates.

At that moment, Petra appeared, wearing a soft grey tracksuit.

"Well, hello. It's my heroic detective."

"Not exactly heroic," he muttered, adding, "It's good to see you looking better. I'm sorry it isn't much here. The apartment doesn't receive many guests."

Petra smiled.

Saana continued, "I'm going to get some food shortly. Perhaps you could think of anything else you may need for tomorrow, Petra? After that, we could bring some of your things here, so you'll be more comfortable."

"Stop fussing; I'll be fine after a shower and a change of clothes. Anything else can wait."

They devoured their breakfast, after which Saana excused herself to go shopping, making a list of groceries and checking Petra's favourite food and drinks before leaving. She announced that she would visit a supermarket and buy some clothes from a local store.

"Are you sure you don't mind staying here for a while?" Saana asked Topias.

"No, not at all. We'll be fine," he replied.

As soon as Saana left the apartment, Petra positively flew across the living room towards him. Topias received her in his arms, and they stood like that for a full minute. After this, their faces touched lightly, which soon became a lengthy kiss.

"My shower?" she reminded him playfully, and they moved towards the bathroom while removing each other's clothes.

Once inside the bathroom, they wrestled clumsily inside the confines of the compact shower unit and soon relocated to the bedroom, after which they made love somewhere between the bed and the floor. It was a frantic encounter as if the two lovers hadn't seen each other for months, spurred on by the knowledge that they didn't have much time.

After this exertion, they sat on the rug on the wooden floor, leaning against the bed to catch their breath.

"It's very nice to see you again, Detective Superintendent Topias Torikka," Petra commented, smiling at the ceiling. She used his full title to mimic their first meeting.

"And you too, Petra. Just nice, though?"

"Mmm-hmm. Maybe a little more than nice. I certainly appreciate the passion that you're putting into your job."

Topias turned and smiled, and they kissed once more.

"We'd better get dressed," he commented, checking his watch.

Saana had been away almost half an hour, and Topias didn't want her walking in on this scene. To this end, they hurriedly donned their clothes and made themselves presentable. Petra returned to the bathroom to dry her hair, and Topias relocated to the kitchen table.

They needn't have rushed as it was a further thirty minutes before Saana opened the door laden with bags.

"Somebody's been busy shopping," remarked Topias.

"Just a bit. Where's Petra?"

"She's in the bathroom. I think she's looking forward to those fresh clothes."

"I managed to find some. Not the most glamorous, I'm afraid, just loungewear and some nice underwear, but I think Petra will be happy with them."

"I'm sure she will."

"Are you staying a while? You're welcome. I thought I'd cook spaghetti for lunch later."

"I'd love to, but I've got some things to do and people to see.

This case still needs solving. I'll just say goodbye to Petra."

"Are you decent?" he called out before popping his head around the living room door into the inner hallway.

"Yes," she replied as she opened the door to the bathroom with a towel around her body and a smaller one wrapped around her hair.

"It's been nice to see you, Petra. Worry not; Saana will take good care of you. I'll check on you again soon."

"I hope so," she replied, blowing him a kiss as the door hid them from view.

Topias left the apartment, with Saana subsequently securing the door behind him.

"You're privileged," Saana joked in Petra's direction. "Detective Superintendent Torikka doesn't usually do house calls."

"Yes," Petra replied, "It was very nice of him," she remarked, trying her utmost to avoid her face flushing red.

TROUBLE

Should I continue seeing Petra? Topias asked himself.

He deliberated that question over coffee that morning. And he didn't reach any definitive conclusion despite reducing a plastic ballpoint pen to shreds. At least he hadn't yet given in and bought a packet of cigarettes; that was something.

In the end, he decided, whatever the case, for appearance's sake, he shouldn't return to the apartment again that day. Another officer would shortly replace Saana for her twenty-four hours off-duty period, meaning the next visit wouldn't make things so obvious.

Maybe I'll go tomorrow?

Topias recalled his feeling as a schoolboy, plotting to meet a girlfriend without her parents noticing. It felt exciting but, at the same time, made him nervous. Considering the delicate status of the case, his relationship with Petra wasn't a good career move either. Besides that, she was shortly to bury her husband. The risks were significant, but he couldn't resist her.

◆ ◆ ◆

On his way to the police station that morning, a thought entered his mind. It was something a little disturbing. He didn't know why it suddenly popped up from nowhere. It may have been previously hidden within his subconscious, but it arose at that moment.

Petra stated that she had hidden the mobile phone in her sock when the kidnappers were occupied elsewhere. When Topias found her in the barn, she wasn't wearing anything on her feet. And today, as always when he met her indoors, she was in bare feet, apparently her habit.

He shook his head, thinking it was probably nothing. Still, it continued to bother him until other matters diverted his attention.

◆ ◆ ◆

On arrival at the station, Topias visited Ina at the forensics laboratory to ask if anything new had surfaced, however small, since their last conversation.

Taking the lift down to the basement floor, he entered the pristine whiteness of the lab. At that moment, Ina was stooped over a table, inspecting an impression of what looked like a partial footprint.

"Topias. Nice of you to visit us down here in the cellar."

"My pleasure. And it's the nicest cellar I've ever been in," he replied, glancing admiringly at the modern surroundings.

She continued, without looking up, "By the way, how are things up there, in the open air?"

Although Ina probably had the most modern premises and expensive facility in the entire Finnish police organisation, she often joked about its location underground.

"Everything's fine upstairs. Except for the problem of people being murdered on a daily basis." He lowered his voice. "Between you and me, I'm beginning to feel the heat."

"Mmm, I'm not surprised, and yes, all this death is most

unsettling. Any promising leads yet?"

"Not much at all; that's why I'm hoping you've found a clue that might help point the finger in the right direction. So, Ina, do you have anything for me?" Topias asked while eyeing the partial print that Ina was studying so carefully.

"Ah, this. Yes, it's part of your case. It's actually from outside the fence of the first victim, close to the tree line. We couldn't recreate it perfectly due to the partial snow covering. Still, I can tell you it's a size 42, standard width, from an outdoor walking boot; you see the deep grips on the sole and circular patterns on the heel. They're quite distinctive. We may be able to find a matching brand."

"No DNA or anything else, I suppose?"

"No recoverable DNA. However, I told you before that we found grains of sand within the probable shooter's print, which we also found in the snow below. It would originally have been attached to the boot. I would say there was quite a lot of it, which probably became attached fairly recently before it gradually fell off. It's not from a beach; it's been filtered and treated somehow. I've seen that kind of sand before, on the sole of the first and second victim's shoes, and it's not naturally produced in Finland."

"Now we're getting somewhere. Perhaps it's from a factory, children's playground, or building site?"

Topias covered all the different options he could think of at that moment.

"Well, yes, any of those. I can't be more specific yet. It had to have come directly from where it was used rather than just being picked up from the ground. Otherwise, it couldn't have made it through the snow to the sole. If it attached itself before winter, this quantity would have fallen off by now unless these were only for occasional use. I would say these prints were from winter boots. This suggests it's being used somewhere in Helsinki as we speak."

"Interesting. Do you have anything else for me while I'm here?"

"As I already mentioned, the victim was shot at close range. From analysing the entry wound, blood spatter, and his final position, we can deduce the first victim was shot from behind the rear fence."

"The shot couldn't have been from any other direction?"

"No, absolutely not."

"Were there any signs of the print anywhere else?"

"Yes. More of the same partial prints around the same area and on the terrace. The ones on the terrace were barely there due to harder-packed snow and ice."

"Right. So, a pre-meditated and silenced shot was made somewhere between the fence and the forest. And either before or afterwards, the same person entered the house to steal the two laptops, probably while Petra was asleep."

"What makes you so sure it was pre-meditated and not spontaneous?"

"It just looks that way. At this point, I have to make some assumptions, and that's assumption number one. It's too much of a coincidence. Why would a random killer be waiting for the moment when Tommi walked out of his sauna. No, this was planned. His wife was the only one inside the house at the time. Did you find evidence of anyone else?"

"No. Petra and Tommi's DNA were all over the house, quite naturally. There weren't any signs of anyone else being recently inside, except the officers involved and traces from the neighbour, Stefan."

Topias studied the footprint again, although it was just an excuse to focus his thoughts squarely on Petra for a moment. After which, he returned to the topic at hand.

"What about Stefan? Does he have boots like this? Was there any evidence to suggest he'd been in the house earlier that night or on previous occasions?"

"No, we checked on the boots. He could've been in the house before that night. It's certainly possible."

"Just to cover all bases: no possibility of suicide, I suppose?"

"No. It's all wrong: firing distance, angle of entry, gunshot residue, blood spatter, no way."

"So, our only suspects, for now, are Stefan, Petra, or both. Or, most likely, a 3rd party who was connected to one or both of them. Although, I don't think Petra was involved, considering she was kidnapped at one stage."

"That's if she was kidnapped at all. Stranger things have happened," Ina commented. "Now, about the second victim. Everything is a carbon copy of the first attack, even down to the sand on his shoes. The exception was that his phone was missing. And, as we know, he was moved to a different place post-mortem."

Topias mulled over Ina's comments about Petra for a few moments.

"What about the break-ins? Anything there?"

"Nothing. Whoever was responsible vandalised the places, except for the third incident, where the wife was staying. That was more deliberate, much less destructive. There was nothing in the way of new DNA to follow up either. They were careful."

"Anything from the neighbour, Stefan, in any other locations?"

"No. Nothing in any of the apartments."

"Anything from the wife, Petra, or the other victim? In Stefan's apartment or in any of the others?"

"No."

Topias reflected for a few moments more and then turned to Ina.

"Thanks for the heads-up. Very useful. I'll update the team. We might need to interview our suspects again."

Topias said goodbye, and took the lift, which brought him up to his floor. As usual, he headed to the kitchen to pour himself a large mug of black coffee. He nudged the door closed and sat at a small table.

Topias needed to think and be able to dismiss Petra from any possible involvement in all of this.

Could Petra have arranged for someone to shoot her husband when he left the sauna? It would be a simple matter for someone to lie in wait in the darkness or be alerted by a text that Tommi was on the terrace. The shooter may even have been the second victim. That would clean it all up nicely, wouldn't it? Who knows, he might even have tried to blackmail her after the murder? She could have designed the burglaries to look like a gang was searching for some fictitious item, thus providing a motive for the killings. The kidnapping could have been staged, as Ina inferred. Perhaps to deflect attention? Remember the phone and the socks, or rather lack of them? The break-in could have been toned down on purpose, so as not to affect her sister's apartment.

What about the deposits into Tommi's account? Did Petra know about the money?

Could Petra and Stefan have been more than friends? Maybe, it was he who had shot Tommi, staging the diversion of a distant shooter afterwards? Could Stefan have even done this alone through his love for Petra?

No. In spite of the numerous questions bombarding him about Petra, she definitely wasn't a killer. He doubted Stefan's capability as well. There was nothing to prevent them from being complicit in the crimes, though, but that seemed unlikely too. After reaching this conclusion, he felt better about his new relationship.

Topias concluded that this was a matter of someone desperately searching for something within the Heikkinen's laptops and being willing to kill anyone who might know. And by the looks of things, they hadn't found what they were looking for as yet.

In addition, the question of the grains of sand re-entered his mind. He remembered standing in it at the building site where Tommi had worked and others who knew him there.

Could it be the same sand?

It was a long shot, but he would ask Ina and her team to check it.

At that point, Topias decided, against his better judgement, that it was time to revisit Petra.

◆ ◆ ◆

On arrival at the safehouse, he rang the bell. There was no response, so he tried knocking at the door. His concern grew as he struck with more effort, and as he did so, the door moved.

That's odd, it's unlocked.

He pushed the door wide open, placing the cardboard tray of coffees he'd brought onto a side table, and instinctively felt for his gun in its holster. Reassured by its presence, he drew carefully and aimed ahead.

"Petra? Saana? Are you there?"

Topias eased into the living area. After checking there was no one there, he cautiously moved to the kitchen and peered behind the breakfast bar. Then he slowly and quietly crept through the inner door, to the bathroom.

Finally, he took a few steps towards the bedrooms, one of which was empty—the other was not.

ATTACK

The bedroom was a shocking sight.

A woman lay face down on the bed, motionless. Around her head was a duvet soaked in dark, congealed blood.

Topias entered the room carefully, gun at the ready, checking that whoever had caused this attack wasn't still there. He gently moved the body's head to one side: it was Saana, the officer assigned to protect Petra. He leant down to examine her for signs of life—she was still breathing.

"Thank God," he uttered under his breath.

He pulled out his mobile phone, called for an ambulance, and then uniformed police support. While on the call, his other hand firmly gripped his pistol lest it be suddenly required.

Satisfied he was alone, he took some towels from the bathroom, placed one under Saana's head and pressed another to the head wound. Sitting on the bed, he examined her. Luckily, the wound looked far worse than it actually was, and he was relieved when she opened her eyes shortly afterwards.

"It's okay. You're going to be fine," Topias reassured her, hoping she wouldn't notice the blood stain surrounding her.

"I'm sorry," she whispered.

"There's nothing to be sorry for, Saana. You're the priority now. We need to concentrate on getting you better."

Topias tried to offer an encouraging smile. This was a struggle as his primary thoughts were of Petra at that moment.

"Can you hold this against your head while I check on Petra?"

Saana lifted her arm and allowed her hand to be guided to a towel.

Satisfied she was stable, Topias quickly searched the bedroom. He knew it would be in vain, but he had to try. He looked inside the cupboard and under the bed; there were few places to check.

He left the room to examine the remainder of the apartment more thoroughly but without success. It was evident that something had, once again, happened to Petra.

He was bothered that his inner voice asked him: *Was it Petra who attacked the officer?*

He dismissed the thought.

No, it couldn't have been her. Petra could never do something like this. More likely, she has been kidnapped again by desperate criminals, eager to get their hands on whatever dangerous secret seemingly links everything.

Topias strode out of the apartment and looked around for traces of a scuffle. He leaned against the railing of the landing, which contained a stairwell and an elevator. There wasn't anything there, so he returned to Saana and began making calls while standing over her, and arranged for Petra's description to be provided to the local patrols.

He was puzzled. It was probable the same person that had done this; the same person that had murdered the two men and possibly the one in prison too. However, those acts were meticulous in their execution, and this one was just messy.

All the apartments had been similarly ransacked, except

for the last one: Petra's sister's address, which had been more carefully searched. The safehouse had only received a cursory check by the look of it.

With different people working in different ways, it was becoming apparent that there were separate criminals at work. Petra had indicated the latter after her kidnapping.

The ambulance team arrived momentarily and administered on-site treatment. Saana became more responsive and explained that she hadn't seen anything. She had only felt a bang on the side of her head, and that was that. The next thing she remembered was waking up with Torikka standing over her. Saana was promptly rushed to the hospital.

When Ina arrived with the forensics team, she quickly moved in to begin work. Katja came next to take charge of door-to-door interviews and persuaded Topias to go home. There was nothing more he could do here, and the search for Petra was now in the hands of uniformed police patrols. She assured Topias that they would call him if anything helpful appeared. He didn't want to go but agreed that home was probably the best place right now.

On his way, Topias received a call from Petri.

"Torikka, I've found something you might be interested in."

"I'm all ears. I need something right now. What've you got?"

"I've been checking into the background of the other people on the board of Advantage Asunto. At first, there didn't seem to be anything suspicious. However, I found some information that it hasn't been doing so well. At one point it was on the verge of bankruptcy and up for sale."

Topias shook his head, not following where this was going.

"The weird thing is, a generous offer was made that would have absorbed it into a larger company. Salonen's debts would have been offset, and he would even have made some money from the sale. Talks began, but suddenly the company was withdrawn from the market."

Topias nodded to himself in the car, waving an unseen hand in the air for Petri to continue.

"Uh-hmm."

"So why would he call off the sale if he was in such financial trouble?" asked Petri.

"Not sure. Unless something happened at the last moment to save the company."

"I thought it might be relevant."

"It might well be. I'm not sure how, though."

"There's one more thing," Petri added.

"Yes?"

"We didn't find it at first, but it turns out that Petra and her deceased husband were members of a local shooting club."

"So, she can fire a gun! Why didn't we know this before?"

"There was nothing online about it. People sign up at the local club and pay, and I found it by checking a company name that I didn't recognise on Petra's bank statement."

"This helps. Thanks, Petri. Have a nice evening."

Topias shook his head again, thinking it was amazing how one simple piece of information could make such a difference.

Ever since the revelation of Petra's phone being hidden in non-existent socks, something had been bugging him about her, despite his other feelings. Now, someone had been bludgeoned at the safe house, and she was gone. And it seemed she was also a competent markswoman. Reluctantly, he had no alternative other than to keep her on the list of suspects.

"What a mess!" Topias exclaimed out loud.

His thoughts wandered to Advantage Asunto and whether Salonen could be involved. This suspicion was reinforced when he received a call from the forensics lab.

The sand sample from the murdered men's boots precisely matched the material used at the building site Topias visited. This was no surprise as the two murder victims had worked there. However, the possible shooter's print also contained these grains of sand. This, together with the suspicious mobile phone bill and Salonen stating he didn't know Tommi, highlighted Advantage Asunto as worthy of further investigation.

As Topias approached home, he noted winter was thawing yet again. The snow melted rapidly as the temperature climbed above zero, leading to poor slushy conditions.

As he concentrated on the road, his stomach growled, and thoughts turned to sustenance. He remembered how little food his fridge and cupboards contained. A pit stop would have to be made at the supermarket.

Redirecting his car to the local store, he began to think about what he might need to survive the following days. His usual motivation to cook had temporarily left him, so he decided only to buy the bare essentials to survive.

◆ ◆ ◆

By the time Topias arrived at the small supermarket, his mentally-prepared list was ready, so he parked his car in the underground parking garage and alighted the vehicle.

It was oddly quiet, considering that most people typically park inside with such a change in the weather. His hunger interrupted this thought, and reminded him he was on a mission.

Topias headed towards the sliding doors but suddenly remembered he had forgotten to set the parking clock that would allow him free parking for the duration of his visit; He had to go back. A parking warden would forgive, not even an off-duty police officer.

Suddenly, a brief whistling sound was followed by a loud ear-splitting bang. Topias twirled around, trying to locate its source, as the noise reverberated around the concrete structure.

Was that a shot?

Then a second one.

Yes, it is.

Topias dropped down against the side of his car and cursed himself for not reacting fast enough; he could have been hit. He carefully opened the car door and waited.

Hearing nothing, he slid horizontally flat across the seats, reaching for the passenger-side glove compartment where his gun and ammunition were concealed.

As he was doing so, he heard a screeching of tyres. He grabbed his pistol and pushed himself out onto the concrete floor again.

Moving swiftly to the car's rear, he aimed his gun at where he thought the shot had come from. By now, the rear red lights of a vehicle were disappearing under the rising automatic shutter. A quick scan informed him that the departing car must contain the shooter, as no one else was visible.

He leapt into his car and accelerated through the garage and out of the exit.

After reaching the top of the slope, he stopped to survey the immediate area for any signs of the car. Already, he knew he'd been too slow.

"Damn," he exclaimed.

There was no sign of a speeding car. The garage had been dimly lit, and the only sure thing in his memory was that the car had been of a dark colour. That was not unusual in Finland, with many vehicles being black.

Topias turned the car around outside the parking area and drove back down the ramp. He alerted the station of the incident by phone, and within minutes, blue lights appeared underground.

A detailed search of the area revealed two bullet casings adjacent to a concrete pillar. These would later be photographed and removed for analysis. Topias wondered if they would match the other bullets recovered from the two murder scenes. Many criminals, either in prison or at large, might wish him ill. He had put several hardened criminals behind bars during his career. Still, he couldn't think of any that would take such a drastic step as to try and kill a senior police officer at a supermarket.

After the initial flurry of activity from uniformed officers, he noted Ina's early arrival on the scene, who gave an initial opinion after a cursory walk around the garage.

"This is a first. There have been a few attempted shootings of police officers when something has been in progress, but never a deliberate attempt to remove one as a sole objective. Could this be a result of your investigation of the murder case? Are you working on anything else that might prompt this behaviour?"

"No. I think you're right. It's all connected. This was a desperate attempt by someone. The criminals must think I'm so close that they see it as the only solution. The thing is, though, I'm not close at all. I don't have anyone in the frame, at least not clearly."

"Do you think Petra is somehow responsible for this?"

"No. Not a chance. There's something else at play here."

Ina nodded.

Olli's car drew up to the kerb, and he jumped out of the driver's seat.

"Are you alright? I was out and didn't get the message right away."

"I'm fine. Thanks, Olli. I'll live to fight another day and to find the son of a bitch who tried to kill me."

The situation was wrapped up quickly, with just the forensics team left to check on the bullets' trajectory and the tyre tracks. Traffic and CCTV footage would be reviewed to try and locate and identify the vehicle used.

Topias left to go home, shunning any suggestion of protection by holding up his gun in reply. He had been fortunate. The shots hadn't even hit the car. He was particularly pleased about that, as it would be a hassle to sort out the insurance and repairs. He hadn't been prepared for this, and would have to be more careful in future.

◆ ◆ ◆

It was a relieved detective that returned home that night. He lost interest in shopping and called a local pizza company to deliver his dinner instead. Otso shared it, eating a slice in addition to his usual meal.

It was an effort to go for their walk that night, and Topias did so by keeping one hand on his gun in his pocket at all times.

CHASE

Topias awoke early and was treated to a spectacular sunset over coffee. So impressive the colours were that he stepped out onto the terrace to admire the view. As he surveyed the landscape, he could see the snow was thawing rapidly now; Spring was definitely in the air.

After breakfast, as a result of his recent encounter, he entered his car more carefully than usual, taking a measured look at the surrounding area before getting into the driver's seat. This paranoia also led him to look under his car in case some device might be lurking. However, he needn't have worried, there was nothing to be concerned about. Topias set off, after waving a customary greeting to a neighbour, and began his commute to the station.

On arrival, he went straight to the kitchen and helped himself to a large mugful of coffee. After a few sips, he headed purposefully to the incident room.

The first task was to update the incident boards with the previous night's experience in the carpark, as he had no doubt it was somehow connected. While he was doing so, Saana knocked on the door and entered. She was in much better spirits than the last time he'd seen her, with the only remaining evidence of her injury being a small bandage on one side of her head.

"May I?" she asked.

"Yes, of course. It's good to see you, Saana. How are you feeling?"

"Much better, thanks. It's good to see you, too, especially alive and well. It's not every day you get shot at in the line of duty."

"This job is getting hazardous for both of us, isn't it? It wasn't even in the line of duty; I was only going shopping for groceries."

"Well, you were probably still thinking about the case," she remarked. "We all know you're never really off duty, and it seems our shooter does as well."

"They tried to catch me off-guard, and the bullets almost hit me too. I was lucky to forget something and return to the car, otherwise, they may have got a direct hit. I need to get more sleep and sharpen up a bit."

"Or drink more coffee?" Saana smiled, gesturing towards his mug.

"I'm not sure that's physically possible," Topias retorted.

"Well, I'm just happy you're still breathing." She reached over and gave his arm a soft squeeze, and smiled. "So, what's up? What should we do to catch these guys?"

"I think it's time for a brainstorm. Can you arrange to get everyone here in two hours? That'll give me time to think."

"Sure. Consider it done, boss."

Saana left, and Topias remained, rooted to the spot, analysing the information on the boards in front of him. He stayed there until his coffee cup was drained. At which point, he collected a refill and returned to precisely the same spot as before.

Just before 11 am, the whole team assembled in the incident room, clutching their coffee mugs and waiting for Topias to begin.

Their leader commenced the meeting by describing the previous evening's events in the supermarket garage. His dramatic story drew some sharp intakes of breath from the assembled audience.

Once this was completed, he explained the news from the forensics lab concerning the sand analyses and the importance of investigating Advantage Asunto. The connections between the construction company and the case couldn't be ignored despite remaining circumstantial.

Next, Olli stood up and updated on the progress of the search for the missing woman, now simply referred to as 'Petra' by all. He explained the crime scene, Saana's injury, Petra's violent disappearance, and the fact that she should still be considered a suspect. However, it was more likely that she had been abducted again by others yet to be identified. Aside from that, he didn't have much else to share, only that CCTV had caught her entering a black Volvo saloon, which had subsequently driven away. There must have been a driver, as she had been seen entering via a rear passenger door. Whether she had been the only passenger or with others couldn't be proven.

Topias stressed that much had occurred in the past twenty-four hours, and there had to be a reason; it looked as if those involved had pressing matters on the table.

The following discussions focused on Petra's involvement in the case. Topias was convinced that she was the key to the mystery. Only by locating her or rescuing her, could they understand the bigger picture. There had to be a reason for her absence or abduction. He couldn't believe she was responsible for any of this, at least not the more severe crimes. To the assembled audience, he was careful in his choice of words. The team couldn't be allowed to think that he might have any other connection with the fugitive other than his professional interest as a police officer.

He was just about to announce a break for coffee when a uniformed officer appeared at the window, gesturing frantically in his direction. Topias waved him in.

"Yes, Matti?" he asked.

"You asked me to check the traffic feed for an old black Volvo in the area of the supermarket where someone took a shot at you."

"And?" Topias asked expectantly.

"I found it, at least I think I have. The plates are from a different car, an old one that was probably left for scrap. It looks like the same car was used in the abduction and the shooting. I haven't found any vehicle ownership details that make sense yet, as it could be from abroad. Still, I managed to track it using traffic cameras on the highway. After that, it ducked off onto a forest track."

"Katja, please, would you put a map on the screen."

"I'm already on it. Here you go."

With Matti's help, she spent a few moments locating the supermarket and slowly traced the route to the highway.

"This is the track it disappears onto," explained Matti. "There are no cameras in the area surrounding the lake or forests, apart from two speed-check points. It's unlikely they would be speeding, though, as it would attract too much attention. There are no signs of the car leaving the area via the next highway or returning to the original one."

"Excellent work. Mind you, it's a wide area, and the criminals could be holed up in any of the cottages there. We need to find out if any of our suspects have a link to one of these cottages. Contact the cottage rental agencies and ownership records to see if one of them lead to anyone, especially Petra, the murder victims, or anyone connected with the construction company, especially Salonen. And don't forget the neighbour, Stefan, just in case."

After distributing various tasks among the assembled group, they scattered to the four corners of the office, feverishly working phones and keyboards. Topias went to the bathroom and splashed cold water over his face, peering in the mirror at his reflection.

"I'm beginning to think I'm getting too old for this," he told himself, pulling his lower lids downwards. "Who are you, Petra? And where are you? Whatever the case—we're coming to find you."

Olli appeared in the doorway.

"Talking to yourself is the first sign of madness, you know?"

"Then, it's well underway. I've been doing it for years."

He walked out of the bathroom, and through the open office, to the kitchen. He needed a coffee now more than ever. Observing his team at work, he felt a sense of pride, with everyone busy doing what they did best together: detecting crime.

Suddenly, Petri looked up at him and shouted across the room.

"Immo Salonen owns a cottage in that area, about fifteen minutes off the highway. It's on the property register."

"Really? That could be it. That's if I'm right about him. Although would he risk using his own cottage? Right, we need to go and check. Katja, send two squad cars after us. It could be a wild goose chase, but we might need backup."

The two detectives left the office and hurried towards the garage. Olli took his car and drove, with Topias occupying the passenger seat, tapping the address into the car's GPS. The time indicated was thirty-two minutes; however, he didn't doubt Olli would cut that down as they sped towards the highway entry road.

"Are you armed?" Topias asked.

"Oh yes. Armed and ready if the need arises, Olli replied, patting his jacket as he did so."

"Me too. Let's hope it doesn't come to that."

They took the highway, and Topias saw blue flashing lights behind them.

Good. We're going in heavy-handed, Topias noted.

"Olli, it's the next turning," he warned as the car sped along, touching one hundred and forty km per hour.

Guided by the GPS, Olli dropped a gear, touched the brake and turned off the slip road into the forest.

"This one," Topias snapped as the car almost overshot the next turning.

Olli swerved the car across the road to the left, and they drove down a track. Some of the snow had melted, and brown slush splattered from the ground onto the windows, reducing visibility, meaning Olli had to decelerate. Topias was okay with that; they had already hit some potholes in the road, and he feared the imminent loss of some essential vehicular part at any moment. He peered through the window as they continued, finding the driveway to the cottage shortly afterwards.

"Stop here," commanded Topias. "Let's get out on foot."

Olli pulled over by the trees and gestured for the car behind to do likewise, which had already turned off its flashing lights. The officers exited the vehicles and, as they gathered in the road's centre, were joined by another unit.

"Right. Block the road here with one of the cars, and you two remain here," Topias instructed the officers who had just arrived. "You two, go left, and we'll go right. Check the outbuildings first, and we'll start towards the main cottage. After that, move around and cover the rear. When we go in from the front, you go in from the back. Does everyone understand?"

They all nodded and proceeded to follow their instructions. Topias approached a gate and climbed over it, with Olli following close behind.

The area in front was laid open to a sizeable clearing, so there wasn't any point in moving slowly, and they covered the distance at speed.

Standing at either side of the front door, Olli tested the handle: locked, of course. They stood there for a minute, watching for any signs of activity, waiting for the other officers to move closer.

"Anything?" Topias asked.

They shook their heads.

"Not even a vehicle anywhere," replied one of them.

"Alright. You two go around the back, and we'll go in the front. Give me one of your radios, and keep the other one on. I'll tell you when to go."

Topias hissed into the radio when everyone was in position, and they burst in, breaking the doors down. The sound of glass smashing accompanied their entry, and they moved through the cottage, shouting warnings as they went.

After checking downstairs, they carefully moved up the steps to a sleeping area in the loft.

"Nothing. Damn. Is there anything in here that might suggest Petra has been here, either of her own free will or not?"

Following a detailed search of the house, it was obvious the property had been unoccupied for a while. The only task remaining was to leave the property and arrange for the repair of the doors.

Unfortunately, Immo Salonen would need to be informed. Topias decided to do it later rather than sooner, as the cabin was obviously unused.

It was a disappointed man that climbed back into the passenger seat of Olli's car. It had been a long shot, but worth a try. Topias let out a big sigh as the car pulled away after directing the other officers to drive around the area in search of the missing vehicle. However, he knew it was a largely pointless exercise. Little else was said until they arrived back at the police station.

"Well, that was a waste of time," Topias commented as they got out of the car.

"Not entirely. Remember what you always say. We've eliminated one possibility, making the other possibilities more probable."

"Yeh. The trouble is that other possibilities aren't exactly dropping from trees right now."

They made their way into the station and headed for the restaurant. Perhaps a break and a hearty lunch would fortify them to continue.

◆ ◆ ◆

After lunch, which had been a comforting beef stew and salad, Topias found a note on his desk, summoning him to the top floor.

"Great. What am I supposed to say now?" he muttered to

himself under his breath as he headed toward the lift.

❖ ❖ ❖

Topias stood alone in the incident room. The conversation with his superior had not been the easiest. Heidi always sided with him in matters of police work, not just professionally but for other reasons known only to the two of them. Right now, she was under considerable pressure from above, and Topias was left under no uncertain impression that progress had to be shown. The police had to demonstrate to the media that there wasn't a manic murderer on the streets with an unstoppable thirst for blood. Add to this, the headlines had not been kind that day and painted the police force as incompetent for not catching the killer.

From bitter experience, Topias knew how these things went. Initially, the killer was blamed, but the police soon took the flak on their behalf.

He did his best to be objective where Petra was concerned, and stood at the boards, rearranging photographs and press cuttings to clarify where they were so far. Using three panels, he arranged the papers into groups around each possible suspect, highlighted with their first name.

On completion, he stepped back to study the boards, hoping the information would clarify his thoughts before the meeting. He began with Petra, in order to rehearse the removal of her from the equation.

Petra had the opportunity and the ability, if not the means to commit these crimes. Still, she had no motive to do so. There was the matter of those payments into Tommi's account—but enough to commit murder for? Unlikely. Besides, she genuinely demonstrated feelings for her ex-husband, at least for a short while.

Topias believed she was not the psychological type to commit these crimes anyway. He believed he knew her well enough now to be sure about that.

Stefan had the opportunity and the ability, but again, there was no apparent motive for him to do so. Despite suspicions about his evasive behaviour regarding Petra, Stefan's involvement remained doubtful.

He didn't seem to have any other connections to the case apart from living next door. Topias was officially comfortable writing him off as a suspect.

Immo Salonen may have had the opportunity to do the deeds or solicited another to do so. He was involved through the victims' employment, and the identical sand linked them and the killer to his construction site. There were also those mobile phone records and his denial of knowing Tommi. Add to this the fact that his business had been miraculously saved from bankruptcy or sale.

In addition, Topias had an odd feeling about Salonen and didn't trust him. His intuition rarely failed him.

There was much to be done. The police had no murder weapon, which would have helped enormously with identifying the culprit. They still didn't know where Tommi's bank account payments originated. Finally, they had little information on Advantage Asunto's apparent rescue.

He leaned against the glass door, continuing to put his mind to work. The exercise had focused his thoughts on the three suspects, and one had moved up his list: Immo Salonen.

Still, questions kept rattling around Topias' head. Questions that he couldn't yet answer.

What was important or valuable enough for the gang to kill? And take the risk of attacking a serving police officer.

In Topias' experience, motives usually involved love, money or betrayal. His mind kept returning to those international payments. There was nothing else for it: someone needed to track down the source of the money.

He dialled the number of his boss. He would need more influence if politicians had to be involved to broker a deal for increased cooperation with the Latvian bank.

EVIDENCE

"Where is it?"

"Where is what? I don't understand what you're saying. I don't have anything!"

Salonen was losing his patience and considering more extreme measures to extract the information he required from Petra. The construction deal was complete, and he was to be a wealthy and successful man. However, the threat of stolen data that could easily incriminate him was still a risk.

Suppose I can't recover and destroy everything, and it ends up in the wrong hands? In that case, it could resurface anytime, landing me in a huge mess.

He planned to hold Petra for as long as necessary. He hadn't gone through all this trouble to allow a young woman to take his success away. No matter the outcome, he decided that the only way to be safe was to ensure she never saw the light of day again.

"Once more. Where is it?" Salonen demanded.

"Please, believe me, I have no idea what you're talking about. If I knew, I would tell you." Petra pleaded.

"I'll give you a little more time to consider your answer. But think on this: you're not getting out of here until I get what I want. This is the last time I'm going to ask nicely."

Salonen walked out of the room, slammed the door, and

turned the key in the lock after him. Petra listened to his footsteps walk away and then down some stairs.

When everything was quiet, Petra looked around, hoping to find something to help her escape her predicament. She had no idea where she was, as she'd been blindfolded during the journey. In addition to this, her hands were tied to a chair. Thankfully they hadn't gagged her, and she could now see, but unfortunately, she couldn't move.

"How did I get myself into this mess?" Petra rebuked herself, feeling the cord that bound her dig into her wrists.

The answer lay in a discovery she had made some months prior.

One evening, while in the bedroom, waiting for her husband to appear from the direction of the sauna, she noticed a memory stick in his laptop. Petra was curious, as she'd never seen her husband use one. As his computer was switched off, she didn't want to go through the whole process of booting it up; it would take too long and make that annoying loud start-up sound. So, she removed the stick and inserted it into her own device.

After the screen came to life, she opened its contents. It was easy enough, as there was no password protection. There was a single folder, unnamed. In that folder was a document that appeared to detail the activities of the construction company Tommi worked for: Advantage Asunto. She thought it odd for him to have such information and read further.

The title of the document read 'Uusi Satama'. Petra had read about this place in the news. It would be a new part of Helsinki, a vast project. There was a list of names. Next to each was a number, opposite which was typed 'Cash', or 'Pay later. As Petra read through the list, she recognised two of the names, men who were relatively senior in local government.

As she scanned downward, copies of plans and documents

concerning parcels of land followed. She didn't understand everything, but there was no doubting what was presented there. This was a deal for a large construction project for which specific individuals had already, or were to receive, large amounts of money. She was studying law and couldn't think of why these people should receive such payments, certainly not those involved in the planning or approval process.

Could this be a list of bribes? And why does Tommi have this?

Suddenly, aware that her husband might appear at any moment, she left her laptop on the bed and walked through the living room to the sauna area to check on him. He was still there, so she hurried back to the bedroom and continued her illicit activity.

As she read, she noted another list of numbers further down the file. These payments had apparently been made to her husband, whose name was alongside them. They were regular amounts, and although not as large as those for the people listed above, added up to a substantial balance. There were also bank account details alongside. Petra recognised it must be his, as it was the same bank as their joint account, with the same set of numbers at the beginning – similar to her own account. They had taken out new accounts at the bank together when they'd arranged their house loan. Petra didn't have access to his personal account, nor did he to hers, so she had no way of checking further, at least not right away.

Why hasn't he told me anything about this money? And what does he intend to do with it?

The information almost certainly detailed illegal activity, and Tommi was either involved or benefited from it somehow. It looked like he could be being paid off or blackmailing someone or some organisation.

Advantage Asunto?

The more she thought about it, the more she worried and felt uncomfortable. She was starting to see the man she'd married in an entirely new light.

Is he a criminal? Should I confront him?

She wasn't sure, but one thing was certain: she wasn't benefitting from this arrangement personally.

Why hasn't he told me anything about this? she asked herself again.

Petra heard a noise from the direction of the bathroom, causing her to quickly close the file, remove the memory stick, and re-insert it into her husband's device. She opened the internet and sat back against a pillow.

A minute later, Tommi entered the bedroom wearing a towel.

"Ahh, that was a great sauna. What are you up to?"

"Just a bit of window shopping. Looking for some new summer shoes."

"Bit early, aren't you?"

"They sell out quickly in the stores in my size. Besides, I can feel summer coming already."

Tommi looked towards the window.

"Ever the optimist, eh?"

◆ ◆ ◆

Over the following few weeks, Petra couldn't stop thinking about what she'd found. She didn't like the idea of confronting her husband directly, hoping he would broach the subject himself. However, she did ask an occasional question to provoke a response in the general area. These questions centred around

Tommi's work, nothing too pushy, just 'matter of interest' questions and some concerning their financial issues.

At one point, she mentioned that the interest rate was increasing on their housing loan, so should they consider paying more of it down? He replied by saying they had no extra money for that and would have to manage for now. Perhaps things would get better later?

This irked her because she knew about the money he'd received, presumably sitting in his account, gaining interest. Was he saving it for them? Or was he stashing it quietly away for his own use?

It was during another sauna evening that things came to a head.

Petra left the shower room and entered their bedroom. Tommi's laptop was once again on the bedside table. This time, it was open. There was no memory stick, which was a shame, as she hadn't completed her research. When she'd opened it before, there had only been time to read some of the documents. However, as the laptop's screen light was on, she had no hesitation in checking for anything interesting. Noting his email tab, she clicked on it and scanned down the list in front of her.

What Petra found astounded her. It was an email address unknown to her, in the name of 'Matka XYZ', not his usual one, which was in his name. Scanning the emails, she found several messages from people she didn't know, plus a few spam emails, promising large payouts for a competition. What she did recognise was the name of a travel company. She clicked open a message, and her mouth fell agape.

The message contained an airline ticket to Mumbai, India, in his name, which was one-way only. There was no ticket visible for her. There was also a reservation for a hotel for two weeks in

Goa; again, it was in his name only for one guest.

Shaking her head and suspecting the worst, she closed the email and scanned further down. She clicked on a message from a Goan Real Estate broker. There were several houses and apartments listed.

What is he doing?

"Petra?" a voice called from the direction of the living room.

She immediately closed the email box and lowered the screen, just managing to replace the device on the bedside cabinet before her husband walked in.

Petra quickly untied the towel from around her chest and dropped it on the floor, leaving her naked, lying on the bed in front of him.

"I'm having another beer. Do you want something?"

"Come on. That's enough beer for you. I have another idea."

That night, she couldn't stop thinking about what she had found, but for some reason didn't confront her husband about it. She didn't quite know why? Perhaps it was disbelief? Or had she misunderstood the whole thing?

Previously, she'd been concerned and even worried for her husband's wellbeing due to suspicions about his dubious activities. However, now, she was angry. Whatever he was involved in might result in him disappearing to live abroad without her, for how long, she didn't know—possibly permanently. She had loved him, but obviously, now, he had other plans.

Petra began to think about what she could do to benefit herself. Whatever the case, she decided she must not allow him to be suspicious about anything, and their life should continue precisely as before. From that moment onward, Petra's perspective of their relationship changed permanently.

Biding her time, she waited until the opportunity arose to access his computer again. Tommi wasn't a computer wizard. He was also not afraid of Petra snooping on him and often left his laptop unguarded and accessible. He knew his wife would never go near it; she had never done it before. Besides, she had her own device, so there was no need.

It was two weeks later when Petra saw her opportunity and took it.

As had happened before, it was during a sauna session. That was the only gap when Petra could guarantee she would have enough time, as she always finished before him.

On this occasion, she left the sauna area, wearing her towel as usual, and found the laptop on his side table, open this time, with the memory stick in place. She took it, plugged it into her machine, downloaded the contents, and deftly replaced it into Tommi's device.

Taking her time, she subsequently downloaded the folder from her computer onto a memory stick she usually used for her books. After this, she placed it where she always kept her backup for her novel, inside one of her books—one with a convenient cut-out hiding place.

After a few minutes, she had a better idea. When Tommi left the sauna to go out onto the terrace, she concealed it inside the sauna, attaching it just behind one of the spotlights. He would never think of looking there. Only she would know where it was hidden, right in plain sight.

That night, something happened that would change her life forever. Tommi was shot dead at the end of that freezing-cold terrace. The couple's laptops were taken, and someone would discover that sensitive information was downloaded.

During the chain of events that followed, Petra decided that there was no way she would reveal the contents of the memory stick to anyone if that information was the reason for Tommi's murder. It could be the only thing standing between her and certain death.

ESCAPE

Think, Petra. Think. How do I get out of this?

Now that she could take in her surroundings, it was evident her prison was a country cottage. It was a recently-built one by the look of it; she could tell by the distinctive smell of new wood.

The room's walls were made of heavy logs, and the last rays of the day's orange sunshine streamed in through a single window on the opposite side of the door. Nothing else but trees were visible. There were only three pieces of furniture in the room, her chair, a single bed, and a small cabinet, where a plastic bottle of water had been placed for her. However, she couldn't drink it as her wrists were bound.

What's the point of that?

Scanning the room, nothing seemed to be inside that might help her escape or raise the alarm. Petra knew the door was locked, as she'd heard the critical turn of the key. She tested her restraints again, found some give in them, and wondered about the possibility of wriggling free if she strained them enough.

Continuing along this train of thought, a plan emerged in her mind. The cabinet looked sturdy enough to smash through the window and its frame, the central struts of which seemed to be more for display purposes than anything else. The bed could be wedged under the door handle to block it or delay anyone's entry to the room.

This plan was no doubt risky, but here she was, a captive in a locked room in a forest—how more treacherous could it get? What was the worst they could do to her if she tried to escape? If she remained and told them what they wanted to know, they might kill her, as they undoubtedly had done to her husband and his friend. She was alive so far because they needed to know what she knew. If she remained here, what might they do to extract the information from her? She didn't want to think about that. Salonen had already warned her that he would not be so pleasant on his return.

No, she wasn't going to wait for that. The only option available to her was to escape, and quickly. Her plan depended on her managing to get free from her restraints. To this end, she began to pull at the cord holding her to the chair. It chafed as she did so, but the pain would be a price worth paying if she could only get free.

❖ ❖ ❖

Topias put down the phone and sighed. He'd finished talking to Maarit, his superior, about tracing the source of the money, and it didn't sound hopeful. He knew that foreign banks were reluctant to reveal details about their dealings, especially ones known to be handling some of the region's more dubious accounts. Still, Maarit had promised to contact the Foreign Ministry and kick them the ball: officially asking the Latvian government for help. There was nothing he could do now. He just hoped for the best and focused on finding another piece of evidence.

He appeared over Katja's shoulder at her nearby desk in the open-plan office. She had headphones on and was concentrating on the screen.

"Anything interesting?" he asked her, lifting one of the

headphone earpieces from her ear.

"Not yet," she replied, looking up and shaking her head. "There are still some possibilities to check."

Katja was reviewing CCTV video footage to track down anything that showed the kidnapping of Petra Heikkinen, or her escape, as had been the other school of thought. In Katja's opinion, the operation had been conducted remarkably professionally, with no helpful video footage or evidence left behind to assist the authorities.

"What have you checked so far, Katja?"

"The safe house area, and the routes that lead from there to the main roads and highway. It was a busy time of day when she was taken. They got in and out of the building without being picked up by any cameras. Let's just say that they knew what they were doing."

"Just in case, check the area around the railway and bus stations, and also the airport, for three hours after she disappeared. Assume she could have either been travelling alone or with others. Remember, we don't know for sure if she was kidnapped. Call me if you find anything."

"Will do," she nodded without removing her eyes from the screen.

◆ ◆ ◆

At the cabin, Petra was progressing with the cable that bound her to the chair. After a while, she had created enough space to withdraw the thumb of her left hand. As Petra wriggled her hand to widen the opening, a sound came from behind the door: it was a key turning in the lock. She silently cursed and hastily sat up straight, clasping her hands together behind her to disguise the fruits of her labour.

The door opened. It was Salonen who entered with an unknown man.

"Petra, I want to introduce you to someone. This is the man that killed your husband."

Petra drew a sharp breath.

"I won't tell you his name but simply inform you that he kills anyone who stands in our way. I want you to consider for one moment if I wouldn't hesitate to ask him to kill you if you don't cooperate? Yes, I would like the evidence back, but ultimately, with you out of the way, it probably doesn't matter so much whether we find it or not. In the meantime, he will try and encourage you to return the information you stole and let's see what happens. Knowing him as I do, I don't expect the experience to be pleasant."

Salonen waited a few moments to allow Petra to digest his words and continued.

"If you remember Petra, I offered to pay you the same amount of money we paid your husband in exchange for the evidence, but you refused. You can still change your mind, you know. Surely you would prefer to enjoy the money and not have dreadful things happen to you? I might even give you a bonus if we can get this out of the way quickly today."

Petra caught a glint in the new visitor's eyes and decided she had better accede to something.

"Alright. I'll take you to it."

"No. You won't, Petra. You'll tell us exactly where it is. For some reason, I don't trust you. You're too clever. So, my offer is simple: tell me where the information is, we'll go and find it, and that's it. You can keep the money, and I'll give you an extra twenty-five thousand euros for your trouble. According to my calculations, that's one hundred thousand in total. Don't tell us, and I'll leave you alone with my friend here in this isolated cabin in the woods."

Salonen nodded to the anonymous male to his side, who leered at the young blonde woman in front of him. Petra was trembling, suddenly more aware of her scant clothing. She was wearing her short lace dress.

"I'll give you one hour to consider this while we have coffee. After that, the gloves are off, and I'm leaving. After that, anything can happen to you."

Petra was in no doubt that the experience that awaited her would be unpleasant and probably result in her death; she just knew too much.

◆ ◆ ◆

After the men left the room and Petra could no longer hear them, it was time to accelerate her plan.

She pulled her wrists apart as hard as she could, extracting the remainder of her left hand from the cable with all her might. She flinched at the painful redness of her wrist caused by stretching and rubbing.

After a short while, her tenacity paid off, and the binding finally came apart and fell away. It was a simple matter to untie her other hand—she was free.

Petra stood up and looked out of the window. It was getting dark outside now. While seated, she didn't realise that the parts of trees she could see were only halfway up, and the room she was in was situated on an upper floor. When she heard the men walking downstairs, it hadn't occurred to her.

Damn. What now?

She looked at the drop below, illuminated by an outside light.

It was too far to jump down, and if she attempted it, she was sure to injure herself. But the trees were very close to the cabin wall. If she could only make it onto one of those trees, she could shimmy down and make a run for it. Would she be able to do all that while the men came after her, though? As soon as they heard the window break, they would immediately check what was happening.

She examined the casement window once more. Although it was locked at the latch, it was only on the inside and looked flimsy. Maybe she wouldn't have to smash the window at all.

Holding the latch firmly, she pulled it sharply upwards. The lever opened, and the handle moved up with a jerk accompanied by the juddering sound of wood freed from wood. She froze and listened for any sound from outside the door, but there was none.

Lucky I'm on the upper floor, after all, she thought to herself.

She carefully opened the window and looked downward; it seemed even higher now. Then, she realised her next problem.

I'm not wearing any shoes.

They had taken her boots. She would have to clamber out, jump over and climb down with nothing on her feet.

Just do it, Petra

Looking back at the bed, she decided not to risk the noise of moving it against the door. She didn't need to now. Placing the chair carefully by the window, Petra climbed on the seat and up to the window frame. Taking hold of the upper section and crouching low, with her bare feet on the bottom of the frame, she could lean outwards and extend an arm, although it was still two metres to the nearest tree. Underneath her, Petra could see large boulders waiting ominously at the bottom. If she fell, the chances are, she would do herself some severe harm.

Knowing there was no choice. Petra stretched as far as she possibly could, readied her legs to push, and left the window sill with one almighty effort. The next few moments blurred as Petra jumped from the window toward the tree.

She hit a branch first, which immediately sagged as she slipped downward. Petra desperately clawed at it so as not to plummet to the ground. As she did so, pine needles pierced her hands and arms, causing her to whimper in pain, but she was determined not to call out, lest her captors should hear.

With her legs flailing in the air, Petra held on as she swung on the branch and hit the tree trunk with a thud. She gasped and tried to hold on but lost her grip and slipped again until she could grab a cluster of smaller branches strong enough to check her fall.

Having made it without dropping to the ground, she used other branches to help her clamber down the tree. Her fragile white dress ripped on sharp twigs, and more needles dug into the flesh of her hands, wrists and arms. Fortunately, despite the pain, she made good time on the descent and stopped for a moment above a small window on the ground floor.

Petra hesitated. If she dropped to the floor, there was a risk of being seen through the window, but there wasn't much else to do at this stage; she would have to jump and hope no one would notice.

Okay. 1, 2, 3.

Petra braced herself and dropped to the ground: a mixture of stones, needles and a light covering of snow. As soon as her feet made contact with the ground, she crouched down and held her breath.

She had made it safely out of her prison.

As she noted the driveway and cars were on the other side,

there was only one direction to go: the opposite way, into the forest. She stopped for a few seconds and looked beneath the building at the gap between its floor and the ground, wondering if she could crawl far enough underneath to hide.

She glanced back at the forest.

No. That's what they'll expect me to do: run. How much progress can I make in bare feet?

Instead, Petra made it look like she'd gone into the forest and deliberately made tracks going towards it, randomly in the snow, snapping and bending tiny branches as she went.

The area had partially melted, so there were areas where the ground was fully exposed, so she decided her plan might work. The partial thaw was lucky, as otherwise, it would be too visible to her pursuers when the footprints in the snow stopped.

When Petra decided she'd gone far enough, she doubled back, tip-toeing in her own prints, and gently stepped over to the space beside the cottage, covering her tracks as she did so. Stooping down, she pushed herself almost flat and crawled underneath. Moving slowly, she went as far as she could and huddled alongside some long-discarded logs.

Petra was freezing now, not surprisingly, as it was still cold, and she was only wearing a flimsy dress now in tatters - and no socks. She tried to stop herself from shivering and her teeth chattering. Petra consoled herself she had outwitted her captors, who had probably thought her to be a fragile, scared young woman. Now, all she had to do was wait.

◆ ◆ ◆

It seemed an interminable time that Petra lay underneath the cottage, trying to think of other things rather than the numbness gradually creeping over her body. She couldn't feel her feet at all now. She was beyond cold, and with the addition of fear, it was impossible to keep her shaking under control.

Then it happened. The men discovered her absence.

A voice shouted from upstairs, and heavy footsteps echoed loudly around the cottage on the wooden floors. Petra could hear the window above flung wide open with an angry bang as it hit the wall.

More shouting and footsteps followed. Now, they were thudding above her head on the ground floor. She heard the door open and someone moving out on the terrace. They felt remarkably close, so she held her breath, worried they might listen to her. Multiple footsteps were audible now, and Petra wondered how many men there were? It sounded like an army marching over her head.

She heard a voice she recognised: it was Salonen.

"She's in the forest. Harri, you and Toni get after her. She isn't wearing any shoes, so she can't get far. Sven, you come with me. We'll take one of the cars and cut her off at the road if she reaches it. Shoot her if you have to; just stop her from getting out of the forest. Let's go."

The last comment made her even more nervous. She tried to concentrate, and by observing the legs and listening to voices, she counted four men, maybe five? No, it was four.

After a couple of minutes, there was silence, and she listened intently for any more footsteps inside the cottage. Everything was quiet above her, so Petra plucked up the courage and crawled under the cottage floor until she reached the other side.

When she pulled herself out, she tried to stand up but her legs had lost all feeling. They buckled, causing her to fall backwards against the wall. Despite her wish to move, Petra had no choice but to lean against the building for a minute. She rubbed her legs hard, after which she pushed herself forward and staggered onto the terrace, and with the aid of a side railing, into the cottage.

It was warm inside the cabin, with the fire blazing in the hearth, so Petra made it to one of the surrounding chairs and sat down to massage her feet. Together with the heat from the flames, this brought them back to some semblance of life, and after a few more minutes, she could stand again. Using items of furniture to push off and propel herself forwards, she found that she could walk again.

Petra was acutely aware that someone might return to the cottage at any time, realising she had tricked them, so she had to work fast. Looking around for anything to use, she searched the living area.

Finding refreshment, she drank water from a cup in the kitchen and found sandwiches on the table, probably freshly purchased, as there was a shopping bag on the counter. She took this and helped herself to a couple of sandwiches and some chocolate, opening one of the bars immediately. Petra was hungry and needed sugar.

Her search was concluded in the hallway, where she found a coat they had bundled her into earlier, and her face lit up when she saw her boots. But the most valuable prize lay in a dish on a table by the door: a set of car keys.

With a clear getaway plan, Petra burst out of the cottage and ran, the best she could muster, to what was the only remaining car, parked twenty metres from the cabin. The drive was floodlit, but she had no choice. She found the old jeep-type vehicle unlocked, and after opening it, she relocked the door and started the engine— it roared to life.

"Yesssss!" she exclaimed, almost in tears of relief.

Pushing her boot down hard, she accelerated away from the

cottage.

Driving down the same track the men had used, she noted it was the only possible exit. She had no idea where she was and continued until a fork in the road appeared in front of her. Unsure whether to go right or left, she shrugged her shoulders and swerved right.

After a few hundred metres, the small track opened onto a larger one. Presented with turning right or left again, Petra chose left and pushed the car faster. She drove hard enough to get away but not so much as she might lose control on what was still a perilously slippy surface.

After a few kilometres, the track abruptly halted, and she found herself at the junction of the main road. This time she turned left, but not before turning the car's heating to full.

"Let's hope for the best," she remarked and sped away.

It wasn't long before she came to a flood-lit sign informing her that it was forty-seven kilometres to drive to Helsinki. She could either continue along the main road or take the highway. She chose the latter and continued her journey at a respectable one hundred and twenty kilometres per hour, well above the speed limit for winter. However, she wouldn't have minded seeing the reflection of blue lights in her rear-view mirror.

ARROGANCE

Fortunately for Petra, Immo Salonen and his men were, as yet, unaware of her escape by car.

The men sent into the forest were still struggling their way through trees, sharp branches, and snowdrifts, cursing Petra at every opportunity. Even though the tracks petered out, some of the forest had lost its blanket of snow, making tracking her impossible. In addition, the winter's early afternoon darkness had fallen, so the gang had to guess the logical direction she might have taken.

Salonen and the man named Sven had driven down the same track as Petra. Fortunately for her, they had turned right and then right again to circle and meet her at the main road, or so they thought.

Remaining with the car, Salonen sent Sven into the forest from its border with the road. He was convinced they would find her before she could flag down a passing motorist for help.

How can a little girl like that evade four men?

Meanwhile, Petra positively flew along the highway in the jeep. As she approached the Helsinki city limits, she allowed herself a brief smile and sigh of relief. But where to go now?

She thought of driving to the police station, but decided against it as she was unwilling to reveal the reason for her abduction: the valuable memory stick. Realistically, there was only one place she could think of where she would feel safe.

Yes, he will know what to do. I must get rid of the car and get to Topias' house.

◆ ◆ ◆

At the station in Helsinki, Katja appeared at Topias' desk.

"Do you have something for me? I hope," he asked.

"We have Mr Salonen downstairs. Apparently, he was out of town, but he received our voice message and has shown up here, as requested."

"Right. Good. Let's see if we can either put Salonen in the frame or move him out of it, one or the other. Did Olli return from meeting with the neighbour again, Paikkala?"

"No, not yet. I know Olli met him at his house, but there's no news. The interview is maybe still ongoing."

"Okay, thanks. Let me know when Olli appears, would you?"

"Will do, boss."

Topias headed for the coffee machine and poured himself a mugful before making his way to the interview room where Salonen was waiting.

Having temporarily given up on finding Petra in the forest, Salonen had returned to the cottage. It was there that he found the other car missing.

Fuming, he and the gang made their way back to Helsinki, and on the way, Salonen thought it wise to respond to a message from the police. He didn't want to be seen as absent at the same time as Petra, as that might jeopardise a future alibi.

Before going in, Topias peered through the blinds at the window to size the man up. Salonen looked every bit as confident as before, if not arrogant. He noticed him check his watch while tapping his fingers. Salonen was impatient. Topias felt for a ballpoint pen in his pocket in case it might be needed and felt its reassuring presence.

Topias opened the door.

"Mr Salonen. Sorry to keep you."

"I'm sure you're a busy man, Inspector. As am I," he replied curtly.

"Quite so. Thank you for coming in; I won't keep you long."

Topias had already decided to keep the objectionable man longer than necessary. He slowly drank some coffee, purposefully setting his mug on the table in just the right place, and proceeded to read his notes as diligently as possible before continuing.

"You are the owner of the construction company named Advantage Asunto. Correct?"

"That's right. I think you know I am."

"Just for the benefit of the tape, that's all."

Topias gestured to the recording device on the table.

"And you are already aware that two of the recent murder victims were employed by you?"

"Yes, in some capacity. The men were not full-time but on flexible contracts, and we utilised their skills when the need arose. I didn't know them very well, but it was a shock in any case. Such a tragedy."

Topias didn't buy the mock sympathy and rehearsed repetition.

"That's right, it was. And Tommi Heikkinen's wife, Petra. Did you ever meet her?"

"No, as I think I told you. I don't generally meet the wives or families of my employees. Unless possibly at some social event at some stage, but I don't remember."

"Do you own a gun, Mr Salonen?"

"No. I don't. Why do you ask?"

"Just procedure. The two men were shot, you see. Then, an acquaintance linked to the two victims was killed in prison. One of my officers was also attacked during an alleged kidnapping—the second kidnapping of the same person. You may have heard about it?"

"Yes, I did. I read it in the paper. Shocking. These things don't usually happen in Helsinki, do they? What's the world coming to?"

"May I ask where you were on these occasions?"

Topias announced the date and time of each incident in turn, and Salonen answered with a clear explanation of where he was, who he was with, and what he was doing in each case.

Again, rehearsed, as he barely needed time to think. Topias analysed Salonen for a few seconds, and his interviewee glibly held his gaze.

That was disappointing. I'll have his alibi checked, but I don't hold out much hope.

Topias continued in another direction.

"Let's talk about your business. It seems quite successful."

"For the moment, yes. There are always things ready to bite you when you aren't looking, but touch wood; it's going in the right direction."

"We have to perform a detailed audit of your company as part of the procedure. Is there anything that we should be aware of?

Any debts? Any new investors? New contracts?"

"As it happens, there is. We've just signed a contract to break ground on a new construction site called 'Uusi Satama'. Here's the press release."

Salonen flushed with pride at his accomplishment.

He fished around in his coat pocket and handed Topias a folded document that outlined the new construction site and its prospects. The paper was glossy and included an artist's impression of the area, with photographs of happy people going about their business and hobbies, promising big smiles and perfect teeth.

"This is quite a coup, is it not?" remarked Topias. "One might have thought the contract would go to a much larger company?"

"Sometimes, it's not just about the size of a company, Detective Inspector," Salonen said with a hint of contempt. "Due to our agility and service level. My company was the best of the bunch when it came down to it."

Topias ignored Salonen's use of a less senior title, which he suspected was done deliberately.

"Congratulations. I imagine this deal will make quite a difference to profitability?"

"Oh yes, indeed."

"You had some problems recently with the company, didn't you?"

"You've obviously read about our financial situation and potential sale."

Salonen leaned forward and spoke more slowly and clearly as if talking to a small child.

"You sometimes ride your horse very close to the wind in this business. Construction carries a lot of debt. Like always, though, I knew we'd bounce back, and now we have plenty of work ahead."

"I better not hold you up then. I'm sure you have plenty to do. Thank you for your time."

"Thank you, Detective Inspector. Have a nice evening."

"Oh. Just one more thing."

Salonen turned around with an impatient sigh.

"The first two victims had sand on their shoes and the same sand on more shoes at their homes. We also found the same sand on the shooter's shoes—the same sand used at your construction site. How do you account for that?"

"I assume many construction sites use the sand, and if you work in construction, you are likely to have sand on your shoes at some point. I probably have some on mine at this very moment. If I am to be a suspect and your case hinges on some sand, a few telephone calls and my bad memory for names, then you have a flimsy case."

Salonen sneered and walked away as Topias watched him thoughtfully, knowing that he had successfully rattled him despite the man's bravado.

SUSPECT

Topias checked his phone and noted a message that Olli had finally returned from the interview. He called his mobile, found he was in the canteen, and happily accepted an invitation to join him.

"What's good today, Olli?"

"The salmon soup is a good choice."

"And the pulla?"

"Of course. I had to get a cinnamon bun for the coffee afterwards."

"Sounds like a good combination to me."

Topias went to the counter to take his lunch, appearing at Olli's table shortly afterwards. He'd managed to hesitate when faced with a rack of freshly baked, sweet-smelling cinnamon pullas but ultimately gave in.

"That interview took a while. How did you get on?" Topias asked.

"Something new came up, but I don't think Stefan is our man."

"Go on," prompted Topias, starting his soup.

"When we began talking, he repeated everything we'd heard before. But when I pushed him, he admitted to being closer to

Petra than we thought. Apparently, they spent time together on several occasions, innocently, or so he says."

Topias looked up from his dish with a curious expression.

"Why didn't he mention that in the first place?"

"I asked him that, and he assured me it was just as 'friendly neighbours' and said he didn't mention it before as he was worried it might look suspicious. Petra didn't volunteer that information either."

"It looks a damn sight more suspicious now."

Topias took a spoonful of salmon soup and paused to give this information his full consideration,

"I think you're right. I don't think Stefan's a serious suspect either."

Olli nodded in agreement and returned to his meal.

"How was your meeting?" Olli inquired. "Katja said you were with the owner of the construction company."

"That was interesting. Salonen didn't say much when we discussed the murders except to reiterate some, quite frankly, thinly-veiled sympathy for the victims. He reeled off a list of perfect alibis when I asked him again about his whereabouts on the dates the crimes were committed. He got them 'word perfect', I'd say. He only became more animated when I asked about his company and showed me the latest business deal."

"Business deal?"

"He proudly showed me a brochure, and I read all about it. It's going to be worth a fortune to him. When I say a fortune, I mean tens of millions. That's probably why he pulled out of selling his company recently. It won't be struggling anymore, that's for sure."

Olli sat back and considered this.

"Something worth murdering for, do you think?"

"I'd say so. Although, three murders—and harming a police officer? A little excessive, don't you think? Mind you; people have been killed for much less than that."

"Hmm. Is Salonen the type? I'm not so sure. Anyway, I assume he remains a suspect. Any news on Petra yet?"

"Nothing. I don't mind telling you that I'm worried, and given the history of this case, I'm beginning to fear the worst."

"We've known each other a long time, Topias. Do you mind if I ask you something about Petra?"

Topias shrugged his shoulders.

"Go ahead."

"Do you have feelings for her? You seem to care about her, and I haven't seen you this interested in anyone since Helene."

"Now you ask me; Yes, I care about Petra, and I feel sorry for everything she's going through. But I have some reservations about her."

"You should do, Topias. Personally, I think Petra is a very clever young woman who can manipulate anyone she chooses. It wouldn't surprise me if she was behind the whole thing. Take care, won't you; you might be in danger."

Olli left the table with a reflective Topias remaining to finish his coffee.

❖ ❖ ❖

Petra made her way toward Topias' house.

She parked the car in an underground supermarket garage

a short walk away—the same one where Topias had taken fire from an unknown assassin. She walked the remaining distance, occasionally asking for directions as she went.

Petra had no money or phone with her and looked quite dishevelled. Aware of her appearance and getting cold with insufficient clothes, she moved quickly with her head down to avoid being noticed.

On arrival at the house, she walked to the rear yard and tried the door. Of course, it was locked, but she felt that Topias was the type to keep a spare key nearby, so she searched in the dark, under flowerpots and mats, shortly locating one under a large stone.

"Here we are. Well done, Topias," she whispered, unlocking and entering the house.

Otso was overjoyed at this surprise visitor and immediately flung himself at Petra as she walked in. She fell backwards against the door and sat on the floor with the large hound on her lap, licking her face in excitement.

"Well, hello, you. And what's your name."

She checked his collar, where a metal tag hung with the name 'Otso' engraved.

"Well, hello, Otso. Very appropriate. I'm Petra."

◆ ◆ ◆

After his somewhat late lunch, Topias ran a brainstorming session at the station.

It was agreed that although Stefan's interest in Petra might not be innocent, he wasn't a serious contender as a suspect. No evidence or visible motive connected him to any of the crimes to support this. To this end, he was removed from the list. Now there were two names on the board: Petra and Salonen.

Ina declared it was improbable for Petra to be the perpetrator of the attack on Saana. According to a broken lock of the bathroom door, it seemed she'd been inside it at the time, possibly for safety. Of course, she could have tampered with his herself, but if the attacker had been Petra, why would she have left her most essential belongings, including a purse and phone?

All evidence pointed to her kidnapping, although, Olli was adamant about her involvement. However, Topias announced that Petra should not be the primary suspect, and the team agreed that the main task to be concerned with was to locate and bring her to safety.

During the meeting, the arrival of a new piece of evidence, courtesy of the Latvian Government, couldn't have appeared at a better time. The small Latvian company paying the funds into Tommi Heikkinen's bank account was owned by none other than a board member of Advantage Asunto. Not Immo Salonen himself, but a known associate. This was not illegal as such, although tax authorities could disagree, but highly suspicious given the circumstances.

The main suspect now was Salonen. The general opinion was that the chain of events had begun when he'd commenced his journey away from bankruptcy toward the acquisition of the 'Uusi Satama' contract and the prospect of massive wealth. Naturally, there would be a solid motive to avoid anything adversely affecting this.

Topias painted a scenario in which Tommi and his friend discovered something to jeopardise the contract for Salonen and used it to their advantage—hence the payments into Heikkinen's bank account. The third victim, the convict, may have learned something about it or been involved in some way, although this connection was tenuous. As insurance, Sommers may have been killed after he was known to have met with the police.

Petra was the only person remaining who could have had access to whatever it was. After a failed first kidnapping, they must have gone after her again. The police officer protecting her was collateral damage.

Questions were raised about the first abduction, the absence of anyone else, or any evidence. Could Petra have done this herself and made it look like a kidnapping? Topias left the question unanswered with a shrug, and neither did he mention his concerns about her phone being hidden in nonexistent socks.

Topias deftly turned the discussion back to the owner of Advantage Asunto, noting that the business deal was concluded, and he was a significant beneficiary. The evidence Salonen could've been blackmailed with had most likely been recovered, or with Petra's disappearance, inconsequential.

The following conversation centred around Advantage Asunto Oy.

According to the latest financial records, the company was now a profitable concern despite its former troubles. They were a small-scale player compared to some of the larger construction firms. Still, they had recently secured some small-scale contracts to continue trading. After acquiring their latest contract, they were set to expand rapidly and become a more prominent player in the sector. In terms of this deal, due to the company's relatively small size, there would be a requirement to utilise a substantial number of sub-contractors—more than usual for such a project. The company's history didn't project a stable and prosperous company, yet they had been successful in their tender.

"Why did the city make this decision?" asked Topias.

It seemed a visit to the planning office would be necessary to investigate the matter further.

After the meeting, Topias felt more optimistic. The more he expanded his current theory, the more team members chipped in with facts and pieces of corroborating evidence to support it. Salonen was the primary target now, not Petra.

Pleased with himself, Topias decided he deserved a coffee.

According to instructions, Saana arranged an urgent meeting with the Chief Planning Officer of Helsinki. He was happy to wait for them before the office closed for the day. Topias decided to go with Olli and determine why Advantage Asunto was awarded the contract rather than its more appropriate competitors.

Perhaps this would shed some light on the situation?

ENOUGH

"Where the hell is she?" Salonen demanded of the others in the room.

There was no answer, just a general shaking of heads.

"Look. You're being paid for this, but here's a little bonus. I will pay the one who recovers the missing information, in whatever form that may be in, the sum of one million euros. And whatever happens, I want you to get rid of Petra Heikkinen, once and for all. Now, are you able to handle this girl? Can you get this done?"

The men glanced at each other and muttered agreements amid a general clamour to leave the room.

After they departed, Salonen sat back in the new, heavily-padded leather chair he'd bought himself. He nodded; now he felt he'd sufficiently motivated the team to finish both the job and the woman.

He never wanted to set eyes on her again.

◆ ◆ ◆

Petra made herself a mug of coffee from Topias' machine and looked out the window. Snow lay on the ground in the yard, with occasional bare patches where spring was desperately trying to appear. As if to support its arrival, the night sky was clear, framed by a perfectly blue sky. Petra felt better than she'd done for some time, safe and secure within her protector's walls.

As she admired the scene, a neighbour appeared on his way to dispose of rubbish. Suddenly feeling exposed with the lights on, she moved to one side, partially closing the Venetian blinds, enough to see the garden yet remain invisible.

Petra felt much better, having taken a shower and washed her hair. She'd also discarded her dishevelled outfit and dressed in some jeans and a polo shirt found in one of the bedroom drawers. They were female clothes. Perhaps, she surmised, left by a former partner of Topias' and not disposed of for sentimental reasons. They were a little big but would suffice. Best of all, she had found some thick woollen socks that were donned immediately.

Petra sat on the sofa and crossed her feet under her in a sitting position, enjoying a mug of coffee. The clock said 4 pm, so perhaps Topias would arrive soon. She clicked the television remote, and a show about renovating houses came on, the type of program she might have enjoyed at home a few weeks before. Leaning back, she finished her drink and placed it on the coffee table, her mind blank, exhausted from her ordeal.

Within a few minutes, Petra stretched out, tilted her head back onto the cushions and drifted off to sleep. The past twenty-four hours had caught up with her.

❖ ❖ ❖

Topias and Olli arrived at the council offices and took the lift to the planning office.

On arrival, they met a polite receptionist who escorted them to the office of the Project Planning Manager for Helsinki: Mr Artemis Laitila.

The man in question was tall and round, positively bursting out of his dress shirt and jeans. He welcomed them as they introduced themselves, immediately after which he began enthusiastically demonstrating the new development in question. It had been lovingly modelled out of wood and sat on a table in the centre of the room.

"This is the next stage in developing our capital city: 'Uusi Satama'. It is a new self-contained district with all the facilities its inhabitants will require. Yet, it is easily commutable to Helsinki's centre to connect with everything the metropolis offers. It's the perfect place to reside."

Artemis Laitila flushed with pride at this statement, seemingly learned by heart from a brochure. He beckoned them to inspect the model.

"It certainly looks impressive. Quite expensive, I imagine, too," remarked Olli.

"We already have tenants lining up for the shopping centre and entertainment complex. We also have buyers ready to purchase almost sixty per cent of the apartments."

"I don't know much about the construction business. How does all this get to happen?" asked Topias.

"How much time have you got? It's a long process, the planning of which takes years. Once a suitable area is identified, a feasibility study commences. We ascertain the project's scope and what can realistically be built according to the land we own or can purchase.

At an early stage, we bring in investors interested in putting money into the development, together with the local council, in this case, Helsinki. In addition to those who wish to buy private dwellings for resale, we also need companies willing to operate local amenities. You know, an anchor supermarket, a play area, perhaps even a shopping centre or multiplex cinema. Once we have secured contracts for living or utilisation in other ways, in this case, a minimum of forty per cent, the detailed planning of buildings and utilities begins. At this stage, we sign agreements with the construction company.

Of course, this is a very brief summary of the process, and from this point, the project detail expands tenfold. We must work in close partnership with everyone to make this a reality. Yes, this will be one of our most exemplary projects."

He beamed at the two detectives to doubtless await the forthcoming gush of praise and bade them take a seat while he plunged his large frame into an equally substantial chair.

"May I ask what your enquiry is concerning? It can't be a new-found interest in the construction business alone?"

"You're very astute," replied Topias. "We're following up on some questions regarding the tendering and awarding of contracts for major construction projects—just like this one."

Topias gestured in the direction of the model.

"Perhaps you could describe the process in detail for us," he asked.

"It is rather complicated."

"Just imagine I have no idea about it, which is mostly true. Please explain it in fundamental terms, for example, as you might to an intern."

"Very well."

Artemis sat up straight and explained the procedure, covering the project release, tendering process, and criteria on which the projects were awarded.

Topias followed with his questions.

"When considering this project, 'Uusi Satama', is it usual for such a large contract to be given to a single and relatively small-scale company?"

"It depends on the development. If a company can demonstrate an efficient and comprehensive service to deliver the project, then yes, why not? It can't be the same two or three massive companies that gain the business every time; otherwise, we risk a monopoly. It's dangerous to rely on the same supplier every time. Of course, the company needs to be stable and managed well enough to complete the project."

We also prefer, where possible, to award the contract to a Finnish company. It keeps the money in the country, in terms of investment, payment, taxation; this way, everyone's a winner."

"With this particular development, did Advantage Asunto meet all of the criteria required?"

"Yes. Honestly, I was surprised they won the tender because it's such a small company. However, it was decided there was no reason not to award the business to them, especially as they were so competitive on the final bid."

"Did they have support from any other direction? Investors? Officials? Politicians?"

"We take this into account, but in the end, the criteria and bid will seal the deal, together with the final vote."

"The final vote?"

"Yes, that's the very last stage. Appointees from this planning office and local government vote on the final selection, a straightforward yes, or no. It's a highly robust process that has resulted in many quality developments for our capital city and will continue to do so."

Topias picked up on his comment.

"Continue to do so?"

"Oh yes. We've used the same process for years and will do so in the future. Several more developments are already lined up. When Advantage Asunto completes a project of this size, they will be in a strong position to bid for future ones."

"Interesting. Well, I think we've taken up enough of your time today. Thank you for fitting us in at such short notice."

Topias stopped and turned around to ask one final question.

"By the way, in terms of representatives, do you vote on the final selection yourself?"

"Oh no. Well, maybe one day. I'm afraid that's above my pay grade right now. That responsibility from this office is down to my superior, the Director of Planning."

After saying their farewells, Topias and Olli convened in the lobby.

"What do you think?" asked Olli.

"I agree they have a robust process, but despite that, only a couple of people make the final decision. It seems to me that a project could be steered through to meet the criteria, with a little help along the way, and then nodded through by whoever is on the final committee."

"Isn't it always a human who makes the final decision about anything? It seems a bit far-fetched to think that Salonen bribed the committee members, or alternatively, they bribed him. How would this come about? I don't see it," said Olli, shaking his head.

"That's the question, or maybe a better question is: who stands to profit from this, apart from Salonen?"

"Let's talk about it over a coffee," proposed Olli, eyeing a café across the road.

They crossed the street and ordered coffee and cinnamon buns, taking a seat by the window to view the council offices as the topic of their conversation. They were apparently the last customers as the café was soon to close.

When the coffee arrived, they returned to the matter at hand. Topias began.

"We know that Immo Salonen himself has plenty to profit by all this. Politicians and planning officers may also have something to gain in terms of pride and satisfaction by creating a landmark development. However, deciding to select a specific construction company that might not otherwise meet their criteria? Now, that might mean that money is being paid to someone or more than one. And for this type of risk, I'm guessing big money."

"That's a big accusation and seems unlikely, don't you think?"

"Maybe. We should check the bank accounts of those involved to be sure. Although we also cannot dismiss the possibility of an inducement in the form of cash in a brown envelope. It's happened before and will continue to do so."

"The old-fashioned ways are sometimes the best," commented Olli with a wry smile.

"Especially as that money will be untraceable and may not even have been paid yet. What if the bribe is conditional on the agreement but isn't payable until the project breaks ground or until it's finished?"

"We'll find nothing then," Olli commented, staring into his empty cup. "I think we need refills," he added, taking both cups and returning to the café's counter.

They sat there for another half an hour, discussing the next steps.

After their conversation, Topias called Petri to begin the application for financial records disclosure of those involved. All being well, a judge would sign it off quickly, and given the gravity of the case, they could get sight of those tomorrow.

In addition, they sent a message to Katja to dig into the background of the planning officer, Artemis Laitila, and his superior. She should also identify everyone else in authority who might have touched the matter, from inception to approval.

The two detectives finished their buns, drained their cups and headed homeward.

SURPRISE

Topias considered the day's events and felt confident things were moving in the right direction. However, it seemed the journey to the truth would take time. If there was no more evidence, they could go no further. At least it was unlikely there would be more deaths. In terms of the blackmailing ring, or what pertained to one—who was left in that circle to be a risk?

There was only one person who remained in peril if she was still alive: Petra.

He thought about her until his arrival and parked his car in the moonlit driveway. He was relieved to see that little new snow had fallen and work on the driveway would be unnecessary that evening.

As he walked to his front door, he thought about food and decided it would be a delivery meal that night. He'd temporarily resigned to postponing his diet; the pulla had prompted that.

Topias opened the door and instantly knew something was wrong: a strange coat hung on one of the hooks by the door, and a pair of boots sat on the floor. He stopped dead and slowly reached for his gun.

Listening intently, he crept through the hall and carefully opened the door to the living area.

On opening the door and looking around, his eyes settled on a slight figure lying across the sofa.

There she was: Petra, and sound asleep.

"How on earth?" he whispered to himself.

Topias stood there for a few moments, unsure of what to do and in a state of considerable amazement.

The police were looking for Petra everywhere, assuming she'd been kidnapped or worse. They'd even considered that she may have absconded at one point, even fled the country, yet here she was, asleep on his sofa in his house.

He thought to wake her, but she looked so pale, angelic and exhausted that another hour or two wouldn't hurt. She would be in better condition to explain things if she was well-rested.

Shaking his head in disbelief, he left her there, returned his gun to his briefcase and placed it on the hall table. He went quietly to the kitchen and, noting the pot of already-brewed coffee, poured himself a mug.

Topias took a delivery menu from a drawer and selected two pizzas: one with goat's cheese, spinach and red onions and a simple Margherita. His favourite was the former, but the latter was plain, just in case Petra didn't like anything exotic. He decided to use the internet to order the food as he didn't want to wake her with his voice, so he tapped out the details on his smartphone.

◆ ◆ ◆

Following the meeting in Salonen's office, his henchmen left the room to pursue different angles in the hunt for Petra Heikkinen.

The four men were currently on loan to him from a dubiously discreet third party, but Salonen was the one paying them. The third party was an investor in the new development. He was a new breed of white-collar criminal who had turned his ill-gotten gains from smuggling in Latvia into a Nordic investment portfolio.

The gang member, Sven Aalto, known simply by his first name, was the team's fixer. He'd been looking forward to spending time with Petra alone at the cabin. If he wasn't determined enough to find her already, the newly-announced bonus motivated him to do whatever was needed. The men would stay in touch to help each other, but he knew he wouldn't need assistance.

Sven was currently to be found in his car, in a garage, with a laptop screen leaning against the steering wheel. He was asking himself a question, the only one for which he needed to know the answer.

Where would she go to feel safe?

The woman had left the cottage with little in the way of clothes or supplies, and to his knowledge, she had no money or phone either. She couldn't hide outside as it was winter, so she would go somewhere secure and warm.

The first place he thought of was her sister's apartment. The next place, although unlikely, as she hadn't been back since the shooting, was her own home. Sven quickly located the address on his mobile. He had been there before and set off to find her.

On his way, he considered other possibilities if she wasn't there. Her neighbour's house was a potential hiding place. They had taken the man to the police station as a witness or possible suspect, and they may have been friends. A visit to Petra's and the neighbour's house could be done in one stop.

As Sven neared the apartment, he remembered the safe house. While observing it, he had seen the detective arrive, carrying coffees. He thought it a bit unusual at the time.

Recalling a comment from one of the gang members. They said the senior detective had spent several hours alone with her and visited her on other occasions. He wondered if she might have simply gone to the police. Sven shook his head. Somehow, it seemed unlikely she would go there. Petra might go to her protector, though: Detective Superintendent Torikka. He decided to tentatively add him to the list.

◆ ◆ ◆

At the Torikka residence, Petra moaned quietly and then yawned, stretching herself across the sofa. She could easily do this to her full length due to her petiteness.

She became aware of being watched and quickly sat bolt upright.

"It's alright; it's only me," Topias reassured her.

"Oh. Thank God for that. I got scared. How long have you been sitting there?"

"About an hour. You seemed tired, and I didn't want to wake you."

Petra rose from the sofa and walked to the armchair where he was sitting. She stood in front of him, regarding him with sleepy eyes.

"Hey you," she greeted him.

"Hey you," Topias replied as Petra got up, sat on his lap and swivelled sideways to face him.

They hugged each other, sitting in each other's arms for some moments before facing each other again. They kissed, briefly at first and then longer.

"It's good to see a friendly face," Petra said.

"You've no idea how happy I am to see you. What happened? I thought you were gone for good."

"Now, that is a long story."

At that moment, the bell rang, and Petra jolted. It was evident to Topias that something was wrong, and she was scared.

"It's okay; I'm here. Is someone after you?"

"Yes," she nodded.

"Really? Okay, not by the pizza guy, though. Anyway, I have a gun. Stay here, and I'll get the door."

Petra moved quickly behind the sofa and lowered herself from view.

When Topias returned, he carried pizza boxes with a tub of chocolate ice cream perched on top.

"It's okay; you can come out now. I thought you might be hungry, so I ordered dinner. This is for your sugar levels," Topias added, holding up the ice cream.

"Thank you. I'm ravenous. Can we eat first and do questions later?"

"Sure. Dig in," Topias replied, opening the boxes and taking the ice cream to the freezer, simultaneously grabbing a couple of cold beers from the fridge.

After consuming much of the pizza, and a second beer each, the couple sat down to talk seriously.

The following conversation was mainly one-sided, with Topias asking the occasional question to prompt Petra to recount the next stage of her story. If she struggled to answer, he merely waited silently, and the gap was filled.

Topias had suspected her of being kidnapped by someone,

but not with this number of people involved. He was relieved she hadn't been responsible for any of the major crimes and felt sympathy for what she'd gone through. It was incredible she had escaped from the cottage and found her way to him.

He sat riveted when she explained the escape from the window and hiding under the cottage floor in the snow. He was amazed when she told him how she entered the cabin, took what she needed, and stole the truck to drive to Helsinki.

Topias asked if she could find the place again if needed, and she nodded that she probably could, with some time to do so.

Petra continued talking until feeling drowsy, at which point she briefly fell asleep again.

When she awoke after her short nap, Topias had more questions.

"Are you prepared to testify that Salonen was at the cottage and involved in the kidnapping?"

"I think so. Yes, I'll try."

"Did you know the other men?"

"I think I've seen one of them before. I thought I recognised one of the voices as well, but it's difficult to be certain."

"Now, here's the killer question. What exactly do they want from you?"

She looked at him for a few moments.

"Petra. You have to trust me. Otherwise, we'll never be able to end this. What do they want from you?"

It was time. Her secret had been hidden long enough.

"Okay. I'll tell you what I know. While Tommi was working for Advantage Asunto, he came across something important, something that Salonen was involved in, and he brought it home.

"What was it?"

"It was a memory stick, but he didn't show me the contents. I found it on his laptop one evening, and I was curious. The information was weird, listing names and amounts of money and about that new development: 'Uusi Satama'. Tommi wouldn't have had access to that stuff normally, and I was worried he might have stolen it."

She drew a deep breath and continued her story.

"Anyway, I didn't come across anything new over the following weeks. I hoped it had gone away or was nothing to worry about."

Petra didn't mention the secret emails regarding her husband's potential escape to India.

"A short while later, Tommi was dead, and I decided to keep quiet about the memory stick, just in case."

"So, let me think out loud for a moment. Salonen had Tommi killed because of what he found, and he had Tommi's friend killed because they threatened him together. But why kill the man in prison?"

"He knew him well, I think. Tommi used to phone him from time to time. I don't know why. He just said he met him in prison, and they looked out for each other."

"So, somehow, he knew about it too. These three got together, perhaps to blackmail Salonen and possibly others, and they were all killed for it. The only one left who might have the information was you. That's why they ransacked those apartments and kidnapped you, but you escaped—twice, now it seems. That's just as well. They would have killed you after getting what they wanted. That memory stick may include information on the business deal: bribes, payments or those involved. It might contain all the evidence we need. No wonder they wanted it so badly."

Everything was becoming more apparent now, and after absorbing her story, he turned toward her.

"Petra, do you still have the memory stick?"

"No. I don't know where it is."

Her lie was convincing. Topias' face fell.

"I never had it. Salonen thought Tommi might have confided in me or given me a copy of it, but he didn't."

"We need to get everything recorded and in a signed statement. I'll call Olli and ask him to make the arrangements at the station. Do you feel ready to do this?"

Petra nodded.

"But I don't want to tell everything in case you get into trouble, Topias."

"Don't worry about me. I'll be fine. Besides, our relationship doesn't have anything to do with the case, so it needn't be mentioned, okay?"

Petra nodded again, feeling a pang of guilt at misleading Topias, but at the same time, deciding to keep her insurance policy safely hidden, at least for the moment.

"Right," continued Topias. "I have one more question for you that's been bugging me for a while. During the first kidnapping, you managed to hide your phone in your sock."

"Yes."

"Petra, you don't wear socks inside. I've never seen you wear them."

He looked down and noticed his thick woollen socks on her

feet.

"Come on, silly. What are these?"

"Ah."

"You should know something, Topias. I have some features that I like to accentuate."

Petra smiled coyly.

"Two of these features are my feet. I was once told I have the most beautiful feet on this earth. Do you know that?"

Petra removed the socks and placed her feet across his knees. Topias had to admit they were indeed, perfect.

"That's why you never see me with socks or stockings. Whenever I see you, I slip them off. I only have your socks on now because my feet were freezing after being outside for so long. By the way, at the same time, I usually undo a button here and there, sit upright, and toss my hair back."

"Ah. Now, I understand."

"But that doesn't explain why you weren't wearing them at the cottage."

"No, because they removed them when I got there, together with my coat and boots, so I couldn't escape. But I did, and it takes more than stones and pine needles to stop me."

Topias didn't buy the explanation entirely, but given his current position, it seemed plausible.

He changed the subject.

"I'll call Olli. Then, we can sit here while I make some fresh coffee and get our stories straight, so to speak. We can't afford to lose our credibility. With you as a witness, at least we can get Salonen and his cronies for kidnapping. We'll work on the murders. If we find some hard evidence, we can charge him with bribery and corruption too."

Topias picked up his mobile phone and dialled Olli, who answered immediately.

"Olli, you're not going to believe this."

◆ ◆ ◆

Sven Aalto loitered outside Petra's sister's apartment block on the premise of having a cigarette. He had to keep up the pretence and smoked three of them before someone finally approached and tapped in a code on a keypad. When the door opened, he nodded to the woman, threw his cigarette away and entered behind her.

As she took the lift, while casting a suspicious eye in his direction, he opened the door to the stairs and ran upward. He hoped a casual observer would accept his action as just casually accessing the building rather than trying to gain access illegally. Just in case, he had to move fast.

As a relatively fit man, he quickly ran up several flights of stairs but had to pause for breath when he reached his destination. He glanced at the lift and noted the woman had exited on the floor below.

With no spectators apparent, he pulled a crowbar from his bag and jammed it into the side of the door. It took a few tries before the wood splintered, but it gave way nonetheless, leaving quite a mess. Sven didn't have time to be gentle.

He entered the apartment and looked around. There was no one visible, but to be thorough, he searched the rooms from top to bottom.

While checking the main bedroom, his phone rang, and he answered.

"Yes. Where? Thanks."

Sven left the bedroom, dived out of the apartment, and flung himself down the stairs, taking them two at a time.

ACTION

"Are you Ready?" Topias asked Petra.

"Yes, I think so. I know what to say. I'm just worried about what happens until Salonen and the others are arrested and behind bars. Will they let me stay with you?"

"Let's cross that bridge when we come to it, shall we? Rest assured, wherever you are—I'll be right by your side."

Petra smiled and rose from her chair.

At that moment, there was a sudden loud crack and shattering of glass.

Topias looked around and shouted to Petra to get down, and did the same himself. It was obviously a gunshot, but he had no idea where the sniper was, so he crawled to the hallway to rescue his gun.

Another shot rang out and thudded into the wall, right by his shoulder this time.

"Petra, get in there, under the stairs and stay hidden," Topias ordered and pointed to the cupboard.

She did as she was told, and Topias worked his way around to a wall cabinet, which he used as protection, and carefully peered around. He couldn't see anyone.

His reconnaissance was interrupted by a crash as the

gunman launched himself through the glass door, rolled onto the floor and levelled his gun.

From the corner of Topias' eye, he saw a shape that propelled itself towards the intruder, after which it found the man's arm and clenched its jaws around it.

"Otso!" Topias shouted.

"Argghh!" the man cried as Otso's teeth clamped down.

The gunman dropped his pistol on the floor as Otso wrestled him to the ground, growling. The man used his left hand to try and push him off, resorting to thumping, but the canine attacker was not going to release its grip.

Topias got to his feet and picked the gun up from the floor. Wrestling, the man managed to break free from the dog's grip, launch himself off the floor and grab for Topias's own gun that he was holding in his other hand.

"Bang!"

One of the guns went off in the struggle, and Sven fell backwards onto the floor.

Topias knelt and looked at the wound. It didn't take much to know it was probably fatal. He moved safely away, took his phone and called 112 for the ambulance service and police.

Pressing a towel against the man's wound, Topias asked, "Who sent you?" as the man lay gasping, unable to speak.

Within a few seconds, Sven's body went limp.

Otso left the intruder and arrived at his owner's side, tail wagging and licking his face.

"Good boy Otso! You saved my bacon, buddy."

Suddenly aware there may be multiple attackers, Topias ran outside with his weapon and proceeded to scour the area surrounding the house.

After a few minutes, secure in the knowledge there were no more assailants, he returned home through the broken back door.

"Come on, Otso, let's check on Petra."

Topias went to the closet and opened it to let her out, but to his shock, she wasn't there.

"Petra?" he called. And then louder: "Petra!"

Topias checked the living area, but she wasn't there either, so he hastily checked the other rooms.

Petra had gone – yet again.

◆ ◆ ◆

Shortly after this activity, the road leading to Topias' house became crowded with vehicles and flashing lights.

The ambulance crew arrived first and confirmed the man was dead. Uniformed police arrived next to cordon off the area and ensure no more shooters were in the vicinity. Finally, detectives arrived, including a concerned Olli and Ina's forensics team.

By this time, Topias was frantic about Petra.

Did someone take her while I was pinned down? Did she run off, scared of what was happening?

He couldn't blame Petra. She had already shown herself to be tremendously resourceful.

With that thought in mind, he commissioned a search and set off in pursuit of her, himself, with Otso in the back seat.

While doing this, he wondered how the assassin had known where Petra was. She could have been anywhere, but the shooter came to his house just in time to prevent them from leaving for the police station. They were to make a statement against Salonen and his crew, and there was only one person who knew she was there at that precise time.

Surely it couldn't have been Olli?

The pen he'd been twirling between his fingers in his pocket snapped under renewed pressure.

Topias didn't believe it. He'd known Olli for years and would trust him with anything. However, the evidence was damning.

Deciding to deal with this thought later, he drove through the local area's streets, scanning them for signs of Petra.

She was nowhere to be found.

After doing this, he returned home, just in case there might be some evidence revealing what had become of her. He found Ina inside, examining the remnants of a bullet shell case.

"Are you okay?" she inquired as soon as he approached.

"Yes, I'm fine, thanks. It'll take much more than a committed assassin to do away with me, even if it's the second time in a week. Anything of interest in here?"

"Only to confirm that one man forcibly entered your property, and the bullet casings we found are from his gun, which might be the gun we're looking for. No one else seems to have been involved. I take it from your expression that you haven't yet found the girl?"

"You guessed right. Petra disappeared almost in front of my eyes. The shooting must have scared her out of her wits, so I guess she ran away. The only other possibility is that she was re-taken by another assailant. Still, you say there are no signs of anyone else?"

"We don't think so, but we're not 100% positive yet."

"If that changes, please let me know immediately, will you?"

Ina placed a hand on his arm.

"I'm sure she'll find a way of contacting you. By the way, we found this near the body; it must have fallen out of his coat pocket."

Ina handed him a mobile phone, and Topias studied it.

"Oh. Go ahead. We've already opened it for you as it was a simple password."

Topias scanned the directory of contacts first and noticed a call had been recently received. It was from a number he recognised: Olli's number. He sighed deeply as he handed the device back to Ina.

"Can you download a list of names and messages from this?"

"Sure. That's an easy one."

Topias took his phone and called Olli.

"Hei, Olli, where are you?"

"At home, just finishing dinner."

"Do me a favour, will you? When you've finished, can you give me a call?"

After the brief conversation, he mobilised a squad car to follow him, and they headed to Olli's house. It was only a short drive from Topias' place, and he'd been there several times before. It was an impressive residence, bought from an inheritance, Olli had once told him.

His former friend answered the door and was surprised to find police officers standing there with weapons raised.

"Is everything okay?" he asked.

"No, Olli, it isn't. I'm charging you as an accessory to kidnapping and murder—namely mine. There's plenty more to add, but that'll do to start with."

Knowing Topias had found him out, it seemed pointless to protest at this point, so a stunned Olli was handcuffed and taken into custody.

As the police entered the house, Topias returned to the car to congratulate his canine companion.

"Got him, Otso. Do you know something? I'll put you up for an award for what you did."

At which point, his faithful hound on the back seat couldn't contain his enthusiasm, and groaned while turning over onto his side for a tickle. Topias laughed at the incongruous sight of a trained police dog reverting to his usual behaviour.

A thorough search of Olli's house commenced, and a request for his financial records was made. It would be the following day before they received the complete information from his bank; however, as it turned out, there was no need for it.

Underneath a table in Olli's home office was a section of wooden flooring that had been carefully cut out and replaced.

Inside, they discovered wads of cash in euros and dollars inside the hole, carefully stacked away. Topias estimated the value to be more than two hundred thousand euros.

"He might have been receiving payoffs for some time," Topias commented to a nearby officer in dismay.

He watched as Olli was taken away, deciding to let him stew in the cells for the night. Perhaps a taste of being behind bars might make him more open to cooperate? He hoped Olli would volunteer some helpful information the following day.

Topias kept checking his messages, but there was no news of

Petra.

Ina called him and advised they had completed their work at his own house. The locksmiths had been to secure the back door until replacement glass arrived. He would get the full results of the mobile phone directory shortly. Already, with both Olli's and Salonen's telephone numbers being in the assassin's phone, it would help prove a connection, which would be valuable evidence.

"Let's go home, Otso," he told the sleepy-looking hound.

Only on his return journey did he realise how Olli had acted against them a second time.

When the assassin found Petra at the safe house, Olli had probably told them of the safe house's location, which was also the cause of Saana being attacked and injured.

Together with the fact that he was almost killed, with Petra, in his own house, Topias' sympathy for Olli, based on their former friendship, was dwindling rapidly.

FLIGHT

Before the shooting incident, while in the safety of Topias' house, many things went through Petra's mind. She not only feared for her life from Salonen's men but also didn't relish the year of probable court appearances that lay ahead of her. Especially, the loss of the wealth that Tommi had accumulated didn't appeal.

In terms of Topias, she enjoyed his company, and he would no doubt look after her, but that wasn't enough; he was no longer useful. She still had the memory stick hidden away and would use it to her advantage if possible.

Therefore, when the bullets began, Petra seized her opportunity and decided with lightning speed that it was time to go. While the fighting pair were preoccupied, she slipped out of the front door and ran without looking back.

She quickly arrived at the old jeep, stolen earlier that day from the cottage, and headed directly to her old house, assuming no one would be there.

When she arrived, Petra went straight to the backyard and vaulted over the fence. She lifted a loose corner of the decking to retrieve her emergency key.

After entering the house, she went to the sauna and stood on the bench to reach one of the highest spotlights. After unscrewing the bulb, her fingers connected with a thin metallic object.

"Here you are," Petra said with relief as she put the memory stick in her pocket.

Next, she needed clothes. She quickly dressed in her favourite black leather trousers, training shoes and a white shirt and black jumper, spending a few moments arranging the cuffs beyond the sleeves.

A quick visit to the bathroom resulted in brushed hair and a hasty makeup application. Now, she felt herself again.

"Welcome back," Petra greeted herself in the mirror.

Taking an overnight bag, she packed it with essentials and a change of clothes. What was missing, was money.

I'm not going to get very far without that.

Petra checked in the couple's document folder and retrieved her passport with relief. Inside was an international payment card used for travel, but she knew little balance was available on it. Without her purse, cash or bank cards, she had no way of getting hold of any funds.

Realising there were no more reasons to stay, especially as Salonen's thugs or police officers could be knocking at the door at any moment. Petra zipped the bag, put on a pair of oversized black sunglasses, and left through the front door.

As she closed the door, her neighbour, Stefan, appeared outside.

"Petra, I almost called the police when I saw the strange car and heard someone on your terrace."

"It's okay; it's only me."

"Are you okay? I heard things from the police and read things in the paper."

"Yes, I'm fine, thanks. Just in a bit of a hurry."

Petra had an idea: it was finally time to make use of Stefan.

"Stefan, I can't explain why, but I need some money to get away for a while. People are trying to hurt me. I promise I'll pay you back. Can you help me, please?"

"Err. I guess so. How much do you need?"

"How much have you got?" asked Petra, her face saddening to gain maximum sympathy.

"Hang on a second."

Stefan went inside as Petra hopped from one foot to the other, wondering if she should drive just away. As she waited, she nervously monitored the road for activity.

A minute later, he was back.

"Here, it's all I have in the house. I don't know if I should be doing this, but...take it."

"Kiitos," Petra said as she accepted the bundle of notes.

She hugged him, promised to pay it back, and left, smiling.

Stefan watched the jeep disappear, wondering why he had just given her his stash of three hundred euros of emergency money to a possible fugitive.

Petra didn't waste a second and made directly for the airport.

◆ ◆ ◆

On arrival at the airport in Vantaa, she stashed the memory stick in a left-luggage locker.

She went to a ticket desk and bought a seat on the next flight to wherever her money would take her. As it happened, this was

Kastrup airport, Copenhagen.

After checking in and passing through security, the next item on her list was a cheap, pre-paid mobile phone and a large glass of wine. However, it wasn't time to leave yet. Before her flight was called, something had to be done.

REVENGE

Immo Salonen was at home.

He poured himself a substantial glass of red wine, and went to the full-length windows of his Helsinki apartment to survey the vista beyond.

The city lights sparkled, and he sipped his drink while waiting for news from his men. Most of all, he wanted to hear that the information was on its way. He was also keen to know that Petra was dead and could bother him no more.

His mobile phone rang, and he answered eagerly.

"Hello, Salonen," the voice greeted him.

"Hello?"

"Don't you recognise me, you bastard?"

"Petra?"

"That's right."

The line went quiet, with Salonen unusually struggling for words.

Why is she phoning me?

"Listen carefully. I have a new deal for you and am giving you only one chance to take it. I have a memory stick containing everything necessary about your activities and bribes to put you away for a long time. Who knows? The police may even connect the dots to the murders you arranged."

"Where is it? If you give it to me, I'll let you live."

Petra repeated the words Salonen had said to her at the cabin in the woods.

"Uh-uh. Well, for some reason, I don't trust you"

"I said this is a new deal," she continued. "This is what you need to do. Deposit one million euros into the account I'm going to give you, and I'll tell you the location of the memory stick. Trust me, there are no copies."

"How can I trust you? Your husband, sorry, ex-husband said there were no copies. Look what happened to him. Do you want to end up the same way?"

"No, I don't. That's why I'm offering you this deal. I don't want your thugs coming after me. I just want to finish this and live my life in peace in comfort. You get the memory stick. I get the money, and you'll never hear from me again."

Salonen thought for a moment, checking the number on display. It was a local Finnish number. Noting she was probably still in Helsinki, he could transfer the money and send his men after her as well.

"Very well. Give me the details, and I'll transfer the money. If you double-cross me, you're a dead woman, and it won't be a good death. Do you understand?"

"Yes. I do. Thanks for that," Petra added sarcastically.

The transaction was made quickly while Petra stayed on the line, after which she dutifully provided him with the location and combination of the locker at the airport. She added that failure to transfer the money would result in the provision of the memory stick to the police instead.

Petra proceeded with her plan and sent a message to Topias about where to find the memory stick and Salonen's men. He notified the airport police immediately.

With the business done, and before Topias could call her on the new phone's number, she removed and snapped the sim card, placing the phone and sim in different waste bins.

Salonen realised Petra would flee, so he called his men to go to the airport, hoping to retrieve the memory stick and stop her before she left the country. He also called his point man, Sven, but he didn't answer, so he left a message telling him to get to the airport, retrieve the memory stick from the locker, and kill that bitch.

Finally, can I concentrate on making money?

◆ ◆ ◆

Salonen's men met in the dim underground carpark and ascended the lift together. The three remaining gang members had joined together to claim the reward money. After all, one-third of a million each was still a nice bonus. They exited the lift and headed to the airport's secure storage area.

By the time they reached it, they were unknowingly being watched from all directions.

Heavily armed airport police waited, as instructed, until the moment the thugs opened the locker and retrieved the memory stick.

Then, they pounced.

Police appeared from all directions, with weapons aimed if the gang should resist. They didn't. Realising they wouldn't stand much of a chance against a team of armoured officers with automatic weapons, they raised their hands and were soon safely in custody.

At this point, Topias and Otso were racing toward the airport in the car.

Topias was keen to interview the men on-site and view the material on the memory stick. If there was enough evidence, even without Petra, they would be able to move on Salonen. He considered calling the airport police and asking them to locate Petra if she was there but decided not to.

Besides, it's too obvious for her to catch a flight from there after leaving the memory stick in an airport locker, isn't it?

He asked himself this question but deliberately didn't search for an answer.

When he arrived, everything was already over, and the gang was in detention.

Topias informed the men that Sven was dead, and Salonen would likely give them up for a more lenient sentence. It didn't take long for one of them to come forward to strike a deal.

Within an hour, Topias had details of the murders and kidnapping. The informer knew nothing about the property corruption element; they were just hired guns. Still, all the necessary evidence was available for that particular charge on the memory stick. Their informant knew nothing about the first kidnapping of Petra but only the one where Saana had been attacked.

Topias was more confident than ever that Petra had orchestrated the first kidnapping herself.

But why? For attention? To appear as the victim? To gain sympathy, or perhaps for protection?

He wasn't entirely sure.

❖ ❖ ❖

Later that night, while Salonen was sleeping peacefully in his Helsinki city apartment, there was a tremendous crash as a battering ram broke open his door.

In seconds, heavily-armed police swept through the apartment and arrested the suspect in his pyjamas. There was no resistance, just indignance on Salonen's part.

Due to the late hour and the operation's success, the interviews of Salonen and Olli were postponed until morning. Topias could have pushed through the night with the suspects, as there were advantages to them being tired. However, he decided with his superior that it was also more beneficial for Salonen to spend a night alone in the cells first. Patience could sometimes pay dividends. Besides that, Topias was exhausted, and it was a relief for him to go home that night.

◆ ◆ ◆

As he entered the house, the sight of the smashed glass door covered with wooden panels reminded him of what the criminals had done to him personally. They had also tried to kill him—twice.

The house was chilly, so he set a fire on his log burner. It was the first time in a while he'd used it, but as the door couldn't be appropriately reglazed until the day after, it would help keep him warm in the meantime.

Opening his wine cabinet, Topias selected a suitable vintage and poured himself a glass. He sat down in his favourite red leather chair, with the flames of the fire leaping in front of him as he reflected on the day's events.

The case could be wrapped up in a week now, at least as far as the charges were concerned. The preparation of evidence and statements for trial would take considerably longer.

He took another sip of wine, satisfied with his choice for the occasion.

His mind returned to the subject of Petra.

Topias had half-expected her to be sitting on the sofa again, waiting for him to arrive. It seemed she was that type of person, full of surprises. However, she hadn't been, so he continued thinking about her, while making progress through the bottle of wine as the evening wore on.

He wondered if she'd been involved from the start; he'd always felt as if she was holding something back, some dark secret that only she knew. The first kidnapping looked as if it had been designed to gain protection and secure her safety. Or possibly to manipulate him? Whatever else she had done, he didn't know.

In her favour, what was for sure was that she was the reason why Salonen and his gang were behind bars, with more arrests to follow.

Most importantly to Topias—she was still alive.

What a remarkable woman!

Topias continued constructing the story in his head, as he had done several times, adding details as he went, each version improving on the last.

There was undoubtedly a high-level conspiracy concerning 'Uusi Satama'. There was evidence that several influential people were receiving large payoffs; the memory stick had revealed their names. More arrests would commence in the morning. The lion's share of the profits would have gone to Salonen, the owner of the construction company; that was why he had taken such drastic steps to secure his wealth.

One thing saddened him immensely. Olli was involved in

this. Judging by the amount of cash under his floorboards, he may have also been involved in other illegal activities over the years. How he became involved with Salonen was a mystery.

Salonen's plan would have worked if it had not been for Tommi, who had discovered vital information and used it to bribe him. Perhaps he had taken it too far, wouldn't stop, or involved too many people? Whatever the case, one day, Salonen and others decided it was time to end it and hired someone to kill those involved and recover the information.

That fateful Saturday night after Tommi's sauna set a chain of dramatic events in motion, eventually resulting in Salonen's demise.

Thinking about Petra again, at some stage, she became involved when she uncovered Tommi's secret and kept the information in a safe place, unfound, despite the ransacking of the homes of those involved. She bravely refused to give up the memory stick when interrogated and threatened with death. Petra hadn't even conceded it to Topias himself. Instead, she'd used it to incriminate Salonen at the right time, from a distance, only when she felt safe to do so.

From a distance?

Another job tomorrow would be to check the sea and airports for signs of her movement.

I wonder why she offered to give Salonen the memory stick in the end? Was it just to have him arrested? Or did she have something else to gain? Topias wondered.

He got up and drained the remnants of red wine from his glass.

Maybe tomorrow will reveal what has happened to Petra?

SUCCESS

Petra arrived at Copenhagen airport, relieved she hadn't been discovered, and no police were waiting for her arrival.

After purchasing a new phone and sim, she set up the international payment card application and tapped into her account. When she saw the figure: One million euros, Petra had to sit down. It was actually there and available to spend—Salonen had transferred it. She drew a deep breath and checked again, quickly logging out and closing her phone in case anyone walking by might notice.

Petra considered her current situation. Even though she hadn't participated in the property fraud, she had undoubtedly profited from it now. In theory, Petra Heikkinen could become a fugitive. She could easily be traced in the Nordic countries, so the best thing was to get away as far as possible. Even with Salonen in prison, Finland would never be safe again for her. It was time to get away, far away.

She opened her phone again, checked the internet's flight pages, and quickly booked an onward journey out of Europe. Her chosen destination was India. Goa had been in her mind for some time, and it seemed the logical place to go.

A flight was leaving for Mumbai that night, so she checked for availability: Yes, there was space. It was expensive, but for the first time in her life, that didn't matter. She booked herself a business class seat and received a boarding pass directly on her mobile phone.

Yes, the card works.

Of course, it worked, but Petra still couldn't believe her situation. She was nervous about going abroad alone, as she had only ever visited Estonia and Sweden, usually on the ferries that ran from Helsinki. However, aside from the fact that India had been Tommi's destination of choice, it had always been on her bucket list since she learned about it at Yoga classes. If ever there was a time to go, this was it. Goa also appealed because it seemed like a place someone could get lost in for a long time. And besides, now, she could go anywhere she wanted whenever she wished. A burst of excitement hit her, and she couldn't wait to get there.

During the booking process, she noticed a hitch.

A visa?

This moment of panic subsided when the booking confirmation advised that Finnish citizens could obtain an E-Visa from the Indian authorities.

Petra clicked on a link to the site and scanned through the information. The website stated that a 'Rush Visa' could be obtained within one business day—if the visit was business-related. A check of the form revealed she could fill in most of the gaps, except the company name and reason for the stay. A memory from her law degree entered her mind, and a solution presented itself.

Petra navigated to the Finnish government site where she could start a simple company online.

Ten minutes later, she was equipped with the name: 'Petra Fashions'. She added it to the visa site, adding a wish to research Indian manufacturers and import clothing to Finland. She finished the transaction with some satisfaction with her deception. However, her entire plan now rested on hoping someone in India would approve her visa before the day's end.

Well, there's nothing I can do about that now. If the worst comes to the worst, I'll book a flight to anywhere else and find another flight to India.

This was not an appealing thought as she wanted to leave the Nordic area, even Europe, as soon as possible.

Moving her mind to other matters, the next thing on Petra's list was her lack of clothes for the trip and almost anything else she might need.

She headed to the airport shops for a shopping spree to build a new wardrobe and accessories. She purchased nothing too lavish or expensive, as she didn't want to stand out, just a range of light, breathable clothes for the heat. A set of cosmetics and perfumes was next.

Petra enjoyed the shopping experience and left the store with several shopping bags, straight to a luggage shop. Fortunately, everything fitted in a couple of new carry-on cases, which she filled after removing the packaging and labels.

After completing this task, she headed to the business lounge and handed her boarding pass to the woman at reception. Every time her details were entered into any computer, Petra became nervous. She could feel people tracking her every move.

The hours spent in the lounge felt interminable but were softened by the consumption of alcohol. At one stage, Petra almost called out in elation when her visa application appeared on her mobile. This prompted another visit to the bar and a glass of champagne. After this news, her eyes focused on the departure screen, where they were glued for the following hours.

Suddenly, it was there. Petra's Goa flight appeared on the

screen, and it was with some trepidation that she left the lounge.

When she neared the departure gate, Petra decided to sit nearby, among a crowd headed for New York. Her plan was to remain concealed until the last possible moment. This way, if any gang members or police officers arrived, there might be a chance of escape, albeit slim. She imagined her entry onto the aircraft seconds before take-off, with the doors closed and locked immediately after her arrival.

It was with considerable relief that, as planned, leaving it as late as possible, Petra walked over to the gate. The flight attendant checked her ticket, and she headed to the plane, after which she was directed to turn left into business class. Petra smiled with relief, located her seat and deposited her carry-ons in the overhead lockers.

Shortly afterwards, a glass of champagne arrived at her seat, which she drank while the plane filled up with other passengers. Petra especially enjoyed this drink, partly for pleasure but also to calm her nerves, as she was keen for the aircraft to depart.

There was nothing else to fear, and within half an hour, she was soaring up into the clouds, away from further danger.

As the plane turned south, Petra breathed an audible sigh of relief. She had escaped to safety. This time, hopefully, for good.

◆ ◆ ◆

Topias awoke early the following morning with a spring in his step. This would be a big day and doubtless result in a landmark case against some influential people.

He breakfasted quickly and even skipped coffee. He intended to drink his fill at the station, all day and even all night if needed; interesting interviews were ahead.

The drive to the station was pleasant, with the sun streaming through the gaps between the clouds as if attempting to dissipate them. Topias had to resort to sunglasses to navigate the rush-hour traffic.

On arrival, he mustered his team together in the Incident Room. Exceptionally, this included his superior, Chief Superintendent Heidi Anttila. She came as an observer, keen to be involved in what could be the final stages of one of Helsinki's most extensive combined corruption and murder cases.

"Ladies and Gentlemen," he began. "Thanks to a message received from Petra Heikkinen, we have five suspects in custody, pending charges. Today, we must construct the cases against these individuals and charge them. The most important being Immo Salonen and, unfortunately, Olli Nieminen."

Topias' voice noticeably dropped in volume when announcing his friend's name, but he continued.

"We also need to identify and build cases against others involved in both the corruption and murder cases and make those arrests today in case of any flight risks. These may include government officials. Finally, we need to ascertain the fate and whereabouts of the missing woman herself: Petra Heikkinen."

Satisfied with his partly-proven theory from the previous evening, he outlined it in some detail, using the incident boards to illustrate individuals or situations as necessary. Questions were raised by the assembled audience, some of which were answered by recent events. The remainder was added to a list.

The team was split into three, with each sub-team focusing on an objective. Topias would take the interviews together with Katja that day, resulting in charges being brought against those already held. Petri would head up the team to identify additional suspects by analysing the memory stick, researching associations, financial details and proximity to decision-making. Finally, Saana was to lead the search for Petra, using ports of entry to Finland, any use of identification for payment or procurement of transit, and relevant CCTV footage.

With everyone updated and on task, they departed from the Incident Room.

Topias and Katja headed to the interview rooms to meet Olli. He decided that if he could gain more information about Salonen and the others involved, he would be in a better position to push for admission from the construction company owner. Topias would also be happy if Olli told all. In that case, the prosecutor might be more lenient with him. Even though Olli had effectively tried to kill him through a third party, for old times' sake, he didn't want to see him locked up forever.

Topias took an extra coffee with him and offered it to Olli on entry. The situation felt decidedly odd. Not surprisingly, Olli had never thought he would be found out, especially not by his long-time friend and colleague. Topias himself couldn't have been sadder to do this. He could have somehow overlooked or minimalised it if it were something minor Olli was involved in. Despite Topias' senior position, he would have done this for his old friend and colleague. However, this situation was impossible to ignore, and a ballpoint pen soon appeared in his hand.

"Would you like to tell me everything, so we can ensure the judge considers your service record, provision of evidence and admission of guilt?"

Olli crumbled immediately. He could do little else, especially as he considered himself a loyal police officer, not a hardened criminal. He couldn't sit there and lie, especially not to Topias.

"Let's set the tape running. I've made some mistakes, and I'd like to correct them."

Topias nodded in agreement and started the interview.

As it turned out, Olli had not been involved in the

broader conspiracy or the murders. His crimes had been in providing information about police activities concerning the case, including the whereabouts of Petra on two occasions. Topias found this fact unforgivable, notwithstanding he had also put his own life at risk. Nevertheless, he remained professional and was supported by Katja. She noted something in Topias' reactions when Petra was mentioned on more than one occasion.

The interview was duly completed, and a statement was drafted. Olli read through it, and approved the document by his signature. He didn't mention any possible relationship between Topias and Petra. The interview went relatively smoothly for all concerned in the circumstances.

Topias, together with Katja, adjourned for a quick snack and coffee, where he prepared his line of questioning for the next suspect. Katja didn't mention her own suspicions.

Before meeting Salonen, he checked in with the sub-teams for any arising information. While there, he provided a short update on Olli's interview. With such cases involving many moving parts, constant communication was vital. Topias firmly believed that each item shared could result in a bigger chance of gaining a leap forward.

Petri struck gold with his research of the memory stick and various confiscated materials found at Salonen's office and apartment.

Three targets had been identified concerning the search for more suspects, including two publicly-appointed council members closely involved in planning decisions and the Director of Planning himself, a civil servant. In addition, several investors were involved. No financial records demonstrated actual bribery transactions, although the memory stick purported such claims. Topias and the team planned to crack one of the suspects involved in the fraud.

One of the civil servants admitted their complicity, being entirely unused to such circumstances. This began a trail that could quickly be followed, leading to more arrests in short order.

Regarding the murders, the forensics team reported on the killer, Sven Aalto's temporary residence.

It was an old cottage, probably rented solely for the task. This led to the recovery of firearms and DNA that proved beyond doubt that he was the killer of Tommi Heikkinen and his friend Jari-Pekka Hämäläinen, and the attempted murder of Topias and Petra.

Topias had to demonstrate a clear link between Sven and Salonen, and the recovered messages helped to do that. The murdered prisoner would remain a mystery for the moment but was doubtless connected to the two first murder victims. Perhaps a more explicit motive for that crime would appear in due course.

The next piece of news was that Petra's movements had been tracked. They had identified her on CCTV footage at Vantaa airport, and knew of her purchase of a ticket to Copenhagen Kastrup airport. Petri was currently liaising with Danish counterparts to ascertain her whereabouts in Denmark or if she had flown elsewhere.

Topias nodded on hearing this, partly happy that she was safe but somewhat sad that she was gone. Ina stood by the briefing room door and noticed an unusually profound reaction from Topias. Somehow detecting her gaze, he looked at her and smiled. Ina could guess what might have happened but kept her mouth closed and averted her eyes.

DEPARTURE

Petra walked through the airport with her bags. Travelling in business class and with carry-on luggage allowed her to leave the plane first and bypass baggage reclaim.

She was the first to be greeted by the waiting Indian passport and immigration officer. For some reason, she felt nervous, wondering if the net of the Finnish police extended this far or if there could be some problem ahead.

As it happened, there was.

As Petra stood at the desk, the official shook his head and asked why she had applied for a business visa the previous day. Her answer was that she'd forgotten to apply for one and became visibly nervous. That was enough for the official, who pressed a buzzer, and momentarily, two guards arrived to escort her into the depths of the terminal.

❖ ❖ ❖

Petra sat nervously in the interview room as one of the guards placed a plastic cup of water in front of her. Judging by his garb, a third guard, obviously more senior, introduced himself as Immigration Supervisor Gurinder Khan and sat down at the vacant chair opposite. Petra took a sip of water and did her best to hold her nerve. With no air conditioning, the room was stifling. An ineffective fan was in the corner, pointlessly pushing hot air around in a circle.

"Why are you trying to enter India with a business visa?" he asked.

"I'm sorry, it was a snap decision. Some time was available, so I took the opportunity to find some clothing suppliers. I'm establishing a fashion business, you see."

"What is your company name?"

Petra replied and tried her best to answer the officer's questions as calmly as possible.

"I'm sorry I did all this last minute, but I've had a lot on my mind. My husband died recently, and I had to do something to take my mind off the situation."

Tears began to roll down Petra's cheeks. This was not all a performance, as she could easily harness her existing emotions linked to Tommi's death and utilise them.

After several more questions and the submission of proof of her hotel address and sufficient funds, it was evident to the supervisor that nothing was untoward. A cursory search was performed on her luggage, but as Petra had removed the labels, there were no further suspicions.

"Alright. I'm satisfied that everything is in order. We must ensure that people are appropriate to visit our country. You were flagged due to your last-minute decision. So, may I ask, are you an appropriate person, Mrs Heikkinen?"

"Yes, I am," she stated smilingly and was escorted back to the terminal with considerable relief.

It was an elated young woman that entered Mumbai after receiving a stamp on her passport.

Petra walked onto Indian concrete to the domestic terminal and booked a seat on the short flight to Goa.

◆ ◆ ◆

Topias entered the interview room with more than a smirk of satisfaction. He didn't get many perks in his job, the main one being the enjoyment of charging arrogant criminals with their just desserts.

He sat looking at Immo Salonen for a few moments, offering him the customary refreshments and enquiring about his health. He was then introduced to Salonen's lawyer, Miss Hanna Tirkkonen. He had met Hanna before and knew she was a competent defence attorney with more than her fair share of successes. However, it was not always for those deserving of such representation.

On this occasion, she wore an elegant black pin-stripe suit and an equally sleek smile that wasn't entirely genuine in Topias' opinion.

He began by outlining the charges.

"Immo Salonen, we have arrested you on suspicion of attempted murder, conspiracy to murder, kidnapping, bribery, and being the beneficiary of a fraudulent business transaction. There are a few other potential charges, but let's start with these and see what happens, shall we?"

There was so much information on the memory stick that Katja had made stacks of document print-outs. Topias took everyone through them in meticulous detail. Although he had been through it already several times, he was amazed at the extent of the information and didn't feel the need to fumble for a pen.

At one point, Miss Tirkonnen sat back in her chair and sighed. Salonen glanced across at her, and she shook her head before leaning forward to whisper something in his ear. When Topias finished, she sat upright, adjusted her suit and asked for some time with her client.

Topias agreed.

When he left the room, the lawyer expressed her opinion in no uncertain terms.

"The evidence they have is overwhelming. Some of it we could question in terms of its authenticity and accuracy. Also, some men have criminal records, and we could question their integrity. However, if you want me to be completely honest with you, that's all a waste of time."

Salonen nodded, stone-faced but accepting of what he had seen.

"We only have one chance: to seek a reduced sentence. If we plead guilty to some offences, they will dismiss the others. If you point fingers and provide information on the other parties involved, they may be inclined to forget about more of the charges. This would also go down well with the judge regarding sentencing. I think we can do a deal."

"That's it. That's my only option?"

"I'm afraid so. All we would do here would be spend money and time to prolong the whole process. If you agree to this and let me do the talking, I think I can get it down to fraud and conspiracy. The kidnapping issues will disappear, as the person involved has fled the country. We can hang some of the corruption charges around the neck of the people you point your finger at. The murderer is already dead, so that's the end of that. If I'm right, we could reduce a potential life sentence to mean you could still be out to enjoy your pension in ten years. Maybe less for good behaviour and in a minimum-security prison."

Salonen stood up and paced the room, thinking. He went on

to ask several questions and ranted into thin air occasionally. Still, He had to admit his lawyer was right. It was not the time to deny; it was the time to mitigate. That was what the next part of the interview entailed.

After lengthy discussions, the two parties agreed on pending charges, those to be dismissed, and admissions of guilt.

Topias had no doubt he could send Salonen away for the rest of his natural life, but he wanted to arrest the others involved. The actual murderer was dead, and the other gang members would be helpful; however, the ring involved in the massive development crime had to be brought to justice too.

He had talked to his superior, Maarit, about the flexibility of charges versus cooperation, and she agreed. The case had to be solved and closed with no loose ends. She was keen to announce progress to the media and for the others to be arrested; otherwise, they could flee the country.

Maarit and Topias discussed Petra at length. Her behaviour at times had been suspicious and downright erratic at times. Worryingly, she was still missing, and it seemed no one had kidnapped her this time. They could only hope of tracing her through her recent travel.

Salonen decided not to mention the bribe he had made to Petra to hand over the evidence. It was true that after some time, the payment might be discovered. However, as it was made to an international payment card of a missing person, it was unlikely there would be an appetite to pursue it.

◆ ◆ ◆

Later that evening, after spending hours in the stiflingly hot immigration officer's office, Petra caught an equally warm flight to Goa, which landed at the airport within the hour.

After waiting to collect her luggage, Petra took a taxi outside the terminal, her bags having been unceremoniously placed in the hold. There followed another uncomfortable journey in a taxi without air conditioning. Still, she didn't mind and was excited to arrive at her hotel.

She was shown to her room, after which she went to the balcony and took in the magnificent views over perfectly manicured lawns and flowerbeds. Beyond that, she could see a turquoise swimming pool and a beach with crashing surf in the distance.

She slipped her clothes off, took a quick shower, and put on a light summer dress, at which point she went straight to the bar and ordered a celebratory drink.

BEGINNING

Some months earlier, Tommi Heikkinen kissed his wife goodbye and left for work. He was to work at the site office in Haaga that day. Some supplies hadn't been delivered, and an inventory was required to check what was urgent from the missing order.

On arrival at the site, he checked in with the supervisor, and they drank coffee in the staff room. This was a portacabin with a few chairs, an electric heater, a fridge and a coffee machine.

After his break, Tommi took a clipboard and went into the building shell to check on the supplies of bricks and struts. He found a few extra cable bundles, so he added those to the list. It was a fine day, so he took his time and returned to the portacabin for another coffee.

He spent the next couple of hours working in and around the site, adding details and discussing requirements with the construction workers. After this, he took the clipboard and headed for the site office, which was another portacabin.

Tommi knocked at the door and entered. He was surprised to see Immo Salonen, the 'Big Boss', as he was referred to, sitting at the desk at the far end. He had met him several times, including on a few occasions at the site office. He knew Salonen generally worked from his downtown Helsinki office or home.

As Tommi entered, Salonen saw him and held up his hand.

Tommi wasn't sure if it was a greeting or a stop sign as Salonen continued talking loudly on the phone.

"I don't care what you have to do; just get him to agree. We've been working for ages on this. If I need to pay a little more, so be it."

Salonen was noticeably aggravated and rose from his chair and strode forward. Tommi had to sidestep for him to leave the office, and he continued the call out of earshot. It was obviously too confidential for his humble ears.

Tommi shrugged his shoulders and put the clipboard down on the first desk, wondering who the person to receive the money was. As he did so, he glanced over to the desk at the far end, the one Salonen used when he visited, and saw an open laptop. He wandered over and wondered what the fuss was about.

His curiosity got the better of him, and he leaned over to glance at the open computer screen. It was a plan for a development he hadn't heard of before. As Tommi was interested, he continued reading. It was clear that this new development was going to be massive. He wondered if it might lead to more work for him or if there were other opportunities to be grasped, such as more work or a permanent job.

He didn't know why, but something made him take a memory stick from the pile of available items in a dish on the desk, put it into the computer, download the file and leave.

Perhaps this information might be useful one day?

Tommi exited the site office, and with his job finished, he left at a pace, walked swiftly to his car, and drove away. He had no idea that the stolen information would result in his death.

He returned home early. Petra was studying law at university that day, no doubt hard at work, so he was alone. He sat on the sofa and opened the memory stick. Inside were plans for a vast development and details of names and payments made: substantial ones to well-known people. Tommi had been around criminals and their activities before and he had a feeling about his discovery—that it could be worth its weight in gold.

Immediately, he called his friend to ensure that what he was looking at was actually what he thought it was. Agreeing so, they conspired on a scheme to threaten Salonen by revealing the information to the police.

Immo Salonen received their call later that evening.

"We want 100,000€ for the memory stick and our silence," Tommi demanded.

After a tense negotiation, Salonen agreed to 75,000€, and a payment schedule was arranged so it wouldn't cause suspicion.

Tommi was delighted when the first payment arrived in his account, and he wasn't about to tell Petra, at least not yet, anyway.

However, after the third payment, the memory stick was not forthcoming. When Salonen requested it, they said they had spoken to a friend, and he had advised them to ask for much more. This friend was in prison, later to be discovered and silenced.

With the expectation of much wealth ahead, Tommi decided to stay silent where Petra was concerned. He had other plans, and these plans were for himself alone.

The following day, Salonen received a new demand, asking for one million euros. This was curtly declined, and that evening, Tommi took his fateful sauna.

ENDING

Petra enjoyed three months of beach life in Goa.

She changed her accommodation from time to time and spread her wealth over several rechargeable payment cards. She now looked completely different, with dark hair and a deep tan.

One particular day, Petra made a decision.

She visited a property agent in Goa, who thankfully spoke good English, and a search began for a house. She spent a week touring the area and settled on an old Portuguese colonial-style house in Baga, near the beach. It would take some time to arrange administrative matters, negotiate permanent residence and finalise the purchase of the old mansion, but she'd made a start.

Petra was delighted.

That evening, she walked to the hotel bar and ordered a drink: one with rum mixed with fruit juice and plenty of ice. The sun was setting and the horizon bathed in a spectacular orange glow.

Petra wandered past the swimming pool to the beach, where she sat on one of the chairs overlooking the ocean. She smiled and kicked off her sandals, placing her bare feet on a stool and raising her cocktail glass in a toast.

"You didn't quite make it, did you, Tommi? So, this one's for you!"

Petra smiled ironically and walked down to the shore, where the surf washed over the sand. She walked further into the sea and felt the waves froth over her feet. Smiling her broadest smile, her eyes sparkled more than they had done in years. She took another sip of her drink, put down her glass and thought of Topias.

Detective Inspector Topias Torikka. The one who kept me safe — my protective detective.

She considered this momentarily and mouthed the words softly, just audibly.

"My protective detective."

What I had to do to convince him to look after me, though. That's the last time I'll kidnap myself. That floor was much too cold.

Petra chuckled to herself and, as she had done with Tommi, Stefan, and many others, proceeded to file Topias away in her mind inside a neat package.

She strolled back to the hotel with her long hair trailing in the breeze.

◆ ◆ ◆

In Helsinki, summer was already well underway.

Topias looked out of the window. The sun was shining brightly, despite it being almost 10 pm.

He went to pour himself a drink, after which he walked out onto his small terrace, which overlooked a forest at its rear. He sat at the small table and took a satisfying drink from his glass of red wine.

Topias' thoughts turned to Petra, as they had often done

these past weeks, and reflected on the more pleasant memories.

Perhaps I'll meet her again someday?

He recalled their brief relationship, and his mind came to dwell on the apparent deceptions. Had he really meant nothing to her?

Then again, he concluded: *it's probably better if I don't.*

Checking his watch, he decided it was almost time for his sauna.

He recalled the sauna in Petra and Tommi's house and the place where everything had started.

Topias still hadn't been able to fill in all the gaps, but despite her dubious handling of certain things, he hoped Petra was finally somewhere safe and could enjoy her life.

The case had been an intriguing experience in more ways than one. Topias had his regrets, but when all was said and done, it was over, and the criminals received justice in one way or another. At least he could turn the page on a successful conclusion.

I need an ice-cold beer and a long, relaxing sauna.

Topias stood up and headed inside. His mobile phone rang, which he retrieved from the table.

It was the police station on the line. He listened for a few moments and replied to an apologetic desk sergeant.

"Yes, I'll be there. Kiitos. I'm glad you called me. I'll be there as soon as I can."

Topias looked across the room at his dog's ears, which were now on full alert.

"Otso, let's go! There's been a murder in Helsinki."

Grabbing his keys and gun from the hall table, he made for the car, with his loyal and newly-resident companion following closely behind.

The End

ABOUT THE AUTHOR

John Swallow

I am originally from Yorkshire, England and have been fortunate to have also lived in countries as diverse as Scotland, Argentina, Latvia and now Finland.

I enjoy writing crime adventures, and the common factor in my stories is that they are usually based in Helsinki or Rauma in Finland.

Thank you for reading my book. If you a few moments to spare, a short review would be greatly appreciated on Amazon or Goodreads. Thank you!

I hope you enjoyed reading this novel as much as I enjoyed writing it!

BOOKS BY THIS AUTHOR

The Paintings Of Rauma

The Paintings of Rauma takes the reader to Finland on a thrilling crime adventure. The story is based in the beautiful coastal city of Rauma and takes Jussi, a local Police Officer, on a journey to investigate connected crimes across Finland, Sweden and Singapore. This Nordic Noir mystery begins with a minor incident that sets in motion a chain of events involving theft, murder, passion and hidden treasure. Jussi Alonen is a local Police Officer whose life is turned upside down when someone from the past comes back into his life. A gang of criminals make their way around Finland, wreaking havoc in search of great wealth. Treasure from the past is found and millions are made and then lost. Jussi finds that there is much more to police work in Rauma than he could ever imagine.

The Waves Of Helsinki

The Waves of Helsinki takes the reader back to Finland for a thrilling new crime adventure. This time, the story is based in Helsinki, the spectacular capital city of Finland. Jussi, is now training to be a detective and becomes involved in an intriguing investigation which quickly develops. This Nordic Noir mystery starts with apparently simple thefts, which if not stopped, will escalate to the spread of major organised crime. Jussi Alonen's career is heading towards his ambition of being a fully-fledged Detective, that's if he can survive the events in Helsinki, Latvia, Russia and his home town of Rauma. Theft and murder on the high seas, combined with a new romance, will challenge Jussi more than he ever thought possible.

The Heat Of Havana

The Heat of Havana finds Detective Jussi Alonen settled down in Rauma once again. However, little does he know that a thrilling new adventure awaits him, one which will not only reconnect him with an old flame but also result in his involvement with international crime once again. Smuggling high-quality Cuban cigars to wealthy Eastern Europeans is a lucrative business. However, when a problem arises, Jussi's old friend Heli finds herself in the wrong place at the wrong time and he unexpectedly finds himself in Havana. Can he save her and return to his life as a detective in Finland? This Nordic Noir mystery gradually evolves into high-octane action as Jussi's new nemesis follows him from Cuba to Finland, with both bent on revenge, in this gripping new story. Cigars, mojitos and rumba turn into kidnapping, smuggling and murder, immersing Jussi in his most exciting adventure yet!

Printed in Great Britain
by Amazon